T0067878

LEAVING THE BORDER

JOSEPH WALTER

authorHOUSE®

AuthorHouse™
1663 Liberty Drive
Bloomington, IN 47403
www.authorhouse.com
Phone: 833-262-8899

© 2022 Joseph Walter. All rights reserved.

No part of this book may be reproduced, stored in a retrieval system, or
transmitted by any means without the written permission of the author.

This book is a work of fiction. Names, characters, places and incidents are a
product of the author's imagination or are used fictitiously. Any resemblance to
actual events, locales or persons, living or dead, is purely coincidental.

Published by AuthorHouse 12/20/2022

ISBN: 978-1-6655-7887-5 (sc)
ISBN: 978-1-6655-7884-4 (e)

Library of Congress Control Number: 2022923644

Print information available on the last page.

Any people depicted in stock imagery provided by Getty Images are models,
and such images are being used for illustrative purposes only.
Certain stock imagery © Getty Images.

This book is printed on acid-free paper.

Because of the dynamic nature of the Internet, any web addresses or links contained in
this book may have changed since publication and may no longer be valid. The views
expressed in this work are solely those of the author and do not necessarily reflect the
views of the publisher, and the publisher hereby disclaims any responsibility for them.

Dedicated to my parents
Bill and Ruth Walter

A special thank you to my wife Judy for her support
and putting up with me through this process.

Contents

Preface

For most of my adult life, I played by the rules. Now at age 58, I'm going to be a rebel. My government has let me down and law enforcement officials say there is not much they can do. My son has been kidnapped by a bunch of low life drug pushers from Mexico and I don't know if I'll ever see him again. I'm not waiting any longer; I've got to try to find him. It's been forty years since I've been to war, but now I am declaring war on the scum who have taken my son and to all of those who may be involved. I may be older, but I am angry, and somebody is going to be on the receiving end of that anger!!

Chapter 1

LIVING THE AMERICAN DREAM

Here I am, living the American dream with a loving wife of thirty-two years and two beautiful children. Our daughter, Kara, is twenty-six, and our son, Vince, is twenty. My wife, Ann, and I own a construction business a little south of Phoenix, Arizona, that is doing well. The business is kept busy building homes, doing excavation work, and installing water and sewer lines.

Kara is married to a fine young man, John, and she is expecting our first grandchild in four months. In my mind the baby has to be a boy, but if Kara knows, she isn't saying. She keeps telling me I just have to wait and see. Kara works part time in the office of our business. John is in his final year of law school and will probably join his father's law firm after he graduates and passes the bar exam.

Kara was always a tomboy growing up. She spent more time playing with toy trucks than dolls and always enjoyed playing sports. She even got it in her head she was going to try out for the junior high school wrestling team when she was in ninth grade. Her mother put an end to that, refusing to sign the papers to allow her to try out for the team. Ann tried her best to interest Kara in girly things as a child, but the interest wasn't there. She was more comfortable playing with boys than other girls. Kara was a very good field hockey player in high school and did very well in track-and-field events as well. After high school she decided not to go to college.

She wanted to come and work for me as a machine operator. With some training, she became a very good backhoe operator.

She worked at that for four years and was accepted by the rest of the crew as one of the boys. All that changed when she met John. All of a sudden, she was putting on makeup and spending an hour doing her hair. She was cleaning the dirt from under her fingernails and letting her nails get longer. She took quite a ribbing from the work crew when she complained about breaking a nail. They would come to me and say, "Bill, can I go home? I just broke a fingernail."

Then one day she came to me and said, "Dad, we need to talk. I want to get off the construction crew. Can I maybe get a job in the office?"

I said, "What's the matter, honey? Did you break another nail?"

She smacked me on the shoulder and said, "No, I just think it's time I learn more of the business part of the business. You are always complaining you don't like that part of it, so maybe I can do some of it for you."

I agreed, and Kara slowly worked her way into becoming the office manager.

To this day, four years later, I have John to thank for turning my daughter into an integral part of our business. Ann and I have often wondered what piece of equipment Kara would be running today if she had not fallen head over heels for John.

Vince is finishing up his sophomore year at the University of Arizona where he is majoring in geological sciences. It looks like his propensity for digging in the dirt since he was a child may pay off for him someday. Vince was always a quiet and sensitive child, maybe because Kara was outgoing and prone to talking for him when they were younger. He excelled in school, especially in science and math. As a child, he and Ann were very close. I was afraid at one point he was going to play with dolls, but that didn't happen—thank God! As he got older, his interest in sports grew, but his love of books and studying always took priority over anything. It was hard for me to understand, but I was grateful he was such a good student. I realized Vince did things like hunting and fishing to please me and often told him it was OK with me if he would rather not do those things. He would always say he was happy to share the time with me. As he got older, Ann and I could see that Vince was definitely college material.

He visited a number of campuses and finally settled on the University of Arizona. He got a scholarship to pay part of his tuition and seemed to really enjoy the college life. I was pretty sure he would end up teaching or doing some kind of research in the field of geology. He had the brains to be anything he wanted to be.

My dream was for Vince to someday take over the business, but I think he may have other ideas. I'm OK with that. I have always taught him to think things through in his own mind before making any decisions. I've come to realize his plans may not be the same as my own. I was very proud of the adults both of my children had become. Although if someone would have told me twenty years ago that my daughter would be running the business instead of my son, I would have said they were crazy. It just goes to show you that you can make plans, but those plans don't always turn out the way you want.

Ann and I have lived in this area for almost thirty years and have seen it grow by leaps and bounds. We were lucky to start a business in an area that is constantly growing and expanding. We started with nothing, and after years of hard work and long hours, things are going well for us.

Our home is on the outskirts of the city on a forty-acre lot overlooking a development our company completed several years ago. We have made a lot of friends over the years and enjoy the lifestyle we have created here. However, I have never quite been able to adopt the laid-back attitude of the southwest. I guess my formative years spent on a dairy farm in the east are embedded in my mind. I guess the farmer's attitude that the work is never done is in my blood.

I grew up on a dairy farm in southern New York. I learned the value of hard work at an early age. By age ten I was driving tractors and milking cows every day. Along with shoveling manure, feeding the stock and chickens, putting hay away in the summer, and anything else my father would want me to do. It wasn't that my father was a slave driver; there was just a lot of work to do, and he could not afford to pay to someone else to do it. Now I am glad my parents gave me a good work ethic; it has served me well in my life. I tried to pass that same work ethic onto my children— although I must admit, Ann and I have spoiled them a bit.

I spent a few years in the military from 1968–70. I served in Vietnam as a scout-sniper and saw quite a bit of action. I saw some things there that I never want to see again. When I came back home, I couldn't decide what I wanted to do with my life and wandered the country for a while. With my military experience, I finally took a job with a private security company. For three more years, I traveled the world working as a "cleaner," as it was known at the time. My job was to eliminate threats to private companies or local governments. This was a very high-pressure job, and after three years I'd had enough of it.

I came back to the States and did not want to be a dairy farmer the rest of my life. Previously, when I was touring the country, I liked the Phoenix area and decided to try to make a life there. That's where I eventually met Ann. She was working at a local restaurant as a waitress, and I was hooked on staying in the area. We dated for a while, and I shared my dreams with her. We were married a year later and started our life together.

I could see potential in this part of the country. The climate was mild, thought hot in the summer, no humidity, and I wasn't too far from a lot of open spaces. The people were friendly and made me feel welcomed. If someone asked you how you were doing, they actually waited for an answer. There were mountains within easy driving distance, and I was fascinated with some of the Indian culture that was prevalent in the area.

We started out with a landscaping business, making lawns and planting trees and shrubs. Ann worked right beside me daylight till dark, seven days a week. Eventually the business grew, she started having babies, and I started hiring help. All the years of our marriage, I have been the dreamer and—thank God—Ann has been the realist. She has had to pull the reins in on me quite often. We both relax by riding horseback and spending time together in the mountains. Now that the kids are grown, we've adopted two new kids, a pair of black labs, Buck and Bo, who keep us company most all of the time.

Ann's mother and father live in the Phoenix area, and overall they are really good people, not the stereotyped in-laws. She has two sisters, Diane and Grace, who live out of the area, and they do keep in touch on a regular basis. Unfortunately, my family has all passed away. Usually we have all of her family here at our place at least once a year for a family reunion, and it's a happy time for Ann. The kids get to know their family and everybody has a chance to catch up on things.

My life is pretty simple, go to work everyday and spend some time with my family. Every year I think about slowing down, but it never seems to happen. Although, at my age, I am beginning to think some of my Mexican employees are right, a mid day siesta is not such a bad idea. For now I am content to spend a few evenings a week walking with Buck and Bo or riding my horse Spook to relax. It's like my Dad used to say "sometimes you have to get along with other people, but I always enjoy getting along with the animals."

After 30 years, I'm still learning Spanish. When I get to thinking I know it all somebody throws some words at me and I just have to say "what?" It reminds of my grandparents who used to speak Dutch when they didn't want us to know what they were saying. I know my Spanish speaking friends mock me because I talk very slow. I've resigned myself to the fact there is no way I could speak as fast as they do. I can always tell when I've pissed one of my employees off, because they walk away from me gibbering as fast as they can in Spanish.

Ann and I have truly been blessed with a wonderful family, good friends and a group of hardworking, dedicated employees. We live in a place that has a varied landscape and a multi-cultural background.

Chapter 2

LIFE TAKES A TURN

While Vince was on summer break, he was working for me running a backhoe and doing some surveying, but mostly still doing what he loved most, digging in the dirt.

One day as I was looking over a house we were building, my excavating foreman called me and asked if Vince was coming in to work that day. It was 9am and he should have been there at 7am. I told Mike the foreman as far as I knew Vince should be on the job. I told Mike I would try to track him down and send him to work shortly. I called Vince's cell phone and got no answer. I then called Ann to see if she knew where he was. She told me he spent the night camping out with a couple of friends, but he should be at work now. I was getting a little pissed because I figured he and his buddies were probably doing some drinking last night and were sleeping it off somewhere.

I drove over to Vince's friend Jeremy's house to see if maybe his parents knew where the boys were camping last night. When I pulled into their driveway, Jeremy was cleaning out the back of his car. Jeremy greeted me and asked what I was doing here? I asked him if he knew where Vince was. He said as far as he knew, at work. He told me Vince left their campsite around 6am saying he had to get to work. Jeremy said he had not seen Vince since then. He told me that he and Josh left around 7am and he then dropped Josh off at his house and got home around 7:45am. I asked

Jeremy to call me if Vince contacted him this morning and he said he sure would. Jeremy told where they were camping and maybe Vince forgot something and went back to get it. I was familiar with the area and said maybe I would check it out later.

I thanked Jeremy and thought to myself, where the hell is that kid screwing off at. Vince was normally very reliable and not prone to going somewhere without telling Ann or me. I figured if he had trouble with his truck he would have called me to come and get him. I was getting a little worried and tried his cell phone again, no answer. I called Josh's house and he told me basically the same thing Jeremy told me. I wasn't sure what to do, so I called Ann back to see if she had heard from him and she said she had not.

I went back to the jobsite and finished up some things I had to do. All the while I was thinking of how I was going to kick Vince's butt when he finally showed up with some lame excuse.

At lunch time I went home and Ann asked me if I found Vince. I said no, I was just about to ask you the same thing. Ann said she was afraid something had happened to him. I told her not to worry; he was a big boy and could take of himself. I said he probably met up with someone and got distracted by something more interesting than work. In my heart I did not believe that, but it seemed to calm her down a bit. I was getting more worried all along.

I drove out to where Jeremy said they were camping and looked around. I found two sets of tire tracks in the sand. One was probably Jeremy's car and the other I knew was Vince's truck because I had just bought him new tires for it a week ago. I could also see that both sets of tracks left the area and out onto an old mining road. Where in the hell did he go? It just didn't feel right. It was out of character for him to just take off without letting someone know what he was doing.

Out of frustration, I drove back to the construction site and immersed myself in some carpentry work. I was hoping this would turn out to be nothing more than a good old fashioned ass chewing on my part and something we would joke about later. In an hour or so, Mike called me back and asked if I found Vince. I said no, I didn't have any idea where he was. Mike said "I just found Vince's truck about a mile from the site where I'm working." I told Mike I would be right over.

When I got to Vince's truck, his water bottle and lunch were still on the front seat along with his hard hat. He must have been on his way to work, but where the hell he is now. Mike and I found several sets of boot prints around the truck, so Vince must have met someone here. Something wasn't right because the keys were still in the ignition and Vince would never let that happen. It was an old truck, but he was proud of it and wouldn't let just anyone mess with his truck. Just then my cell phone rang, it was Ann, and she said I needed to come home right away. She was sobbing and I asked her what was wrong. She said "Someone just called and said they have our son and were holding him for ransom and they would call back in 30 minutes with some instructions."

I told Mike I had to go and would call him later. I told him to lock up Vince's truck and I would pick it up later. My mind was racing; why Vince, why my family, we weren't wealthy. Did I piss somebody off bad enough to kidnap my son? Was Vince ok, should I call the police?

When I arrived home 20 minutes later, Ann was waiting for me in the driveway. She was crying and asking me what we were going to do? We both hugged and cried and I honestly didn't know what to do.

In 10 minutes the phone rang. I answered and the voice on the other end asked if this was Bill Wright? I said it is who is this? He said we have your son and if you ever want to see him again we want $100,000 cash, in small bills, by noon tomorrow. I told him we didn't have that kind of cash. His response was "get it". The caller said he would call back tomorrow morning at 10am with instructions. If I wanted to see my son alive again, get the money and don't bring any cops into this deal.

This just didn't seem real. I kept thinking someone was playing a sick practical joke. I was known for playing practical jokes on other people, but nothing like this. This was real, finding Vince's truck, him not showing up for work, and it all added up now. Someone must have grabbed him on his way to work this morning. My head was spinning. I could come with maybe $50,000 - 60,000 cash but not a$100,000. Where was I going to get another $40,000? Ann and I debated about calling the police. I knew the local sheriff very well and decided to give him a call. I'd known Bob Tucker for over 20 years. We hunted together over the years and had become good friends. After explaining things to Bob, he said he would be right over.

It was about 4pm when Bob arrived. He was a straight shooter and didn't mince words. He gave Ann and me a hug and said "Let's get moving on this." I told Bob the caller had a heavy Hispanic accent and I couldn't here any background noises. A Hispanic accent in this area is not unusual. Half of my 18 employees were Hispanic and they were good people. Bob asked if I fired anyone lately or pissed someone off really bad. I said I had not fired anyone in over a year and didn't think I got anyone mad enough to kidnap my son.

Bob said he had worked on some of these cases before and would like to bring in some help, but only if we agreed. I trusted Bob and asked him "Please, be honest with me; what are the odds we will see Vince alive again if we pay the ransom?" Bob said it would depend on who we were dealing with, maybe a 50% chance. That hit hard, it also meant a 50% chance these people would kill him.

Ann and I talked it over, between the tears and choking them back, we both agreed to let Bob make the phone call for more help. Bob made a call to the FBI and told us to try our best to stay calm. He said he would not leave until the FBI agents arrived.

I decided to make a few calls to try to raise the additional money I needed. I called my bank and they verified I had $62,000 in cash reserves from the business and $10,000 in savings from our personal account. I still needed an additional $28,000 to meet the kidnappers demand. I spoke with the bank manager and told her I would need to borrow $28,000 by tomorrow morning to buy some equipment at a sale. Bob told me earlier not say anything to anyone else about what was going on. The bank manager, Carol and I had done business together for years and she said no problem, she would draw up the papers

Today and have them ready for me to sign in the morning. She asked me what I was buying and I told her some excavating equipment. I thanked her and said I would see her at 9am sharp tomorrow morning. I felt at least I was doing something to help this situation.

It was now 5:15pm and two FBI agents had just arrived. Agents Hanson and Nicolas introduced themselves. Ann and I went through the same question and answer period as we did with Bob. They were very professional and to the point. They asked us if we intended to pay the ransom. I told the agents I could have the money by tomorrow morning and asked their advice on paying the ransom. Agent Hanson echoed Bob's quote that we would have a 50% chance of getting Vince back alive if we paid the ransom. He did say "If we are dealing with a ring of kidnappers working out of Mexico, the odds may be higher. These guys are interested in keeping a reputation of returning their victims. In a twisted way, it is better for their business if the word got out to the families of the victims that when they paid, they would see their loved ones again."

There had been a rash of kidnappings in the Phoenix area in the past year or so. The police and the FBI had not been able to crack the ring thus far. A lot of the kidnappings appeared to be drug related according to police reports. I was confident Vince was not involved in any drug dealing, but I also knew the FBI had to look at all the possibilities. They questioned Ann and I about Vince perhaps using or selling drugs and also if Ann or I had any dealings with drugs. We were a bit offended and denied any knowledge of drug use ourselves and by Vince as well. The agents promised they would do everything they could to get our son back to us safe and sound. They seemed sincere in their words, but came up short of promising they would get our son back alive. I did not like having to depend on other people to take care of my family. I was feeling pretty helpless and left out as the agents were busy coordinating their efforts. They were in contact with the state police and I don't know who else. When I asked if I could do anything, they just told me to try to stay calm.

Earlier in life I had some very intensive training as an Army Ranger and felt I should do something on my own, but what? The waiting and not knowing if Vince was alright was nerve wracking. Bob was trying his best to console us and keep our hopes up. Kara and John stopped by and we all hugged and cried and asked once again, why this family? Kara brought clothes along for both of them and said they were staying until this was over. It was comforting to have them both here. John's father was an attorney and John had one more year of law school and would probably join his father's law firm when he graduated. John offered to call his father to come over, but realistically, there wasn't much an attorney could do right now. I told him thanks, but not right now.

It was now 7pm and the FBI had some communications equipment set up, my living room looked like a military command post. They seemed busy planning and preparing. Agent Hanson looked at me and said "We are ready for when the kidnappers call."

Hanson said "My people will try to get a fix on the caller's location. All we can do right now is waiting. We were all pacing the house, not able to sit down or willing to act the fact that there was nothing we could do at the moment. Ann made coffee and ice tea, Kara and John just held onto each other. I went into my office and looked at photo's on the wall of Vince from past hunting trips. His first deer, when he was 10 years old and a bear he shot in British Columbia. Photo's of him from playing football, wrestling and baseball from little league to college. I went to my gun safe and checked inside. I had a pretty extensive collection of guns, but right now they were useless. I had no idea who to use them on. My thoughts at the moment were if this turned out bad, which gun would I use to take out the people who kidnapped my son. I was trying to remain positive about the situation but I'm also a realist and had to look at both sides. There was this constant nagging in my mind; why my son? I could not figure it out.

At 9pm the phone rang. We all jumped at the sound of the ring. On the third ring the agents gave the signal to answer it. The voice on the other end asked "Do you have the money?" I told him I would have it by 10am tomorrow morning. The caller asked if I was familiar with an abandoned mine at the end of Cooper road west of Phoenix. I said I was familiar with the location. He told me to drop the money in a black plastic garbage can by the old mine entrance. He also said to come alone and no cops or I would never see my son again. He told me to be there at 12 noon and there would be directions of where to find my son. I asked to speak to Vince and there was a pause. Then I heard Vince's voice "Dad, Dad I'm ok". Then the phone went dead.

My knees went weak as the caller hung up and I had to sit down. The reality of this thing hit me all at once. I'd been trying to be strong for the rest of my family but now the emotions I was holding back came bursting out of me. Ann, Kara, John and I just hugged without saying a word. After a few minutes the agents broke the silence and said they could only narrow the origin of the call to a half mile radius of western Phoenix. That was a big area to cover. The agents asked me to describe the area for them. I let Bob describe it for them because he and I had hunted in that area quite often. Bob told them "It was 6-7 miles west of town, very isolated. There was one drivable dirt road leading into the mine and from there it was several four wheeler or horse trails leading into the back country." It was going to be a long, sleepless night.

Chapter 3

DEALING WITH CRIMINALS

None of us slept very much during the night. Bob went home to get some sleep, the two agents slept in the living room. Ann and I just held each other in bed and talked about the kids and what we would do after Vince came home. I would spend more time with them and maybe let Mike take on more responsibility with the business. I could hear Kara and John talking in the next room; I doubt they got much sleep either.

We were up at 5am and Ann made breakfast for everyone. I called Mike and told him he was in charge today, I would not be in to work today. He asked me "Did you find Vince and is everything alright?" I couldn't tell him all the details but I trusted Mike completely. I told him Vince was ok and there were some things I needed to deal with today. I told Mike "Bring Vince's truck back to the job site and we will pick it up later. I'll call you later today and explain what is happening and please keep this to yourself until I can explain it to you." He assured me he would.

The agents explained to us what they would like to do. Hanson said "One of them would ride with me to the drop site, hidden in the back seat of my truck. There would be other agents around the perimeter of the area, hopefully cutting off the trails leading away from the old mine. They would have a State Police helicopter standing by to track any movement away from the mine after Vince was safe. Bob and two of his deputies were going to come in from the mountain behind the mine on horseback to cut off any of trails leading in that direction. No one would take any action until they knew Vince and I were safe." We agreed to try it their way and we all agreed there would be no attempt to stop the kidnappers until Vince was safe. Agent Hanson assured me the other agents were already in place. They went in under the cover of darkness last night so as to leave no dust trail this morning.

It was nearing 7am and I could not wait any longer. I had Carol, the bank managers home phone number and called her to see if we could meet at the bank in an hour. She agreed and said I must be real anxious to get to the sale. I told her yes, I was real anxious.

I met with Carol at the bank and everything went well there. I now had the $100,000 the kidnappers demanded. It was a lot of money, but it seemed insignificant compared to my son's life. I arrived back home and now we had to wait again. I kept thinking of all the things that could go wrong and it was incredibly difficult to think positive about this whole deal. I asked the agent if I could take one of my own guns with me. He said absolutely not, there would be enough fire power at the scene if needed. He didn't know I had a handgun in the console of my truck already and I guessed at this point I would not tell him.

At 11:30am agent Hanson and I got in my truck and headed out to the old mine. We got there about ten minutes early. I eased up the old dirt road and didn't see anyone around. I saw the black garbage can sitting outside the mine entrance. My stomach was churning and my heart felt like it was going to blow out of my chest. I stopped 100 yards from the garbage can and looked around, nothing but sand, brush and a bunch of old timbers from the mine. This was it; I pulled up to the garbage can and put the money inside. On the inside of the lid there was an envelope taped to it. My name was on the envelope. Hanson whispered to me to save the tape when I peeled it off, there could be finger prints on the tape. I crawled back into my truck and opened the envelope. The note inside said to drive away and don't look back or stop. It also said I would find my son standing along the highway one mile east of Phoenix, if everything went as planned and I didn't bring any cops with me. I handed the note to Hanson and after reading it, he said lets go. It would take 25 minutes to get back to the highway normally; I was going to make it a lot quicker than that. I told Hanson to hang on it might get bumpy.

On the way out we noticed two dirt bikes heading into the old mine area. Hanson said don't worry my men will take care of them. We made it back into Phoenix in 15 minutes and got to where the note said Vince would be. I pulled off along the side of the road and looked around and didn't see him anywhere. My heart was still racing and I was starting to panic! We drove further down the road and didn't see him anywhere. We then circled back and drove back into town and found no sign of Vince.

While I was driving, Hanson was on his phone to the other officers and discussing something but I couldn't hear what he was saying. I pulled off and looked around at Hanson and asked "now what the hell are we going to do?" Hanson said "The two people on the bikes were not the kidnappers; they were just a couple of kids out riding. The other officers may have blown their cover when they stopped the kids on the bikes. If the kidnappers were watching they may have seen the other officers pull the kids over. His men were holding the kids just in case they were part of the scam." I told him I didn't give a damn about two kids on dirt bikes, I wanted my son back.

Hanson called the state police to have a car positioned where we were supposed to pick up Vince, in case he showed up. He told me to head back to the drop site. My mind was racing, I was questioning the wisdom of bringing the police into this, I just should have handled it myself and maybe Vince would be sitting in the truck with me now, instead of some damn FBI agent. Part of the way into the mine, we met Agent Nicholas along the road. He said there was no activity around the garbage can and no one reported any activity in the area. The two boys admitted a guy paid them $20 each to ride their dirt bikes out here at 12 noon today. They described the man as Hispanic maybe 5 ½ feet tall. That narrowed it down to a few thousand men.

I was about ready to explode. We had no idea where these kidnappers were and worst of all no idea where Vince was. It was now after 1pm, an hour after I dropped the money and no one saw anything but the two kids. Hanson said "Let's drive up to the garbage can and check on the money." When he opened the lid, all we saw was a hole in the ground. The can was about 6 feet from the mine entrance and apparently they dug a tunnel from the mine to under the can. I was sure there was a bottom in the can when I put the money in it. They must have had a false bottom in the can. These guys were pretty smart and obviously had given this location a lot of thought. They took the money right out from under everybody's noses and no one ever saw a thing. Hanson called the state police to see if they found Vince yet. Nobody had seen him. They must have had a spotter somewhere who saw the agents go after the kids on the bikes. The kids were a perfect diversion. Bob and his deputies reported seeing nothing on the ridge behind the mine. I had this sickening feeling that because I brought in the police my son may be dead.

Two of the agents went back into the mine shaft and found where they had dug out a tunnel to the garbage can. The agents continued back the mineshaft and found a passage way to the outside along a drainage ditch at the bottom of the ridge. The ditch was probably not visible from higher up where Bob and his deputies were posted. The deputies followed one set of foot prints out around the ridge to a spot where he must have gotten away on horseback.

They got their damn money, why didn't they give me my son back? What purpose would they have for keeping him? I asked Hanson the same questions. He told me not to give up we may still find Vince. Chances were the guy on horseback ditched the horse and was long gone by now. We'd been out foxed. Hanson was back and forth on his phone and radio to different people, some of whom I had not even met. What seemed like a good plan sure didn't turn out the way we planned. I was angry and sad at the same time, feeling more helpless today than yesterday. Now I had to explain to my family why I wasn't bringing Vince home and face the reality that maybe he wasn't coming home. Hanson told me to go home and be with my family. He and his men would continue to search the area for any evidence they could find and he would see me later in the day to keep us updated. He was right, but in a way I hated to go home without Vince. I felt like I failed my son and the rest of my family today.

Chapter 4

A FAMILY UNITED

When I pulled into the driveway, Ann, Kara and John came running out of the house to greet me. The disappointment on their faces was obvious when they didn't see Vince in the truck. Before I even got out of the truck, Ann asked "What happened?" I explained the situation to them and I know we were all thinking now what. We all went inside the house and it was like no one wanted to ask the next question, what if Vince was dead? Ann said "I refuse to give up; I will not believe Vince is gone." We all agreed we were going to live by the belief that Vince was still alive. We would have to have proof that he was dead.

A few minutes later Bob pulled in and for the first time, I broke down and cried. Bob was doing his best to encourage all of us. He said the law enforcement officials apparently underestimated these kidnappers; they appeared to be very organized. They obviously had their own surveillance out there. It was apparent they planned to send in the two kids on the dirt bikes to try to draw out anybody staking out the drop site. When the agents revealed their positions they decided to not give Vince up. Bob said there was still a chance we could get Vince back. Maybe the kidnappers would contact us again, maybe they dropped Vince at another location and we just haven't found him yet. I told Bob we were not giving up; we were going to do whatever it took to get Vince back. Bob agreed he would do all he could.

There was a knock at the door and when I answered it, it was Mike, my foreman. Mike asked "what the hell is going on?" I stepped outside with Mike and explained things to him. Mike said "Damn it Bill, why didn't you tell me what was going on yesterday? You know I love that boy like he was my own kid." I said I was sorry but we needed to keep the number of people involved to a minimum. Mike said he understood but now what could he do to help. I told him the best way he could help us right now was to keep the business running and make sure everything was going smooth. I asked him to please not let anyone else know about this just yet, at least until we found Vince. Mike said he would be back this evening after work and we could talk some more.

I trusted Mike Warren completely; he'd been working for me a long time and he was a friend as well. His son Matt and Vince grew up together and until Matt went away to college they spent a lot of time together. I felt the same way about Matt; he was part of our family. It was nice to know that people cared, but this thing was far from over and we needed to be careful who we talked to about it. We had no idea who was involved in this kidnapping. It could possibly be someone we know. I still felt so damn helpless and unable to control this situation, it was driving me crazy. I know Ann was feeling the same way.

Mike was pulling out of the driveway and another car pulled in. It was John's father Greg. Greg gave me a hug and asked is there was anything he could do. I said "You just did it man. I told him that was the hardest part; not knowing what to do." Greg said "I have a couple of private investigators I can call on to take a look at things if I wanted him to do so." I told him to keep that on the back burner for today; I wanted to talk to the FBI agents first before doing anything on my own. He told me it would only take a phone call from me and he would put these guys on it. Greg and I went inside and we all talked about some of the goofy things Vince did over the years and also about our new grandchild that was on the way. It would be the first for both of our families. Greg and I joked about who was going to spoil it the most. It was a bit of a relief to laugh about something.

About 4:30pm agent Hanson stopped in to report on what they found. He told us "Unfortunately they didn't find much. They found where the man on horseback was picked up but from there the trail ended. They stopped several vehicles pulling horse trailers to search them but found nothing." In this part of the country vehicles pulling horse trailers were pretty common. He admitted the kidnappers were more organized than they gave them credit for. They had a forensics team going over the area for any evidence they could find. Hopefully they would come up with fingerprints, shoe prints, garbage or anything that would give them some leads. Maybe even the horseshoe prints if they could match them to the horse. I was very frustrated and tried my best not to say what I was thinking. I was feeling the FBI bungled this stake out. For now placing blame on someone wasn't going to get Vince back. I'd just lost $100,000 and perhaps my son. I really didn't need someone to tell me to relax and they would handle everything.

Guess what, agent Hanson said "we are doing all we can at the moment, hopefully our forensics team will come up with some evidence we can work with. I understand your frustration Mr. Wright. You and your family need to try to relax and allow us to do our job." I could feel the anger welling up in me and I told agent Hanson it would be best if he left our house right now before I say or do something I might regret later. Greg stepped in and said "look we are all a bit on edge right now; how about if we step outside and give everyone some space." Greg took Hanson by the arm and they both walked out the door. I realized the FBI was doing their best and that they knew they screwed up, but this was not the time to play nice. It was time to take the initiative and do something positive to get our son back. I also realized that it was quite possible the kidnappers may have never intended to return Vince.

Ann grabbed my arm and said "I know you well enough to see the wheels turning inside your head. What are you thinking?" I said "It's time we had a family pow-wow."

I said "We need to think about the fact that Vince may not be coming back and maybe we need to go get him. I don't know how or even where to begin but as a family we need to accept that reality. I need to know from the rest of you what you think. The way I see it either we all agree on a plan or the plan does not happen." Ann spoke first and said we need to give the FBI and police more time to do their job. She said "I know you Bill; you want to grab your guns and go hell bent after somebody. But you don't even know who you're going after!" Kara said she agreed with her Mom. As much as she would like to kick the tar out of somebody; we should give the police more time to do their job. She said besides Dad; you're no spring chicken anymore. John of course agreed with Kara despite my looking at him with my meanest scowl.

I said "ok, ok I know when I'm out voted; the three of you win for now. We will give the police more time. But we all need to think about our options if they can't find Vince. I told them I would be right back; there was something I needed to do outside."

Greg and Hanson were still outside talking when I went out. I said excuse me guys but agent Hanson I owe you an apology. I had no right to be rude to you. I know you were doing the best you could. The fact of the matter is we all underestimated these guys and they just plain out smarted us today. Hanson said there was no apology necessary. He could not imagine the stress we were under right now and promised he would do all he could to help us. We shook hands and I told him that was all I could ask of him.

Hanson excused himself and said he was going to the lab to see if they had anything for him. I told Greg of our decision and he said fine, he thought that was the sensible thing to do right now. I also said I would keep those private detectives in mind if the police could not find Vince. Greg offered to do anything he could to help and hugged me and said we will get through this together. He said his goodbyes to the others and left for the evening.

We were finally alone and I know we all felt alone without Vince there. We ate a little bit and I know at least for me I kept staring at the phone to make sure it wasn't off the hook in case the kidnappers would call back. Or, maybe Vince would call to say hey come and get me. For now I was thankful we had each other.

The next morning I woke up about 5am after sleeping maybe 2 or 3 hours. It seems I do my best thinking in bed when I should be asleep. I kept thinking of things I should be doing to get Vince back. Some of the ideas I had were pretty stupid, like renting an airplane and bombing some of the known hideouts of these criminals or setting up at the border with my long range rifle and shooting illegals as they crossed the border.

One thought kept making sense to me; putting a team together to go get Vince. I had some old friends who would probably go for it. With all the experience we had from the military and beyond we could do the job. But maybe we were too old for such an undertaking and maybe I was letting my ego get in the way of common sense. I really hated being so indecisive.

About 6am Bob stopped by to see how we were doing. He told me the crime lab did get some fingerprints and they matched a known criminal who had been arrested and deported back to Mexico two years ago. The FBI had suspected he was working with a kidnapping ring for some time but so far they had not been able to track him down. They had some leads as to where he was living but again those leads did not pan out. Bob told me to hang in there, they might get this guy figured out and maybe he could lead them to the other members of the gang and also to Vince. Bob said "I know you, Bill, and I know you're already thinking of doing something on your own. Please, give us some more time." I promised Bob I wouldn't do anything in the next few days but beyond that there were no guarantees.

Mike stopped in to check on us later and he asked "What are we going to do about Vince boss?" I told Mike for now we are going to let the law handle it; I just promised Bob Tucker I would give him a few more days to find my boy. Mike said a couple of the guys on the job are from Mexico and if that's where Vince was maybe they could help us locate him. Maybe they could get some information that could help us. I asked Mike again to keep things quiet for now. He agreed, but I know the wheels were turning inside his head as well. I told Mike to go to work and he would probably see me later in the day at one of the job sites.

After breakfast John and I went to get Vince's truck and bring it home. On the way John asked what I was planning to do. I asked him why everybody thinks I'm going to do something. He said because I'm the kind of guy who doesn't like sitting around waiting for somebody else to do something. I told John, I guess your right but I promised Sheriff Tucker I would wait and give them a chance to find Vince. For now that's what I was planning to do. John asked "When you decide to do something will you include me in on it?" I said I don't know.

When we got to Vince's truck, my chest got tight and I felt a lot of anger. I wanted to see these bastards fry for taking my son. I told John to take my vehicle back to the house and I would be along shortly. I crawled in Vince's truck and just closed my eyes for a minute. I remembered the day we bought this truck for him. He was so proud of it. He promised he would work all summer for nothing to help pay for it. I told him "damn right you will!" I could see him in the driveway washing and polishing it. I swore he'd rub the paint off of it.

He is a good kid and like any Dad I am very proud of him. He turned out to be a fine young man mostly because of his mother's teachings. He is more sensitive than me and always very polite. Ann would always joke she was going to knock off the rough edges on Vince before he grew up to be like me. I envision him becoming a teacher or something like that because of his gentle nature. This old truck is a part of him and right now I needed something of his to hold onto.

When I got back home, Ann was on the phone and for a minute I thought she was talking to the kidnappers. Then I realized she was talking to agent Hanson. When she hung up she repeated what Bob told us earlier in the morning. He also gave her all the rah-rah stuff; hang in there, don't lose hope and were working hard on this case. The four of us gathered in the kitchen and prayed for Vince's safe return, just as we'd done several times before. It was easy to blame God or ask God why he allowed something like this to happen. I didn't blame God; he didn't have anything to do with it. There were evil people in the world just as there were good people in the world.

If it was one thing I learned in life; it was to not get too comfortable because life is always changing and life will always throw some curveballs at you. It was what I was taught and what I believed; we were put in this life to help each other deal with those curveballs. We all shed a few tears as we closed in prayer and I know I felt God's presence upon me. It was almost two days since this whole thing began and it was physically and emotionally draining for all of us.

I told Ann, Kara and John I was going to go out to one of the job sites and check in on things just to get my mind off this mess. I suggested maybe they each find something to do as well. John and Kara decided to go to their house and do some painting in their nursery. Ann said she would do some baking and stick around the house just in case the phone would ring. I got to the job site where we were installing some new water and sewer lines. I talked with a few of the guys and it seemed the job was going well. One of the guys asked me where Vince was screwing off today and I just said "ah, you know these kids; he must have had a long night." We both laughed and he went about his work. I then went to the new home my crew was building and helped out with some carpentry work for a couple of hours and it did help me to focus on something else for a while. The other guys joked I must be getting old; I was only good for a couple of hours work a day.

As I was leaving, agent Nicholas stopped by and asked me if I had a few minutes. I said "Sure, what's on your mind." He told me "We have eliminated most of the suspects in the case and they believed they had it narrowed down to a Mexican gang that operated in the area. They interviewed several individuals and had a few more to track down. At this time they couldn't pin anything on anyone." He went on to say sooner or later someone would talk.

He asked me again if I was sure Vince was not involved in any kind of drug use or dealing. I told him I would be shocked if I found out Vince was dealing drugs. Nicholas said ok; we have to look at all the angles. He left after giving me assurances they were making progress on the case. Damn it; now they had me questioning whether I knew my own son well enough. I was sure Vince wasn't into drugs and I wasn't going to allow some strangers to tell me otherwise.

I was having trouble focusing on any one thing; my mind kept going back to Vince. I went home and looked up an old friend's phone number. Jay McMurray lived in Idaho and I had not talked to him for almost a year. Jay and I served in the military together in 1969-70 while doing our duty in Viet Nam. We became good friends and after the military we both were employed for some private security firms throughout Southeast Asia. We both went through a lot of rough times together and we both owed our lives to one another. Over the last forty years we got together for some hunting trips and family vacations. Jay and I had a bond that could not be broken. Two years ago Jay's son Ryan was killed in action in Afghanistan and it took an awful toll on Jay. I spent some time with him after Ryan's death and we became even closer. Jay now lived alone in the mountains as his wife Mary died of cancer the year before Ryan.

When I called Jay, he answered with his usual gruff voice saying "I don't want any of your damn stuff; quit calling me!!" I said "McMurray, you miserable old bastard, you haven't changed a bit!!" There was a pause and then he asked "Bill, you old SOB is that you?" He said he was sorry he thought it was some damn salesman that kept calling him. I asked how he was doing and he said "you're right, just as miserable as ever." Jay asked how things were in Arizona and I replied not so good.

I explained to him what was happening and his immediate response was what can I do to help. I told him I wasn't sure but I had this burn in my gut to take some action on my own. Jay said sounds like your ready to call up the old unit again. You know we ain't done that for forty years and we might be a little rusty. I told Jay that was why I was calling; to ask him if he thought I was crazy for thinking I could go kick some ass and get my son back. Jay's response was "yes Billy, I do think you're crazy if you think your going after Vince without me! You and I are a team even after all these years. We put a hurtin' on old Charlie a long time ago; I figure we can do the same now to some punk ass Mexicans."

I said hold on now; I'm just thinking about this and I promised the local sheriff I would give him a couple of more days to sort this out. Jay said it will take me a couple of days to get my stuff together; I'll be flying down there in two days. You know I got more money than brains; I'll get my old plane juiced up and be in Phoenix day after tomorrow.

He asked if he should bring his old reliable model 700 along. I said why not. Jay was right he did have more money than brains some times. He owned a big timber company and a couple thousand acres of ranch land he sold to a fellow from California for a lot of money. He had his own airplane and airstrip and he traveled pretty much wherever he wanted to go. I knew if he said he was coming to Phoenix there was no talking him out of it. I simply told him to call me when he got to town.

I told Ann Jay was coming down in a couple of days and she just rolled her eyes. She knew it didn't take a whole lot for the two of us to get into some trouble from time to time. She asked what I was planning and I told her nothing yet. Ann said I don't want you two old farts going off half cocked and getting yourselves killed. I assured her we would not go off half cocked; we would be prepared if we decided to do anything. Besides I thought Jay just needed an excuse to come and visit.

From the first day I met him, Jay was quite a character. That day was in boot camp when our drill sergeant decided to make an example of Jay. The D.I. heard a wise crack Jay made and called him on it. He made Jay do 50 pushups and told him he was a wise ass sissy. The D.I. said to Jay "Isn't that right, you are a wise ass sissy?" Jay responded "No Sir." Wrong thing to say, Jay!! The D.I. put his foot in the middle of Jay's back and pushed down while Jay was trying to do his pushups. The D.I. barked "Are you a smart ass sissy now?" All I could here was a very weak "Yes, Sir." That was Jay; he had a tendency to put his mouth in gear before his brain.

Jay was the brother I never had and even though he was a bit eccentric; I trusted him with my life and that of my family. He saved my butt a few times in the Nam. Once when I was pinned down from enemy fire; he moved in behind them and took out a nest of four men with a couple of grenades. Another time he covered my back when our camp was overrun with the enemy. Jay took out two NVA soldiers who had a lock on my position.

For a few minutes, I was reflecting on the past and not Vince. It was reassuring to know I had such good friends to count on, if I needed them. I was beginning to realize I needed to formulate a plan if the police could not find my son. I made up my mind I was going to give them two more days to do their job.

The first step in my plan was to call our local legislators office to see if there was anything they could do. I was given the whole rah-rah political crap; we sympathize with you but there is not much we can do. Next I called the congressman's office for this area and basically was told the same thing and was reminded to not to try to take matters into my own hands. I was assured the federal government was aware of the seriousness of this problem, and was working on efforts between the Mexican government and the US officials to bring down these kidnapping rings. Both offices said they were aware the FBI was working on my son's case and they would advise me to let the FBI handle it.

Later that evening, I called Mike Warren and asked him to contact Raul Martinez, one of my other employees. Raul was from Mexico and went back periodically to visit family. I thought he might be able to help us find our way around down there if we needed to go. Mike called me back and said he and Raul could meet with me tonight if I wanted. I told Mike, I would meet them at the new home site, not my house. At 8pm I met Mike and Raul and discussed my tentative plans.

Raul told Mike and me he grew up near a town called Madera. It was an isolated area on the edge of the mountains, maybe two hours south of the border. He said he had some family that still lived in the area and he also had relatives that lived in Chihuahua. Raul said he knew there were some gangs that operated out of Chihuahua, but he didn't know much about them. He told us he could make some phone calls to his relatives in Chihuahua and get some information, but he needed to be careful, he did not want his relatives to be hurt for providing information. I told them both, at this point I did not want either of them to do anything. I would try to get some suspected locations where these kidnappers might be hanging out from the FBI. Both Mike and Raul said they would do anything they could to help. I told them to sit tight and I would let them know if I needed them.

I was feeling like maybe I was already getting too many fingers in the pie. We couldn't drag too many people down to Mexico, it would just complicate things. I was also feeling like at least I was doing something positive. Tomorrow, I will contact the FBI and try to get some information on where they thought these guys were holed up. When I went back home, Ann looked at me and asked 'What are you up to?' I told her I still owed Bob Tucker two more days to find Vince after that I was going to get Vince on my own. I shared with Ann the little bit of planning I had done. I also told her there was a lot of information I needed to gather between now and then.

I'd been so busy today, it felt really good to sit on the sofa and just hug Ann. We sat in silence for a while; I guess both of us trying to make sense of this situation. Buck and Bo came over to us and both put their heads on our laps, sensing as only dogs can do, the pain in our hearts.

Chapter 5

THE WAITING GAME

The next morning Bob Tucker and agent Hanson stopped by around 8am. Bob said "We have gathered some more information that we want to share with you. We located an individual who we believe was involved in Vince's kidnapping. This person rented a horse to the man who picked up the money. We have a description of the man who rented the horse and we are circulating a picture of him throughout the area. We also found some fingerprints on the saddle and traced them to a known criminal who is in their system. As yet they have not found the man and unfortunately they still had not found any sign of Vince."

We thanked them for the information and it was good to know they were making some headway. I asked Hanson "Do you have any idea of where this gang was operating from?" He said "We have a few leads and most likely it is one of two areas. The first is a coastal town named Cabo Lobos along the California Gulf and the second is in the Sierra Madre Mountains southwest of Chihuahua."

Agent Hanson said he had to leave but he would be in touch later in the day to update us on any new developments. Bob stuck around after Hanson left and asked how we were doing? He said "He knew this must be incredibly difficult for us and he wished he could do more for us." Ann asked "Bob do you think Vince is still alive?" Bob said there was still hope and we should not give up. He said he was hoping these guys were greedy enough to ask for another ransom after things cooled down. I asked Bob what we could do to help. He told us to make sure one of us was close to the phone all day, just in case someone did call. Beyond that, everything else was being handled. Bob hugged us all and said he and his family were praying for us and he would keep in touch.

As Bob was leaving, our pastor Paul stopped by. Paul is a young man with a good heart and we were glad to see him. He prayed with us for Vince's safe return, for Kara's baby to be healthy and for God to watch over all of us through this time of trouble. Paul offered his help and that of the congregation and we were grateful for that. We simply asked that he and the others in our congregation continue to pray for all of us, especially for Vince. Paul's words were comforting. For such a young man he always seemed to know the right thing to say.

After the pastor left, I suggested to Ann she get out of the house for a while today. She had not been anywhere since Vince was taken. She guessed she would go do some grocery shopping and maybe stop by her parents place before doing that. I said I would stick around the house in case the phone would ring. John had some classes today and he left for school early today.

Kara went into the office this morning to take care of some paperwork and to do this week's payroll. Although our world stopped the last few days, the rest of the world was still moving along.

I liked being home alone; it gave me some time to think. I'd been avoiding the chances of Vince still being alive. The odds were not good. I'd dealt with killers before and they didn't think like normal people. A human life meant nothing to them. Hell, I got paid to kill people at one time in my life and the main reason I got out of it was I couldn't take the killing anymore. I could remember a time when I simply viewed it as my job and felt very little remorse in taking someone else's life.

I read the statistics on kidnappings in this part of the country and according to police reports; most all of them were drug related. I just could not bring myself to believe Vince was hooked up with drug dealers. Maybe they took Vince by mistake; maybe they thought he was someone else. I kept staring at the phone – come on damn it – ring. I kept thinking how I was going to live my life without my son. This was the third day and

I still had no answers to my questions. The waiting, not knowing what happened, not knowing what to do was eating me up inside!

I decided to go to the barn and work off some of this nervous energy. I took the phone with me, but the damn thing wouldn't ring. I cleaned up the stables and curried the horses, filled their grain buckets and put down some fresh straw. After working up a good sweat, I felt a little better. Bo and Buck were full of energy and chased sticks I was throwing for them outside the barn. I suspected they were missing Vince as well because he was the one who played with them the most when he was home.

I decided to go into my office and check out some of my guns and maybe do a little inventory. I had a gun safe built into one of the walls. The wall panel would slide open with the flip of an electric switch; something Mike designed for me a number of years ago. I took out my favorite, an old model 70 Winchester with a custom target barrel chambered in 30-06. That gun I had made for me in 1975 and it was like an extension of my body. I had plenty of other guns; but this old model 70 was a shooter. As I was sifting through some of my things; I found stuff I forgot I even had. A pair of infrared binoculars I bought in Australia years ago, some forty year old metal ammo boxes, rocket type flares and a box of MRE's (meals ready to eat). Now these delicacies I had to try. This box had 1972 stamped on the side and was never opened. I must admit that there was a time in my life when these were the only thing I had to eat; they tasted pretty good. My devious mind thought; tonight I'm going to prepare a special meal for my family. I pulled out five packs of roast beef for tonight's dinner. Ann and the kids would get the rare opportunity to experience the US Army's gourmet meals.

Ann came home and said she had a nice day away, but she was anxiously waiting for me to call with some news throughout the day. When Tara and John got home, I told them all that I was preparing a special surprise for dinner tonight and they could all be seated at the dinning room table. I brought out the four steaming packets and gave each person one. The looks on their faces was priceless. John who was normally very quiet asked "What the hell is this?" I told him it was roast beef, mashed potatoes and gravy, enjoy!! Ann asked if I was sure they were ok to eat. I assured her I tried one for lunch and thought it was fine. I then reminded them that thousands of troops all over the world had eaten them and survived quite well. They all tried it and in unison said it wasn't too bad. Tara asked "Is this all we are having, this little bag of stuff?" I excused myself and went to the basement and got a pizza out the oven; I put the pizza in earlier as a backup. When I got back upstairs with the pizza there was a big cheer from the dinner table. Tara reminded me she was eating for two and that little bag of stuff was not going to cut it. We all had a good laugh about the MRE's for dinner and for a little while it was a happy house again.

Around 8:45 the next morning the phone rang, it was Jay McMurray. He said he would be touching down at the Phoenix airport in an hour. I told him I would be there to pick him up. I told Ann Jay was coming in and she just rolled her eyes. I was glad my old friend was coming. Although Ann liked Jay; she knew when we got together things seemed to happen, some good, some not so good.

Jay was a throwback to the old west; one of those guys that was born 100 years too late. He was a man of his word and a handshake was as good to him as any legal document an attorney could draw up. Speaking of handshakes; his was the most powerful I'd ever encountered. His hands were big and strong from years of tossing logs and cattle. Jay loved to approach some unsuspecting young man with an arrogant attitude and offer to shake his hand. Jay delighted in putting a man on his knees with one big squeeze. I'd seen him do it countless times over the years and never saw anyone who was not put to their knees, including me. If Jay liked you, you had a friend for life. Likewise if he didn't like you, he would not have a problem telling you so right up front. When we first met, he looked at my hands and said "you have the hands of a working man Bill and I like that." It would be good to have my old friend with me again, maybe between the two of us we could get my son back.

I got to the airport and found out where I could find Jay. When I got to the terminal, I could see him talking to one of the security people. Jay was trying to talk the guy into letting me drive my truck to his plane to unload his things. The security guy told Jay he would have to allow him to check his luggage before he could take it from the airport. I could see that Jay was not going to allow that to happen and I had a pretty good idea why.

I suggested to Jay that he make arrangements to take his plane to a private airport a few miles away. The security officer said that might be a good idea, because there was no way Jay was unloading this stuff here without it being checked first. Jay made a few phone calls and I called a friend I knew at the other airport and the arrangements were made. An hour later I met Jay at the other airport. I was able to drive my truck to his plane and we unloaded his things into my truck. I thanked my friend at the airport and Jay said let's get the hell out of here. When we got to my house and started unloading Jay's things, there was a big black old beat up trunk with a lock on it that we unloaded last and it was heavy. I looked at Jay and asked "OK, what is in here?" Jay said "just a few essentials." He unlocked the trunk and inside was an arsenal. Two semi-automatic rifles, hand grenades, claymore mines, a hand held rocket launcher with rockets, his trusty old model 70 Winchester and a lot of ammo!! I knew that's why he didn't want to have this stuff checked at the airport.

Jay looked at me, winked and asked with a grin "You think I forgot anything?" I just shook my head and told him to not let Ann see all this stuff or she won't let us go outside to play. We both hugged and laughed and we left the old trunk locked in the back of my truck. We went inside and Ann greeted Jay with a hug and a kiss and showed him to his room.

I was so glad to see Jay, for a little while I forgot why he came here in the first place. I called Bob Tucker to see if he had any news for us. Bob said they were still digging but at this point they really didn't have anything new. Bob said he knew me well enough to know I was getting frustrated and he asked me to try to be patient and let them do their job. I didn't say anything to Bob, but in my mind I was thinking you've got one more day. While I was on the phone, Jay and Ann were catching up and talking about old times. When I walked into the room, Ann looked at me and asked "OK, what are you two going to do?" Jay echoed her words and asked "Yeah, what are we going to do?" I said "I don't know but we are going to make some plans and we are going to get our son back." Ann said "I know you are going to try something and I want to be in on the plan. I want to know where you are going and am included in any plans you guys make." I assured her we would include her in whatever we decided.

I called Mike Warren, my foreman, and asked if he would check with Raul to see if the two of them could come over to the house this evening. Mike said "hang on a minute, Raul is working with me right now and I will ask him." Mike said "ok boss, we'll be over tonight around seven o'clock.

Later that afternoon when Kara and John came home, Jay entertained them with some stories of my past. Jay was known to embellish things a bit and he hadn't lost his touch. He related a story of how he and I got into some trouble while in South America and how he saved my butt from being cut up by a couple of rebels. According to Jay, he jumped in to save the day. It's not exactly the way I remember it, but I let him have his fun. The facts were over the course of a few years we saved each others butts more than a few times. There was no one I would trust my life to more than Jay. Besides, over the years I'm sure I told quite a few Jay stories to my family as well.

After dinner that evening, Mike and Raul stopped by to talk. Raul brought some maps and contact information along with him about the part of Mexico he grew up in. Raul also mentioned he knew some people in Phoenix who could maybe help us. These people had been burned by some of the gang activity in the area, but would not talk to the police about it. They feared some kind of retaliation by the gangs. He said he would set up a meeting with them if I liked. Obviously, I said "set it up." Mike told me there were several other employees who came to him willing to help in any way they could. Two of them were former gang members who could possibly provide us with some information.

Just like that things were starting to come together. Jay winked at me and said "For some reason these here Mexicans seem to like you Billy." I told him maybe it was because I paid their wages. Raul said "No sir boss, you treat us with respect and we respect you as well, we want to help." I thanked him for that.

I could see a truck pull in the driveway and then another one. It seemed there was several more parking out around the horse barn. I looked at Ann and said "what the hell is going on!" We all went outside and there was 15-20 people making their way to the house. I recognized some of the guys who worked for my company and their families and some of the people I didn't know. Mike stepped in and said "Everybody is concerned and wants to help, so I hope you don't mind I told them to stop by tonight." I was so humbled all I could do was cry. Ann and I hugged and cried together and we invited everyone to come inside.

Most of the people brought food, all of them offered to help in any way they could. Some of the men offered to act as guides for us in Mexico, some of them even offered to fight beside us if we chose to do so. We prayed together, cried together and I know my family was deeply touched by this showing of concern. I think I even saw a tear from old Jay that he quickly tried to hide. My faith in my fellow man was renewed a bit this night.

It appears we have a lot more support and resources than we were aware of having. One of my other employees, Sammy, has a brother who works at the border crossing as an inspector for Mexican customs. Sammy said he would be glad to talk to his brother about helping us get across the border. I told Sammy to make it happen. This was a big piece of the puzzle I was concerned about. With the gear that Jay brought and my own gear; we could easily be arrested as terrorists trying to cross the border in either direction. We had enough explosives and weapons to start a small war. In my mind at least, this may be a war until I got my son back.

Some of the people hung around until almost midnight and it turned out to be an inspirational day. After they all left and everyone else went to bed, I sat in my office alone contemplating the task ahead of us. My mind was racing with different scenarios, what might work, what wouldn't work, could I control myself and Jay to think clearly and methodically like we were taught, were we too old for this mission and worst of all was I fooling myself into thinking Vince was still alive.

I had to remain positive and I was not ready to admit that Vince was probably dead. Tomorrow we would begin to plan in earnest. Tomorrow would be our last day of waiting. Hopefully, tomorrow the FBI would bring Vince home to us. If not, we would be ready to take some action on our own.

At 9:00 the following morning there was a knock at the front door. Ann and I looked at each other and I know she was thinking the same thing I was; this is it, they found Vince. My stomach tightened and we answered the door holding hands, hoping for the best and fearing the worst. John and Kara were right behind us and I could hear Kara sobbing.

When I answered the door it was agents Hanson, Nicholas and Bob Tucker, alone. My heart sank as I said "I hope you have some good news for us." Hanson said "I'm sorry we have not found your son yet, but we need to talk." We invited them all in and we sat down in the living room.

Hanson said they had information that I might be planning to take matters into my own hands. I asked them what information they had. Hanson said they knew Jay McMurray was here and that the two of us had extensive training in the military and beyond. He said they knew we have been meeting with various people to set up a rescue plan. Bob said "Look Bill, I know you and I know you are a take charge kind of guy. You have been patient so far and I know it must be killing you inside. Please, allow us to follow through with this case.

Hanson said "We are continuing to investigate every lead we have and the Mexican authorities are doing the same, but it's just going to take some more time." He added "I would hate to have to arrest you for obstructing our investigation."

I did not like to be threatened. I walked to the door, opened it and asked them to leave. As they were leaving I told them they would have to do what they had to do and I would do the same. That was it; I guess we each played our cards. Ann looked at me and said "Let's do it!" We all held hands, including old tough guy Jay and we prayed for guidance.

Chapter 6

NO MORE WAITING

After we prayed, Ann said "You guys are going to need someone to coordinate things for you and have a base of operations and I am that person!" Jay and I stood and saluted Ann and said "Yes Mam!!" in unison. Our coordinator got out a note pad and said we were going to make a list of supplies. First was communications, I had a pair of satellite phones and Jay had one of his own. I would take my laptop with me as well. Our next issue with communication was to set up a network of contacts from Phoenix into Mexico. We would need the help of some of my employees and their friends and families for that to happen. Ann has more of a gift of gab than I do, so we left her handle that assignment also.

The next was personnel. Jay and I were in charge of that department. Although we had a number of volunteers like John and Mike, Raul and a few of his friends, some of whom we didn't even know, we were both adamant it would only be the two of us. John who was sitting in the same room listening to all of this objected and said "I really want to help get Vince back and I really want to go along with you guys." I said "Look John, I know you want to help but you don't have the skills that Jay and have. I don't want to be responsible for something happening to you. These are probably some nasty people we will be dealing with and Jay and I have dealt with their types before. Besides after this thing is over we may need you and your fathers' legal skills and I am counting on you for that." John hung his head and said softly, "I guess your right."

Next on the list was equipment. I felt like I should get my truck reinforced a bit in case we had to travel some rough terrain. Maybe put some steel plates on the undercarriage to protect the oil pan and transfer case, a couple of extra tires and wheels and a reinforced front bumper. I figured I could have all this done tomorrow at the welding shop I did business with.

I had a tent and sleeping bags, extra five gallon water jugs and fuel containers and a camping stove. We would need to buy some food and a couple of cots for keeping our old bodies off the ground, if we had to sleep outside for a few nights. I already had flashlights and tools in the truck, so by tomorrow night we would be ready.

Ann said "There's one thing we haven't discussed yet." I looked at her and asked "What's that?" She said "All that fire power in the back of the truck. Do you really think your going to need all that stuff? You guys even have bombs in there!!" Jay said "Oh Annie, they're not bombs, they're land mines." She hated being called Annie and Jay knew he just screwed up. Ann asked "What the hell would you use land mines for?" Jay was trying his best to smooth things over and said "Those mines are our back up. If we get in a jam, they might cover our butts for us. I've had those things forever and never had to use them." Ann just shook her head, knowing there was no use in trying to argue with Jay. I should have known better than trying to keep that stuff a secret from her. Ann told us to go out and make sure we had all the weapons we needed and she would get on the phone to start lining up the contacts we needed along the way.

John came along outside with us and asked to see the land mines because he had never seen one before except for on television. Jay was more than happy to show him. John asked Jay where he got them and the only thing he would say was from a friend. Jay said they were old but they still worked. He sat John up perfectly for John to ask the next question "How do you know that?"

Jay went on to say about six months ago he was bored and decided to see if they still worked. He took one out in one of his fields and planted it. He then rigged up a rock tied to a heavy rope with a big knot tied above the rock. He suspended the rock directly over the mine and tied the rope off to a nearby tree. He then walked back about 100 yards and settled in behind a big tree and took aim with his rifle at the big knot tied above the rock. He shot the knot off, the rock dropped on the mine and in Jay's words "There was one hell of an explosion!" I asked Jay how big the knot was and he said about the size of a baseball. Then I asked how many shots it took. He said two, it was a windy day! John was duly impressed. I don't know if the story is true or not but that is classic Jay.

Jay and I walked out to the horse barn. We sat down on some hay bales and he looked at me and asked "What the hell are we going to do?" I told Jay my first thoughts are we need to gather as much intell as we can about where these guys hole up when they are in this country. I think we can use our own contacts to find that out. Between Raul and Sammy and their families, we have an edge the police don't. They can get us the information from these people they won't give to the police. We may have to crack some heads to find where they operate across the border but I think we can handle that.

I got on the phone to Sammy and Raul and told them what we needed. They both agreed to get on it and they would get back to me as soon as they had any information. Jay and I knew we had enough fire power to do whatever we needed to do, the question was could these old bodies take and give a beating like they used to do. We both joked about it but for me at least there was some doubt.

We discussed taking either Sammy or Raul with us if we had to cross the border to interpret for us. My Spanish was not good enough to carry on conversations with strangers. I didn't want to put either one of them in any danger, but we both felt we needed someone to speak the language for us and maybe help to open some doors for us as well. If things went well maybe we wouldn't even have to cross the border. I also decided I was going to approach Bob Tucker for whatever he could give me as far as intell he had. He may or may not give me anything; it would be up to him. He would still be my friend either way.

Jay felt it would make sense to focus on some of the gangs locally and get as much out of them as we could; I agreed. We would wait for Sammy and Raul to call back. I called Sheriff Bob Tucker and after a big sigh from him; Bob told us to come into his office and we would talk. I had no idea whether Bob was going to give us anything or preach to us but we were about to find out.

On the way to Bob's office, Jay asked me what kind of guy this Sheriff was. I told Jay he was one of us; but I didn't think he would put his job on the line to help us. We went into Bob's office and he just shook his head and said "I knew we would be having this conversation at some point. What are you guys planning to do?" I told Bob we just needed some names to work with in this area. I told him we had people who could open some doors that were probably closed to him and the FBI. Bob asked if we planned to work with him and keep him abreast of what we were up to or not. I assured him we would keep him in the loop. He asked what kind of weapons we had and Jay simply answered "Adequate." Bob scratched his head and went to a filing cabinet and dug out a file and handed it to me. He handed me a piece of paper and told me to write down the four names that were on the top page in the file. He then took the file back and put it in the filing cabinet. Bob told us they were sure that one or all of these four men were involved in Vince's kidnapping, but they have been unable to locate any of them. Bob looked me straight in the eyes and said "Don't make me regret doing this." I thanked Bob and we left his office.

I called Sammy and Raul and gave them the names. Sammy said he recognized two of the names as some bad dudes who hung around his neighborhood. Jay and I went back to the house to wait for the phone to ring.

When we got home, Ann was busy talking on the phone and setting up a network of contacts from Phoenix to the Mexican border. She told us she had three other women making calls to Mexico to line up a network for us across the border. When she got off the phone, she showed us what she had mapped out for us so far. She had done a great job of setting up contacts and check points for us. Apparently a number of these contacts had family or friends who had been affected by these kidnappings and were willing to help to do whatever they could to stop them.

Jay and I decided to round up the supplies we might need. We dug through my stuff and found a tent and some sleeping bags, some cooking utensils, lanterns, satellite phones, walkie talkies and a bag full of possibles. A possibles bag contains things you might possibly need sometime, tools, duct tape, glue, etc. Most of this stuff I only use during hunting season when we move into a back country camp for a week or two.

While we were rooting through my things I found an old knife Jay bought for me when we were working in Africa. He bought it from an old man in a local village we were trying to help liberate. I asked Jay if he remembered the old man's name. He said he would never forget. His name was Albert Albert, and when the old man introduced himself he would say "You can call me Albert."

As were gathering things together, Mike, Raul and Sammy pulled in. They told us they located one of the men who were on the list and he was in Phoenix as of 45 minutes ago. Sammy said the guy was hanging out with some gang members at a downtown club and they were probably drinking and most likely armed. All three men said they wanted to go with us if we were going after this man. I told them "We are most assuredly going after this man but I wasn't too sure I wanted the three of them involved." Mike said "I'm not asking permission to go with you; we are going." Raul and Sammy agreed. I reluctantly said ok but they would back up Jay and me if we got into trouble. We all piled into Mike's truck and headed for town.

When we arrived at the club there were a bunch of guys standing around outside and they all checked us out when we pulled in. Sammy identified the guy we were looking for as soon as we stopped. He was dressed in jeans and a faded leather vest and drinking a beer. His name was Jimmie and he was surrounded by five or six other guys. We could see some of the other men were carrying handguns but could not see one on Jimmie. Jay asked "How we gonna play this?" Sammy told me on the way in that Jimmie was a truck driver who was laid off his job, so I told Jay I was going to offer him a job. Jay looked at me like I was nuts.

I walked across the street and asked if anybody here was looking for a job driving truck. One of the guys asked who wants to know. I told them I owned a rig that was loaded and ready to go to Chicago and it had to be there the day after tomorrow. The pay was good and it would be cash. One fellow said he might be interested and I asked if he had his CDL (commercial driver's license) and he asked "what's that?" I asked if there was anyone else and Jimmie said "Yeh, maybe I might be interested, what's the pay?" I told him $2000.00 cash. I told Jimmie if he was interested I would like him to come with me now to make sure he was capable of driving the rig. I told him I would bring him back when we were done. Jimmie looked at his buddies and they slapped each other's hands, Jimmie looked at me and said "Let's go."

That was almost too easy, maybe these guys were not as smart as we thought they were. Jimmie walked across the street with me and looked inside and hesitated when he saw four other men inside. He asked me who these guys were and I told him the three men in the back were all applying for the truck driving job as well as him and introduced him to my friend Jay in the front seat. I told Jimmie to sit upfront with Jay and me. He got in but I could see he was a little nervous riding with these other men. Jay made small talk and joked with Jimmie and he seemed to settle down as we left town.

I drove towards the old mine shaft where we dropped the money earlier and when we got to an old ranch road; I turned off and traveled back to an old abandoned ranch house. I parked the truck and before Jimmie could get out; Jay stuck a handgun in Jimmie's ribs and told him not to move. Jimmie said "What the hell is this, where's the truck." Before anyone answered; Mike had another handgun stuck in the back of Jimmie's neck and we all heard the unmistakable click of the gun being cocked.

I got out and walked over to Jimmie's door and opened it. I said to Jimmie "Now that we have your attention; I'm only going to ask you one time "What do you know about the kidnapping that took place at the old mine shaft four days ago? Before you answer; know that the boy you took is my son and I will do anything to get him back. My friends and I will not think twice about killing you and leaving you here for the coyotes and buzzards to pick you clean."

Jimmie said he had nothing to do with that kidnapping. I asked him who did. He said he was not sure. At that point the click of Jay's handgun being cocked got Jimmie's attention. He said "Ok, ok, I might know someone who was involved." I told him to give me a name. Jimmie said "If I do, they will kill me." I explain to him, if he didn't I would kill him right now. He asked "If I tell you, will you let me go?" I said "I will."

He told me the man I wanted was Juan Cruz. He said Juan was a bad dude who ran a drug and kidnapping gang that operated in this area. The name Juan Cruz was the first one on the list of names Sheriff Bob gave to me. I asked where I could find Juan Cruz and Jimmie said he didn't know for sure. I asked where he hung out and Jimmie said sometimes at the club where we picked him up and sometimes he spent time down in Chihuahua, Mexico. Jimmie said Cruz had a house in Phoenix but he didn't know where it was located. I asked him when the last time was he saw Cruz and Jimmie said about 3 or 4 days ago.

I told Jimmie to get out of the truck. I had to know if he was telling me the truth. Between Jay and me; we'd interrogated enough people to learn body language and speech patterns to figure out what was true or not. I pulled out my handgun and stuck it in Jimmie's face. I asked him again if he had anything to do with my son's kidnapping. He pleaded with me to not shoot him and swore he did not. As I looked at him, I could see urine dropping out the bottom of his pants onto his shoes. For me that was the sign he was telling the truth.

We left Jimmie where we parked; tied to the front porch of the old ranch house. I called Sheriff Tucker and let him know we had a present waiting for him at the ranch. Jimmie supplied us with the names and descriptions of three other men who were now at the club who could give us the information we needed to find Cruz.

We went back into town and picked up Sammy's car and drove back to the club. We parked a couple of blocks away so nobody would recognize us. Sammy called a couple of his friends to meet him at the club and they would help Sammy identify any of the men we were looking for. This time it may not be as easy; Jay and I figured we may have to pick up one of these guys after they leave the club. It would probably be a long wait as these guys were partying pretty hard. We weren't too concerned about Jimmie ratting us out because the sheriff should keep him occupied for a while. The four of us settled into Sammy's car and left the others to find the men we were looking for. This was a pretty bad part of town and there were a number of gang punks walking by the car making stupid comments and gestures. After an hour or so, we were all getting tired of it. We all got out of the car to stretch our legs and it seemed to bring more of these clowns out of the woodwork.

One group of enterprising young men came up to us and asked what we were doing here. One loud mouth poked his finger in Jay's chest and asked "You deaf old man, what you doing here?" While the kid was waving his hand in front of Jay's face; Jay grabbed his hand and bent it behind the kids back and put him to his knees. Jay calmly said "I'm looking for someone to shine my shoes; while you're down there; you interested." The group of young men drifted away from us.

We figured we better stay in the car and behave because we didn't want to draw too much attention to ourselves.

It was now 1am and it seemed we'd been waiting for ever. We saw Sammy and one of his friends come out of the club and follow two men down the street away from us. Sammy motioned for us to follow these guys. I pulled the car out onto the street and drove past the men and turned into a side street and stopped in front of them. They both pounded on the hood of the car and were hollering for me to get out of the way. One of them said "You don't want to mess with us, man!" We all got out of the car and surrounded the two men and I said to them "You're wrong, we do want to mess with you."

We disarmed them and escorted the two men into a back alley and sat them down on an old back seat of a car that was leaning against a brick wall. The mouthpiece of the two asked "Who are you, man? What do you want?" I told him I wanted information and I was not going to play games. They had two choices; either tell me what I wanted to know or die. The mouthpiece said "You must be crazy man, this is our turf, and we will kill you people."

I looked at the quiet one and said "Listen carefully; I'm only giving you one chance to answer correctly." I pulled out my handgun and pointed at his head. "Four days ago you were part of a gang who kidnapped my son; I want him back. I also want Juan Cruz. Tell me where my son and Cruz are and you live. Lie to me and you will both die right here, right now." At the same time there were four more guns pointed at the two men. The quiet one said "Yes, yes senor, I was part of the kidnapping but I don't know where your son is and I don't know where Cruz is right now. All I know is something went wrong and Cruz took your son away. He probably took him across the border." I asked him where across the border. He told me Cruz had two or three places. Two of them were in the mountains east of Chihuahua and the third was in a valley south of the Chihuahua. I handed him a piece of paper and told him to draw me a map. His hands were shaking so bad I didn't know if he could draw or not. He started to draw and his buddy spit on him and called a dead man in Spanish.

I turned to the bigmouth and said "Now it's your turn. I want to know how many men Cruz has with him and also where his house is located here in Phoenix." He spit on me and called me a dead man in Spanish also. I shot him in the calf of his right leg and while he was writhing in pain in the alley, I grabbed his hair and said "Last chance; answer my question." He gave me the address of Cruz's house and told me he had between 6-8 men with him most of the time.

Jay looked at me and asked "You want me to kill them?" Both men got wide eyed and pleaded for their lives. I had no intention of killing them but I did want them to maybe feel some of the fear Vince felt when he was taken. I took the map and said we would tie them up here and call the Sheriff's office to pick them up. I was sure Sheriff Bob would be calling me before too long. I wiped the gun clean and wrapped the quiet man's hand around the handgun I used to shoot the bigmouth with so his fingerprints would be on the gun. I knew the gun was untraceable. I figured that would keep the police busy for a while trying to figure out what happened. I waited until we were quite a distance from the alley and called the Sheriff's office to report a shooting.

Our next stop was Cruz's house. We parked some distance away from the house and Jay and I moved in on foot. There was a car parked outside and we could see a couple of people moving around inside. Jay said "Let me handle this one, you can't have all the fun!" Jay knocked on the front door and a young woman answered. He told her his car broke down and wondered if there was anybody here who could help him jump his battery.

The woman said she and her sister were the only one's here and they didn't know how to jump a battery. Jay thanked her for her time and he moved off the porch to the side walk where I was waiting. We watched from outside for a while and concluded she was probably telling the truth as we didn't see anyone else around. We figured with two nice looking young females here; if there were any men around they would be close by. It appeared the fellow was right when he told us earlier that Cruz was in Mexico.

When we got back to the truck, Mike said "You had a phone call on your cell while we gone." I gave Mike my phone so I wouldn't be disturbed while we were checking out Cruz's house. The call was from Bob Tucker.

We decided to go back to my house and everybody would go home for tonight before I would call Bob back. When we arrived back at my place, I told Mike, Sammy and Raul to head out so they wouldn't be involved in this, if things got ugly.

Jay and I went inside and we explained most of what went on tonight to Ann. I told her I needed to call Bob Tucker back and we would talk some more. Bob answered his phone and said "You've been a busy bee today. We picked up your package earlier today and he said you threatened to kill him. He also said you were a crazy s.o.b. It turned out the state police had several warrants on him, so I guess I should thank you for that." I said "You're welcome."

Bob asked me "What do you know about two men found in an alley a couple of hours ago. He said one of them had a gunshot wound to his leg." I didn't like lying to Bob but I was in this too far now. I told Bob "I don't know anything about that." Bob said the two of them were known associates of Juan Cruz's. Bob also told me "Look Bill, these guys are not talking to us, which is probably good for you. You can't be shooting up people in my town. Friendship aside, if I find evidence of your involvement I'm going to have to arrest you and anyone else involved." I told Bob I understood and would not expect anything less. Bob asked "Off the record, did you find out where Cruz is?" I gave Bob the address of Cruz's house and told him he wasn't home right now. Bob ended the conversation telling me to be careful.

It had been a long day and we decided to go to bed. Ann and I talked most of the night in bed. We both knew from here on out it was going to get tougher to get Vince back, but we had to try. We both had this ache inside our hearts that Vince was probably dead but we would not give up until we had the truth.

Chapter 7

THE HUNT IS ON

John and Tara joined the three of us for breakfast the next morning. We discussed the previous day's events and we needed to make plans for us to head down to Mexico. John asked "How can you guys get the information that the police cannot?" I explained "The police had to operate within the confines of the law; Jay and I did not. We could use more creative ways to get people to give us information. As my attorney, that's all he needs to know for now." I told John "We have reached the point where we may now need his and his father's expertise to get us through this deal. I asked him to check with his father to see if he had any legal contacts in Mexico." John told me "That was already taken care of. Here are the names of an attorney and private investigator in Mexico should we need their services." John also indicated they were both willing to donate their time to help us. I knew there was a reason I liked this kid!

I asked Ann to touch base with the P.I. and let him know I would be contacting him shortly. He could certainly help us in tracking down this scum. Jay and I double checked our equipment and we felt we were ready to go. Jay poked me in the ribs and asked "Are you seeing what I am seeing?" I said "If you mean the car that has been parked about ¼ mile away all morning, yes, I see it." Usually the first thing I did when I got up in the morning was look around outside from my bedroom window with my binoculars. Normally, I was looking for deer or antelope, but lately I was looking for people looking at me. We both knew it was the FBI keeping tabs on us. Jay got his spotting scope out and crouched behind the truck to check them out. Jay said "These guys need to get some better equipment; all they have is a pair of 10 or 12mm binoculars. With this spotting scope I can see the guy with the bino's didn't shave this morning!" We decided to pull my truck over by the horse barn to make it more difficult for the agents to see us and maybe have a little fun with them.

I backed up to the horse trailer and we pulled it around to the barn to load up some grain, hay and water for the horses. Around here you don't go anywhere without water, it can get pretty dry.

I decided to take Spook, a big white gelding who was great on mountain trails and Manny, a paint mare who was good on trails as long as she could follow Spook. She did not like to lead and Spook did not like to follow; as long as we remembered that we should be fine. We loaded the saddles and other tack we would need onto the trailer and decided to hold off on loading the horses until we were ready to go.

Jay and I needed to decide if we wanted to take Raul along to interpret for us. Sammy couldn't go as his wife was expecting a baby shortly and we had no idea how long we would be gone. After booting it around for a while, we both felt we needed someone to speak for us and help open some doors. Raul would go with us. We decided against another horse because we needed someone to guard the truck and equipment if we took off on horseback. I called Raul on his cellphone and told him to get his things ready; we would be picking him up later today. He seemed happy he was going along. Except for the horses and Raul we were ready to rock and roll.

Back at the house, Ann told us our contact at the border crossing would be working the 3-11pm shift and we should call him on his cellphone when we were approaching the border. Jay looked out the window and said our watchdogs were still out there. At this point, they had only suspicions of what we were doing and they had no proof we'd done anything wrong. We were both sure they would somehow try to stop us, probably at the border. I called John's father Greg to see if he knew anyone who could smooth out our crossing into Mexico. We only needed help to get past US customs because we had Mexican customs covered. Greg told me to sit tight he would make a call.

We waited about an hour and Greg called back. It turned out he knew a customs official who had an ax to grind with the FBI and he assured Greg the FBI would not use customs to interfere with our crossing. I thanked Greg and it looked like we had smooth sailing. It looked like this was one time a politician could actually help us.

We went back out to the barn and loaded Spook and Manny on the trailer and I called Raul and told him we would pick him in 15 minutes. We all held hands and said a prayer for safety and the safe return of Vince. Ann and Tara gave me a hug and a kiss and we said our goodbyes. Ann even hugged Jay and told him to bring me back safe.

As Jay and I were pulling out of the driveway; a flood of memories came into my mind. The two of us had been through a lot together; we both trusted each other with our lives. Jay slapped me on the knee and said "Well partner, it feels good to be back in the saddle with you again!" I agreed. I knew there was a Jay story coming! "Remember that time in the Congo when we got our jeep blown out from under us? Those rebels thought they killed us but all they did was piss us off." Jay slapped his knee and laughed. "Remember the look on their faces when they came sneakin' in to make sure we were dead? They looked real shit faced when we rolled out from under the jeep and mowed 'em down with our AK-47's!" I reminded Jay that as much fun as that seemed, he ended up with a broken arm and I had concussion from that little escapade. Jay's comment was "Well ya', but that was a long time ago." I could only shake my head.

We stopped by Raul's place to pick him up and he was ready to go. I told Raul there would be no hard feelings if he chose not to go with us. He said "No way, Senor Bill, I am pleased to help you." We were ready to head south. I was glad to get on the road, to finally be taking action to get my son back. I had no idea what to expect. All I was sure of was I was prepared to do whatever it took to see Vince again.

While we were heading south, Jay was keeping Raul entertained with some stories of our past. Jay had a way of romancing his stories and making them more colorful over time. Raul was soaking it all in. He said to me "Senor Bill, I see why you are such a good shot and you never seem to be afraid of anything." I told him "That's not true; I'd been afraid many times. Like the time Jay told me he knew how to fly a helicopter. It was only after we were airborne that he told me this was the first time he actually flew one. Or the time we were pinned down by enemy fire and he was spotting for me as I was shooting. I asked him how many North Vietnamese he could see. He told me there were only three or four; keep shooting. It turned out there were actually 30 or 40. We ended up crawling on our bellies for 500 yards through elephant grass and spent the night hiding in the tree tops while the NVA were searching for us on the ground beneath us." Jay chuckled and said "I never was very good at math!"

As we were approaching the border, I asked Jay to call our contact on the Mexican side and give him a description of our vehicle and an ETA of crossing. I was very nervous about US Customs pulling us out of line and searching our vehicle and trailer. As we pulled up there were the usual questions; where we were headed, was this business or pleasure, did we have any weapons and so on. The agent told me to go ahead and have a nice trip. When we pulled up to Mexican customs it was the same usual questions and we were told welcome to Mexico, proceed. There was a big sigh of relief from all of us. I told Raul "You just witnessed another time I was afraid!! We went a couple of miles down the road and I pulled over to let Raul drive. My knees were weak from nerves and when I stepped out of the truck and I stumbled a bit when I hit the ground.

Raul knew this country better than I did and I thought I would try to catch a little sleep. We had a couple of hours drive until we got to Raul's family. I couldn't really sleep but it was nice to rest my eyes. Jay was quiet except for the occasional snoring. I remembered that snoring almost got us in trouble a couple of times.

A lot of our former job was reconnaissance. Our lives depended on being quiet and being able to slip in and out of situations undetected. Many times we would spend days moving a short distance or we would spend days in one location. Jay snored when he slept on his back and it was my job back then to make sure he never slept on his back. Right now I didn't care if he snored but maybe later I would.

It was 10pm and we pulled into a little truck stop to grab a bite to eat and get some fuel. I checked on the horses and they were doing fine. I was really glad we brought Raul along because he could talk fluently with these people. I was struggling to understand a lot of what was being said because to me they talked so fast. Although most of them could speak

English obviously they preferred to speak Spanish. Jay didn't understand much Spanish and was constantly asking me "What did he say?"

We hit the road and in another hour we reached Raul's brother Paul's house. His brother had a small ranch where he raised horses and cattle. Raul and his brother rattled off in Spanish to each other and fortunately for Jay and me, Paul could also speak English very well. He showed us to a bunk house where we could spend the night and we put Spook and Manny in a small corral for the night.

The next morning we had breakfast and we decided to make a trip into Chihuahua to check a known location that Cruz was supposed to frequent. We left the horses and trailer at Paul's place. We had an address and we drove by the location. We didn't see anyone around and decided to park a block away and just watch the house for a while. It was a large old house with a chain link fence around the perimeter. There was a pickup truck and a car in the driveway but no sign of anyone being around. Raul said he would find out if anyone locally saw any activity around the house the last day or two. He had family that lived in the area and they always knew when these guys were around. Jay and I stayed in the truck as we would probably stick out like a couple of sore thumbs in this neighborhood.

We could see Raul hugging and talking with a number of people, it was obvious they knew him well. He came back to the truck and said there has been no one around for the last week. He said his friends and family would watch the house for us and would let him know when anyone came back. They did not like these men and would be happy if they would be arrested and taken away. They bullied the neighborhood residents and unfortunately the people who lived here were afraid of them and afraid of retaliation if someone turned them in.

Our next step was to find the mountain hideout where Cruz and his men were probably holed up. We dug out the map the guy from Phoenix made for us and double checked it with a local map for accuracy. It was surprisingly accurate; we must have gotten the guy's attention. We thought we were able to find a way to get into the area without using the horses. We wouldn't know that for sure until we tried it. We went back to Paul's ranch and he went along with us into the mountains to help to show us the way. He told us there were a number of unmarked roads we could probably use to get into the spot where Cruz's camp was supposed to be.

I felt good about finally doing something positive to find Vince. He had to be here because we eliminated the other two places where these clowns hung out. Paul guided us into the back country on some roads we had no idea were even there. We twisted and turned and squeezed in and around some spots I wasn't sure we could make. After an hour of following Paul's directions, we drove to the top of a ridge and parked the truck. Paul felt the spot we were looking for was in a ravine at the bottom of this ridge. We got out the spotting scope and binoculars and scoured the area for any sign of a building or vehicles. Jay spotted a flash of light from a reflection of the sun off of something down it the ravine. The area had some heavy cover of thick brush and it was difficult to see much. Jay put the spotting scope on the object and he could tell it was a pickup truck. Game on!!

Jay and I decided to move in closer to get a better look. We both loaded up with a handgun and optics. Paul and Raul remained at the truck; I did not want them involved in any gunfight if it came to that. We were just going to assess the situation, but things do go wrong. We eased down the hill to a spot where we had a better vantage point. There were two small cabins and two full size pickup trucks parked nearby. Two men were sitting outside one of the cabins and we could see they were each armed with an automatic rifle. There were probably more men inside and possibly Vince as well. We needed to get a closer look.

Jay looked at me and said "we best wait for dark." I agreed. We were probably out manned and we were obviously able to move around undetected after dark. Both of us headed back to the truck to wait until it was dark. Back at the truck we filled in Paul and Raul what we planned to do. They wanted to help but I told them when they heard us coming back, get the truck fired up and ready to bug out of here. There were still a couple of hours until it got dark, so we would just have to wait. Waiting was torture, those couple of hours seemed like a day. I sensed we were close and had to remind myself to be patient. I busied myself packing odds and ends of things in my backpack. I double checked my handgun and rifle. I stuffed a couple of grenades in my coat pocket. I had extra magazines for my handgun loaded and ready, Jay was doing the same thing.

It was peaceful and quiet out here. Under other circumstances, it would be exactly the setting I would enjoy. Some birds singing and squirrels scurrying in the dried leaves always looking for something to eat were about the only sounds we heard. Occasionally we could hear a truck door slam or somebody talking below us but it was too far away to understand what they were saying. I was kind of nervous; it had been a long time since I was involved in a situation like this. I knew my reflexes were not as quick as they used to be. On the other hand I believed I was more level headed and methodical then when I was 20 years old. I wasn't sure about Jay; I knew he could handle the pressure, but was he physically able to handle it. I also remembered my instructors telling me there was no room for doubt. Doubt and fear were what got people killed.

It was finally time to move; the sun was down and it was getting dark down in the valley below us. Jay and I decided we would check out the two cabins first and come up with a game plan based on what we saw. From here on we would only communicate with hand signals. As we eased down the ridge my heart was pounding so hard I was afraid someone else would hear it. For the first time in 40 years we were stalking people not elk or deer. It was both scary and exhilarating. I could feel those old instincts coming back. Go slow; use the cover available, move like there was someone behind each tree. When we reached the valley floor; we could not see anyone outside. We split up. Jay moved towards the cabin on the left and I moved to the one on the right. Each cabin had a small window on each end. I eased into position to look inside. I could see two men and a young girl maybe 15 or 16 years old seated at a table. They were all eating. The men each had a handgun strapped to their side and I could see the girl had been tied at her wrists, by the rope burns around her wrists. They must have untied her to allow her to eat. She had a bandana hanging around her neck, probably used as a gag when she wasn't eating. I saw two beds in the one room cabin and I could see the lights were gas operated. There was an outhouse about 40 feet behind the two cabins.

I crept back to the place Jay and I decided to meet and waited for him to come back. Jay crawled in on his hands and knees and said there were two armed men in the cabin and he didn't see anyone else around. No sign of Vince. He told me there was a closet or some room with a closed door he couldn't see into. We decided to keep the gunplay to a minimum because of the hostage or hostages that might get injured. Jay said the two men were eating at a table right now. We figured with everybody eating right now; sooner or later somebody was going to need to use the outhouse. Hopefully it would be sooner.

We both moved around to the back of the cabins and waited for someone to come out the back door of either one. We needed to be quiet and quick with our actions. We waited for about 40 minutes and the back door of the cabin with the two men opened. One of the men made his way to the outhouse. Jay intercepted him and with one quick twist of the man's neck he was done for. Jay dragged him into the bushes and hid the body then came back to the rear of the cabin.

After waiting for 30 minutes; the second man came out of the back of the cabin and hollered in Spanish "Hey, did you fall in or did you fall asleep!" He grumbled something and stepped off the porch towards the outhouse. I jumped him and used the same maneuver to quiet him. Now we had to get the two men out of the other cabin; away from the girl. I whispered to Jay "Go into the empty cabin and start groaning like he was sick and be ready to take down whoever came in. I would try to draw them out." I went outside the front of the cabin dressed in the dead man's clothes and hollered for some help. My Spanish was good enough to tell them I needed help in the other cabin, my friend was very sick. Both men came out and headed for the cabin Jay was in. They told me to watch the girl. When the first man opened the door; Jay laid one on him with his big right hand. I jumped the second man before he got to the other cabin and knocked him out with a tree branch that was lying on the ground. We tied the two of them together and gagged them both to keep them quiet.

Jay went in to find the girl and released her from being tied to her bed and assured her we were here to help her. I went to the other cabin hoping Vince was in there. He was not. My heart sank. The door Jay saw earlier through the window was an empty closet. I tore through the cabin trying to find some clue that Vince was here or at least he had been here. I found nothing of Vince's.

I headed back out to the two men we tied up; they were going to give me the information I needed or they would die. The anger was boiling inside me and no one was going to stop me. I pulled out a picture of Vince and asked the first man "Have you seen this boy?" I took his gag off and he bit me on my arm. I lost it, my mind turned to rage and I beat the man until he was unconscious. Jay pulled me away from him or I probably would have killed him. I pulled the gag out of the second man's mouth and showed him Vince's picture and asked him if he ever saw him. He said "Si, si Senor, three days ago, the boy was here but he was taken away." He said he did not know where he was taken. I told the man if he wanted to live he would tell me the location of any places he knew of that my son could be. He gave me three locations that he said he knew of; none of which were familiar to me.

I wrote down the locations and told him if he was lying I would come back and hunt down his family and him and kill them all. I asked him his name and he said it was Gorge Gonzales. I also asked him if he knew a man named Juan Cruz. He said he knew Cruz but had not seen him for several days. I asked him if Cruz was the one who took my son away. He hung his head and reluctantly said "Si Senor." I put the gag back in his mouth.

While I was talking with this man; Jay was making sure the girl was ok and trying to calm her down. I was sure my actions did not make her confident we were the kind of people she could feel safe with.

I apologized to the girl for having to witness my anger. I asked her what her name was and she said it was Maria Turner. She said she lived in Phoenix and was taken from her family four days ago. I assured her we would see she got back to her family safe and sound. I showed her my picture of Vince and asked if she had seen him. She said no, she never saw him. Maria said "I'm sorry I can't help you" and then she cried in my arms. I told her it was ok, we would be glad to help her get back home. It felt good to be able to console someone; I only wished it would have been my son.

We left the two men tied to a tree. We figured sooner or later somebody would find them. Maybe the coyote's would find them first. I left a note attached to the tree "Juan, Cruz – I'm coming for you!" We then burned both of the cabins.

Jay and I took Maria back up the mountain to the truck. She was weak from exhaustion and we ended up taking turns carrying her up the steep hillside. She only weighed 100-110 pounds and our adrenalin was still pumping from our encounter. When Paul and Raul saw us coming they came and helped carry Maria the last 100 yards or so. They were both eager to hear what happened and if we found any sign of Vince. I told them Jay could give them the details, as I knew he would paint a colorful picture. They gave Maria some water and wrapped a blanket around her to keep her warm.

I needed some time to reflect on what just happened and make some plans for our next move. I was really disappointed we did not find Vince. I guess I was a little overly confident he would be here. The doubts were starting to creep into my mind; maybe we were not going to find him, maybe he's already dead. For now, I need to focus on the moment; we need to focus on getting Maria back to her family.

I asked Maria for her parent's home phone number and their names. I dialed her parent's phone number on my satellite phone and her father answered. I simply said Mr. Turner there is someone here who wants to speak to you. Maria grabbed the phone and said "Daddy, Daddy, it's me and I'm ok!!" Those few words brought tears to my eyes. I was happy we could help this family; I even noticed old Jay wiping a tear from his eye. After talking with her father a bit Maria's father asked to talk to me. I identified myself and we made tentative plans to meet at the border tomorrow. We all climbed into the truck and headed back to Paul's ranch. On the way Jay was enlightening Paul and Raul of how we took care of the four hombres down in the valley and how he was getting tired carrying Maria all the way up the mountain by himself! Imagine that!

Chapter 8

ONE FAMILY REUNITED

When we got back to the ranch, I called Ann with the news and I could hear the disappointment in her voice that we didn't find Vince. We both agreed to keep on trying and I really needed the reinforcement from her. I guess that was one of the reasons our marriage has survived as long as it has. We were always there to support each other, no matter what. I filled Ann in with what little information I had about Maria and she seemed genuinely happy we could help. Ann reminded me that we went on this trip for one purpose but perhaps God had a different purpose in store for us. I would have to think about that. It was time to turn in for the day; it had been a long one.

The next morning, we decided I would take Maria back to the border and the rest of the guys would look over some maps and try to figure out what our next move was. On the ride back, Maria couldn't thank me enough for what we did for her. I told her that's what people do for each other, help when they can.

She told me she was a high school senior and she was taken from a street while she was walking home from school. Two men stopped to ask directions and while she was giving directions someone grabbed her from behind and forced her into the car they were driving. A man forced her onto the floor of the back seat and put a blind fold on her and gagged her after tying her hands behind her back. She said she didn't see anything for a few hours after that. They took her to the cabin where we found her. Maria said she wasn't sure why they took her.

She hung her head and said "I probably shouldn't tell you this but my brother has a drug problem and he hangs out with some bad people. I was thinking maybe the people who took me were trying to get even with my brother for something." Maria went on to say "My parents tried putting my brother into rehab. but he would always fall back into the same rut. My parents spent a lot of money on him and although they can afford it, it kind of made me mad that they wasted so much on him."

It all made sense to me. This girl was pretty smart. Maria asked me why I thought these men took her and my son. I told her there was only one thing, money. She asked me if I was rich. I said I didn't think I was but maybe some people thought I was. She said her Dad owned a bunch of car washes and she thought he was rich. Maria dozed off after a quiet period of driving. We were about 45 minutes from the border and I gave her father a call to let him know we would soon be there. I asked him to meet us on the Mexican side because I didn't want to have to deal with customs. I still had a lot of stuff in the back of my truck I really didn't want to show anyone.

We agreed to meet at a truck stop a few miles from the border. I pulled into the truck stop and Maria didn't recognize her father's car anywhere. We drove around for a few minutes and then she saw his car pulling into the truck stop. We pulled up beside them and before I got the truck stopped Maria had the door open and jumped out to go to them. There were big smiles and hugs and kisses from her mother and father. There was a young man in the back seat that got out slowly and seemed hesitant to approach Maria. Maria looked at him and opened her arms to him and they both hugged. I assumed it was her brother. Mr. Turner came over and shook my hand before I could get out of the truck. After I crawled out, Mrs. Turner hugged me and kissed me on the cheek and said "I don't how to thank you!" Maria said "Mom and Dad, this is Mr. Wright, my hero!" She then hugged me and gave me a big kiss on the cheek as well. I told them to please call me Bill. Maria then introduced her brother Chris to me. He responded with "Nice to meet you sir."

Mrs. Turner asked "Who are you and how did you find Maria? You're like the Lone Ranger to us, you saved our daughter!" I couldn't help but think, if I was the Lone Ranger, wouldn't that make Jay - Tonto? I would keep that one for the future. I explained the situation to them and that I had some help. I told them that I was going to continue my search for my son when I left here. They both asked what they could do to help. I said, "These are some nasty people and my friend and I had some special skills that will allow us to deal with them." I suggested that when they got back home they might consider creating more awareness in the community about these kidnappings and try to build some kind of political and community support to stop these things from happening.

They both seemed willing to attempt something.

While we adults were talking, I noticed Maria and her brother talking in the car. I saw they were both crying. Chris got out of the car and walked over to a trash can and tossed a bag of something into it. He walked back to his parents and fell to his knees and said he was sorry for all the trouble he caused. He knew it was his fault that Maria was kidnapped and he thought they would kill her. He said he owed these people a lot of money and they took Maria to get back the money he owed from his parents. Chris promised his parents and sister he would get clean and do whatever he could to bring these guys to justice. Chris looked at me and said "Mr. Wright, take me with you, I know these guys and I can help you." I told Chris he could not go with me, it would be too dangerous. I gave him a piece of paper and a pen and told him to give me names and places, who was in charge and anything he knew about where they hid out. Chris started writing.

I told the Turners I did not want my name mentioned in connection with Maria's rescue. I needed to remain anonymous so I could continue with my search. I did not want the FBI or any law enforcement agency getting in my way until I found my son. I knew these agencies were aware my friends and I were here but we'd be ok as long as they didn't know where we were. For me the look on their faces was reward enough. If they wanted to say the Lone Ranger found their daughter; that was ok with me. Mr. Turner reached in his pocket and handed me a fist full of cash. He said he wanted me to have it, he knew I would have expenses and he would be offended if I didn't accept it. I felt strange about accepting the money then

Maria looked at me and said "Go ahead; take it, my Dad's rich." We all laughed and I thought; what the hell and stuck the money in my pocket.

They offered to buy me lunch, but I was anxious to get back. Chris handed me the piece of paper I gave him earlier and surprise, surprise Juan Cruz's name was on the top of the list. I recognized two other names on the list, one of whom we just eliminated yesterday. I did not mention any of that to the Turners. We hugged and agreed to meet again after I found Vince back in the States. Maria hugged me and whispered in my ear "I hope you find your son soon and God bless you."

I saddled up and moved south again. I had a renewed confidence and was feeling good about what we had done. I was pleased with the way Jay and I handled things yesterday and even though we were older, the old instincts seemed to be there. I know I wasn't supposed to but I enjoyed sneaking around and taking down those four men. It was always an adrenalin rush years ago and that rush was still there.

I stopped to relieve myself and was reminded of the lump of cash in my pocket. I crawled back in the truck and pulled the money out of my pocket. There was $4000.00 in that wad. That would buy us a few steaks and some apples for the horses.

Chapter 9

THE HUNT CONTINUES

I arrived back at Paul's ranch at midafternoon. The boys had a game plan laid out and ran it by me. It sounded good to me. Our next step was to check out a location given to us by the guy at the cabins. It was obvious Juan Cruz was running things and we needed to keep chipping away at his organization. It appeared they were using a series of small and isolated locations and that suited us just fine. Paul and Raul mapped out a circle of sorts where we could move from location to location quickly and silently. One of the locations we could only safely move in on with the horses, it would be our last stop if we needed to go that far. I could see Jay was getting pumped. He was talking faster and his body language was more animated.

I told the guys "It looks like a good plan. However, tonight Paul, I want you to pick out the finest restaurant in the area and I am going to treat us all to a good meal." Jay asked if I had a winning lottery ticket. I said sort of and pulled the wad of cash from my pocket. I had not really thought of it before, it worked out to $1000.00 per man. I counted out $1000.00 for each man and handed it to them. I then explained that Maria's father gave it to me to help cover some expenses. Jay looked at me and winked "Does that mean we are Merc's (Mercenaries) again?" I just said I guess so.

Paul took us to a little cantina a few miles from his place. The owner allowed us to pick out our own steak from a case behind the counter. They had big 2 inch thick western cuts and smaller girly cuts as we called them. We all picked the big ones. Steaks were one of the few things Jay and I didn't agree on. I like mine rare and he likes his well done. I always enjoy grossing him out with my bloody plate. He always makes a big production out of it.

This time Paul and Raul also ordered their steaks rare. Jay just rolled his eyes when we ordered. Sure enough, when our waitress brought out our dinners, Jay started moowing like a cow. He told the waitress "Be careful; them steaks might poop on you, they're not dead yet!" He moaned and groaned through most of the meal about the blood on our plates and that we were vampires and on and on. After we finish our meal, the waitress asked if we were ready for the house specialty dessert. Jay asked "What is it?" The waitress looked at him, never cracked a smile and said "Blood pudding, Senor!" I almost fell off my chair laughing. Jay even had to laugh and he handed the waitress a $20.00 tip.

All of us hit the sack early tonight, we knew tomorrow was going to be a long day. My thoughts were about Vince and maybe tomorrow would be the day we would find him.

I was awake before daylight the next morning. It wasn't long before the rest were up and stirring around. I'd made up my mind that each camp we encountered we would destroy. If we had trouble finding Cruz maybe we could piss him off enough to come looking for us. Either way I was determined to have an encounter with this man.

We left Paul behind today; he had a ranch to run and I didn't like putting him in any danger. The three of us took off for the mountains to the southwest of his ranch. Paul gave us good directions and Raul was very familiar with the area. In addition they had other family members along the way who were willing to help us if we needed it. We drove for about an hour before we started to climb an old road up into a mountain pass. We followed the road down into a valley and up the opposite side. The road was narrow and we could see where someone was running smaller vehicles, probably 4 wheelers on this road. There were ruts in the road every place there was a turn that would show a narrow wheel based vehicle. We drove very slowly so as not raise much dust to alert anyone who might be watching the road.

We came to a Y in the road; one direction the 4 wheeler tracks were using heavily; the other direction was not used very much. Instincts told me to go easy; we might be close. We pulled the truck onto the less used trail and got out to follow the other trail on foot. We paralleled the trail for a mile or so. It went up and over the other side and almost down into the next valley where we could see a cabin. There were two 4 wheelers parked outside the cabin. My heart started beating faster, maybe this was it, maybe Vince was here, and maybe I would have my showdown with Mr. Cruz. Jay and I decided to move in closer to check things out. There wasn't a lot of cover, so we would have to be careful to use the cover we had. I sent Raul back to get the truck off the trail we parked on and make sure it was turned around and ready to go if we needed to make a fast get away. It was something we should have done to start with. In our haste to check things out we'd made a mistake. I told him to conceal the truck as best he could and keep a rifle ready in case he needed it.

Jay and I eased down to within 150 yards of the cabin and glassed the area with our binoculars. We could see scabbards on the 4 wheelers, so we knew they had a least two rifles. There was a small barn about 50 yards from the cabin and a corral with three horses. We split up and circled the cabin to see how many doors and windows we could see. When we met later we determined there was one window on all four sides, one front door and one rear door. We had not seen anyone moving around to this point. We would once again have to wait until dark to move in. It was a long wait. Fortunately, we were in the shade and the sun was setting behind us.

We watched and waited, then we waited and watched, in the worst way I wanted to go take a peek into the cabin. But it just wasn't safe. There was not enough cover to conceal us; we would have to wait another hour for darkness. Jay and I took turns watching and while I was resting my thoughts turned to Vince. I was remembering the times we spent together. The first time I took him fishing and how proud he was of his first fish. Even though it was only 3 inches long, he smiled from ear to ear. I remembered the first time he hit a home run in little league, I think I was more proud of him than he was of himself. When as a one year old, he first discovered dirt and how upset his mother got when he took his first mouthful and I just laughed. I hoped we were going to have more memories in the future.

It finally got dark enough for us to move in. It seemed strange we had not seen any activity at all around the cabin. Jay took one side of the cabin and I took the other. The cabin was empty. We checked out the barn and there was no one there either. All that waiting for nothing, it seemed we'd wasted a lot of time.

I went inside the cabin to look around for any clues, Jay stood watch outside. It was obvious someone had been here recently; no dust on the chairs or table, there was a washcloth on the sink that was still damp. In this dry country things dried out quickly. While I was looking around I found ½ of one of my business cards lying under a bed. My pulse quickened; it was a clue from Vince. A few years ago I mistakenly double ordered the cards and Vince and I would use a card torn in half as a sign we were at that spot. We mostly used that sign when we were hunting and got separated. Praise the Lord, this was the first indication Vince was alive in over a week. My spirits rose 100% at that moment. I ran out the door and showed the card to Jay and he looked at me like I was crazy. I explained the whole signal thing to him and he got excited as well.

We decided to have a little fun and leave our own calling card for these guys. The keys were still in the 4 wheelers so we each drove one onto the porch of the cabin. There were gas lights inside the cabin, so we turned them all on and beat it out the door. There was a metal box just inside the door and we flipped a coin to see who would make the shot. Jay won and one shot from his old Winchester through that metal box made enough sparks to make one hell of an explosion. We went over to the corral and let the horses out and then we high tailed it back to the truck.

Once we were back at the truck; Raul said "What the hell did you guys do? I felt the earth shake with that explosion." I told him it was one less camp we would have to check out anymore. I showed Raul the card I found and he knew the meaning of it. Raul said "Senor Bill, this is a good thing!" It sure was. We all had some adrenalin flowing and we were ready to move onto the next camp. As near as we could tell, the next camp was about 5 or 6 miles away. We had to travel over a couple of mountain passes and a bunch of switchbacks to get close and it would be slow going.

We were all hungry, so Jay dug out some hotdogs and wrapped them in aluminum foil and put them on the manifold of the truck's engine to heat them up. We made like Willie Nelson and were on the road again. While we were moving off the mountain where we parked the truck we saw some headlights bouncing towards us in the distance; it was the first vehicle we'd encountered in the mountains. We had no idea who it might be so we prepared for the worst. We stopped the truck and got a couple of rifles out of the back just in case it got ugly. The headlights got closer and it appeared we were both on the same road. As we approached the other vehicle I found a spot to pull off along the side of the road. It was a one track road and there was no way two vehicles could pass each other side by side. The pickup truck pulled up beside us and I heard the action of Jay's handgun chamber a round. The driver stopped and rolled down his window; I could see there were two men in the truck and the driver said "Ola Senor." I heard Raul chuckle and he said to me "It's ok Senor Bill, it's my brother David."

There was a big sigh of relief from all of us. We all got out of our vehicles and Raul introduced us to his brother David and guess what his other brother Jesse. I looked at Raul and asked "How many damn brothers do you have?" He said six brothers and four sisters. Jay looked at me and said "Holy shit, the hot dogs!" I opened the hood and he grabbed the foil and opened it, they smelled really good. Jay dug out some buns and we all had a couple of hot dogs. David reached in the back seat of his truck and pulled out a cooler with some sandwiches and cold beer in it. We had a little picnic on the spot. These were good people.

Raul asked his brothers what they were doing here. David said Paul called him and was concerned he could not come with us and asked David if he and Jesse could check up on us. David said on their way in here they saw a bright light like a big fire on the other side of the mountain and wondered if we were in trouble. I told him there was no trouble for us. David said "Senor Bill, you are messing with some very bad people." I told David these guys pissed off the wrong people and they needed to be stopped. Raul and his brothers talked in Spanish to each other for a few minutes and I only understood half of it. Jesse was asking where we were headed and Raul explained our plan to both of them. Jesse told us in English he knew the location of the next camp we were headed for and would be glad to show us how to get to it. He said he stumbled onto it last year while he was doing some hunting in the area.

I agreed we would follow them into the area tomorrow morning. It was after midnight and we needed to get some rest. Driving around out here at night with our lights on made me feel like a beacon light from a lighthouse; we could be seen for miles around. We moved away from the mountain and into a valley where we found a secluded spot to park both vehicles for the rest of the night. When we settled in, Jay was entertaining the boys with old war stories and cowboy tales and they seemed to enjoy them. We drank all of David's beer and Jay wanted to go back into town to get some more but we didn't have time for that. I didn't sleep much but it felt good to stretch out and rest. I did fall asleep for a bit and the last thing I remember hearing was Jay telling a story about tracking a wounded mountain lion up in Idaho. I think everyone else was asleep at the time.

The next morning we were on the move again by daylight. Jesse thought it would take an hour or more to get to the next spot. In my heart I just knew we were getting closer to Vince and maybe this would be the day we would find him. I asked Jay how he was holding up and he told me just fine. He said his old bones were a little stiff but this is what he was born to do. The two of us often talked about that. We both believed that it was no accident our paths crossed and we were given the skills we have for a purpose. Neither of us was ever sure what specific purpose God intended for us, but we knew it had something to do with helping people in distress. Maybe it was to prepare us for this moment or something in the future. A long time ago we quit trying to figure it out. We both loved sneaking around trying to outsmart people or animals. There was a time in our youth, we enjoyed the killing, we kept score and we didn't care. I would kill to protect my family but I had no desire to do it for money anymore. I had a fear welling up inside me that I might cross that line and start to enjoy it again. I needed to talk to Jay about that subject; I wasn't sure if he had the same feelings. But now was not the time.

We eased up and around twists and turns in the road and it was slow going. This area was a little more flat with more sage brush and mesquite, not too many big trees. It was very thick with brush; one would have trouble seeing 10 feet into the brush at some spots.

Jesse said there were some very big mule deer in this area but they were hard to find. We moved into an area that was a little more open and Jesse said "We better pull over; I think we are getting close." We got out of the truck and climbed up on a big rock outcropping. From the top of it we could see an old ranch house maybe ½ a mile away through our binoculars. There were a few outbuildings that were falling down, a pickup truck and a motorcycle parked outside the house. It was really open around the house; like someone mowed the brush to keep it short. The mowed area was probably 75 yards around the perimeter of the house. It seemed odd that someone would do that for any reason other than to be able to see company coming. More than likely they didn't like company. Jay said "Holy shit!" when he spotted a big Rottweiler dog chained to the front porch.

Jay looked at me and said "You know I don't like any of them damn German dogs. You remember what happened the last time I ran into one of them don't you?" I nodded yes, I did remember. In Cambodia Jay stumbled into a Rottweiler that almost took his leg off until I was able to shoot the dog. I reminded Jay that I carried his fat ass for over a mile until we got some help for him. How could I forget that! It took him three months to heal from that encounter.

We glassed the area pretty thoroughly and found a way to get close to the house along a gully that ran almost up to one of the old outbuildings. The problem was the gully and buildings were on the opposite side of the house from where we were. We all went back to the truck to look at some topographical maps to see if we could find a way around to the other side. Jesse said there were a couple of old roads that wound around and came out a mile or two on the other side of the house. He said the main road into the house came in from that direction; somebody used the road a lot and kept it in good shape. It looked like that was our best shot at getting in there. We could only go a few hundred feet more on this road and we would be totally exposed to the house. I backed the truck around and we circled around to the other side of the house.

When we came out to the well-used road; we had no idea how far from the house we were. Jesse said he would walk along the road to see how far away we were. I believe he was thinking he would cut the two old guys a break and that was ok with me. It was a hot, dry, dusty day. Jesse came back in about ½ an hour. He said it was roughly a mile to the house and there was a spot a couple of hundred yards closer we could pull the truck into and nobody would see it. We headed to that spot. I pulled into the spot and Jesse was right; the truck was hidden by some tall brush.

Jay and I loaded up with some gear and weapons. David and Jesse wanted to go with us but I said no. They did what we asked them to do by getting us here. I told them "Sit tight." I gave them each a walkie-talkie and told them I would call them if and when we needed their help. The two of us started up the road towards the house. We got to a point where we could see the house and we moved off the road to do some more glassing. We could see two men loading some cardboard boxes into the back of the truck. Jay asked "What do you think is in them boxes?" I said "I didn't think it was candy." Before long the two men jumped into the truck and headed down the road towards us. I asked Jay what he wanted to do. He said "I'm not jumping out in front of that truck if that's what you're asking." We let the truck drive past us. There were only the two men in the cab and the bed was full of boxes, neither of the men was Vince.

We slowly moved in towards the outbuildings to get a closer look. The gully allowed us to get within 25 yards of the house. The smell coming from the house was unmistakable. It was a smell from our past – cocaine. This house must be their cooking house. We knew what was in the boxes. I looked at Jay and said let's see if anybody else is home. Jay said "Whoa partner, what about that damn dog?" I told him to wait here, I liked dogs. I bellied up closer to the dog and he was sleeping. I had a couple of raw hot dogs in my pocket and slipped one under his nose. One gulp and it was gone. I gave him the second hot dog and he was licking my hand. I motioned for Jay to come up and he was shaking his head. He whispered to me "How the hell did you do that?" I just told him "I told you before, I like dogs!" I untied the dog and left him run.

We bellied up to the house and could not see anyone around. All the windows were boarded shut so I eased up to the front door. It had a pad lock on it and of course it was locked. Jay shot the lock off and we went inside. It was a cocaine factory, processing, packaging, and shipping. We looked the place over and there was no one else in the house. I found no sign of Vince.

Jay looked at me and smiled. "What are we going to do now, Billy boy, light her up?" I said you bet, partner. But first give the boys a call; they might want to see the fireworks. Jay radioed Jesse and told them to come on up. When they arrived Jay dug some grenades out of the back of the truck and said to Jesse and David "Wanna help?" He showed them how to pull the pins and said have at it. Jesse and David each lobbed a grenade into the house and we all ran away from the house. We all dove into the gully near the house. I felt something wiggle under my leg and there was the dog sniffing my pocket for another hot dog. There were pieces of wood and tin roof flying everywhere. Somebody was going to be pissed when they discovered this mess. Jesse said "That was wild!!"

We all had little nicks and cuts from flying debris but it was good to know we put this place out of business. We all piled into the truck including the dog and beat it out of there, back to the road we originally came in on. We drove back to the area we parked at last night. I was disappointed Vince was not at that house. We had one more spot to check out and we would need to go back to Paul's ranch and get the horses. On the way to Paul's place Jesse said "You guys have opened a big can of worms. When Cruz finds out what you have done, he will come after you." I said that was ok with me, it would save us the time of having to find him. Jesse said "You don't understand Senor Bill; he will not stop until you are dead." Jay said "Let them try, he has no idea who he's coming after."

It was time for us to disassociate ourselves with Raul's family. They lived here and Cruz would come after them if he found out they were involved. Jay and I loaded up all of our gear and the horses while Raul was saying goodbye. We hugged Raul's brothers and thanked them for their help. I told them when this was all over we would not come back here, so there would be no connection between them and us.

The three of us headed for our next rendezvous. Hopefully this would be the one. I was getting concerned but I had to keep going. This next location was not quite as isolated. There was a frequently used road going by within 200 yards of the house. The only way we could reach this place was to move in from behind the property where there was some brush to cover our approach. There were no roads behind the property so we would need the horses to get close. We could not take the horse trailer into some of the spots we did earlier with only the truck. From Paul's ranch it was about a 2 hour drive and it seemed strange to be traveling with other traffic on the road.

We reached the road that ran by the house we were looking for. Raul thought we were a few miles from the house. We drove down the road looking for a place to pull the truck and trailer into where we could hide it. According to the map there was a camping area about a ½ mile from where we got on the road. We came to the camping area and there were two campers there. One had a tent pitched and the other was a small camper. We pulled in and found a spot. We were not completely hidden from the road but we felt we blended in enough to not be conspicuous. Obviously people who used this road were used to seeing campers here and would not think much about it. We backed the horse trailer into a group of trees so it wouldn't be easy to see from the road.

Jay and I had to load our gear into saddle bags and we each had a scabbard to put our rifles into. The horses were well rested and ready to go. There was a ridge line behind us and we decided we would climb the ridge to get a better look at the lay of the land. Raul and the dog would remain behind to guard the truck and set up a little camp to make things look good. If anyone asked, his story would be two of his friends were doing some scouting for deer season and he was doing the cooking for them.

We headed up the ridge and the horses were eager to go. When we reached the top we dismounted and did some glassing to get our bearings. The ridge ran about a ¼ mile behind the house. The valley where the house was located was very flat with only the one road traveling up the middle of it. We had to move closer to get a better look at things. We stayed off the top of the ridge to keep us from being skylined and easy to see. Once we were within a 1/4 mile of the house we got off and did some more glassing. It appeared the house was empty. We could not see any vehicles or anyone moving around.

My hopes fell. This was the last location we knew of and if Vince wasn't here, we were back to square one. Jay looked at me and apparently saw the disappointment on my face and said "You know as well as I do, things are not what they always seem to be. Let's move in and take a closer look. It's the only game in town." I agreed.

We closed the distance to the house by half and dismounted the horses. The horses were tied and left to graze a little grass for a while. We glassed for quite a long time. Finally, I saw a flash of something shinny through one of the windows. The flash was there and then it wasn't; like someone moving past the window. I didn't know what it was. Maybe something fell or it could be a fan inside blowing something. Or just maybe somebody was inside. Whatever I saw, I knew I saw it. The game just changed!! Now we had to proceed as if there was someone in there.

Jay looked at me and said "Maybe we got Mr. Cruz's attention and he's waiting for us." We both knew we were playing with fire and they could be waiting to ambush us. I figured by now he knew the drug house was gone and we cost him a pile of money. We settled in and glassed every square inch of the property. Jay was looking through the spotting scope and spit on the ground right next to my foot. "What the hell you do that for?" I asked. "It's an experiment. I can see a wet spot down there in front of the house, right where some vehicle tracks end. I wanna see how long it takes for my spit to dry in this hot sand." In a couple of minutes Jay's spit was dried up. It was another hot, dry day and if that wet spot was water it would have evaporated quickly. There was a hot breeze blowing so even if it was oil or transmission fluid; the wind blowing the sandy soil would have covered it over in an hour or so. That told us someone parked there recently.

Once again, we would have to wait for the cover of darkness. If there was someone in there, we were sure they would be heavily armed. We had a few hours to wait, so we both laid back and rested. I was reminded about the old days, how a lot of our time was spent just like this. Glassing and waiting, spending hours, sometime days for a few minutes of action. I recalled reading stories that glorified snipers and other military adventures but most of them did not dwell on the waiting and watching, it didn't make good copy.

After some time of not saying a word, Jay poked me in the ribs and asked "Ok Billy, we're alone now, how do you really feel about the situation?" I looked at the best friend I ever had and I had to choke back the tears. I told him "I thought we were too late, I was afraid Vince was already dead." Jay wiped a tear from his eye and said "I believe we have to face that reality. However we do have one more option and it's that house right down there. Let's get our act together and do this thing right."

Jay threw an empty handgun magazine at me and said "Let's rock and roll one more time partner." We refilled our packs and checked our extra mags to make sure they were full. Jay made sure the horses were secured and old Spook looked at me as if to say, I'm ready to go again. I stroked his muzzle and told him not yet, we would be going the rest of the way on foot. The sun was setting as we eased off the ridge. I wasn't crazy about the notion of having to crawl on my hand and knees again. This part of the country had thorns everywhere. My hands and knees were sore from being stuck by everything I brushed against. Yes, I even had some stuck on my butt.

Moving slow and steady, there was still no sign of activity around the house. We worked our way closer using a dry creek bed for cover. I said a little prayer asking God to please let us find Vince in that house alive and to keep us safe once again.

It was totally dark now, no moonlight. It always intrigued me how our eyes adjusted to the lack of light. Even in the darkness there were still shapes and landmarks visible. I could make out the outline of the house 100 yards away.

We decided earlier to stay together and move in tandem. We would belly crawl the rest of the way, slowly moving from bush to bush, watching, listening, our two bodies moving as one. We were 20 yards from the back of the house behind a clump of brush when a spotlight beam hit us in the face! It was blinding for an instant and I closed my eyes. It was definitely an "oh shit" moment. I was expecting gunfire but there wasn't any. When I regained my focus, I could see there were spotlights shining all around the perimeter of the house. Jay whispered "Motion sensors?" Maybe, but just before the lights came on I heard a floor board creak inside the house. Someone was inside! I whispered to my partner "You wanna rush 'em?" "You nuts?" he responded.

After 30 minutes of not moving a muscle, we were confident we had not been spotted. There were a couple of bushes between us and the house and we slithered like snakes with our faces to the ground. It was painstakingly slow moving a few inches at a time. My old legs were cramping. Jay had his head almost in my crotch and I was tempted to fart, but this was no time to fool around. I was dying to stretch my legs out straight but with him between them it was impossible. Forty years ago we could go for a mile like this but now it was torture. It took us an hour to go that last 20 yards. When we finally reached the back of the house, standing up never felt so good. We both had to take a few minutes to get the circulation going in our legs again. I was sweating so bad my camo face paint was dripping off.

We could hear two people talking inside; I heard one of them mention the name Juan. My blood pressure rose 20 points! "Those Gringo's will pay for messing with Juan Cruz" the other man said. I looked at Jay and said "Lock and load – Mr. Cruz is home and waiting for our arrival."

Our next step would be to create a diversion to draw them out just in case Vince was in- side. Jay seemed to know what I was thinking and tapped me on the shoulder and pointed to those damn firecrackers he dragged along everywhere we went. I looked at him and snapped "What?" Jay whispered "You work your way around to the front and when they come out, take them down. Let the rest up to me. It's gonna take me a while to move around but you'll know when I'm ready." He patted me on the shoulder and slithered back into the cover of the bushes.

It was easy for me to move around to the front of the house because of a dark spot from the spotlights next to the house. Jay on the other hand had to move slowly to get past the beam of light and back into the bushes and then circle around to the front in the darkness. I had no idea what he was up to but apparently he did. I waited and waited for an hour and a half. All at once the sky lit up with showers of sparks raining down on the top of the house. The firecrackers all had the distinct whistle of a missile.

Two men came running out the front door each carrying a semi-automatic rifle. I dropped each of them with a shot in the leg area. Rushing over to them, I kicked their weapons out of their reach. Jay came running past me and burst into the house while I kept the two men pinned down. There was a burst of fire from inside the house and some moans. I could hear some shuffling around and then it was quiet. I wanted to go in and check on Jay but I had to watch the two men on the ground. Finally I heard Jay holler "Billy, I'm coming out!" Boy was I glad to hear that gravelly voice.

Jay came out dragging another man behind him. I could see Jay was hit in the arm and he said he was ok. He looked at me and said "You need to meet this son-of-a-bitch before he dies!" I knew from the pictures of him I'd seen earlier, it was Cruz. Jay turned to guard the two men on the ground and I pointed my flashlight into Cruz's face. He looked into my eyes and asked "Who are you?"

I grabbed his shirt and asked him "Where is my son, you bastard?" Cruz spit in my face and said "I killed your boy last week and I enjoyed it." I wanted to put a bullet in him and then thought no, let him suffer. I could see Jay hit him twice in the belly and I knew he was dying. I'd seen too many of those wounds before and the outcome was never good. I think he wanted me to end it for him.

I asked Jay how bad he was hit and he said "I'm not hit; I fell against the damn table when I went in and cut my arm a little bit, its ok."

I turned to the other two men and asked them where my son was. I cocked my .45 and said "Last chance – where is my son?" One of them said Cruz killed him last week because he tried to escape. The second man said "Si Senor that is the truth."

Jay said "Billy, you need to go inside." I walked through the door and I could see Vince's old varsity jacket hanging over a chair. The jacket had his name on it and there was a bullet hole in the chest and the back.

My knees went weak. I dropped to the floor and all the emotions of the past two weeks came pouring out of me. I held Vince's jacket and wept openly for the first time since we started this search. I feared this moment from the day he was kidnapped. How was I going to tell Ann and Tara? Their hearts would be broken as mine now was. I took a few moments to collect myself and the anger began to boil inside me.

I stepped outside and looked at Cruz, he was dead. I looked at the other two and thought about killing them but I had no more taste for it. Jay asked me if I wanted him to finish it. I said no, tie them up.

While Jay was tying them up he asked one of them what my son looked like. The man said my son was very tall and skinny with blonde hair. Jay looked at him and asked "As tall as me?" The man said "No Senor, much taller" and he reached his hands as high as he could. Jay looked at me with wide eyes and a big smile and said "Man, did you hear that?" I did. Jay was 6' 2", Vince was 6' and very muscular in build with dark brown hair. It wasn't Vince that they killed!!

Vince must have given his jacket to someone else. It was a long shot, but there was still hope. Maybe, just maybe he was still alive. I didn't have to make that phone call to Ann!

After securing the two men, we went back inside the house to look for more clues. We tore the place apart trying to find anything. I looked closer at the coat and found a few blonde hairs on the collar. We found a few more items of clothing but I could not identify any of them as belonging to Vince. I knew what I was looking for but could not find it. Jay found a metal lock box under the cushion of a stuffed chair and pried it open. Inside was $10,000.00 cash. That was 10% of what these guys took from me. It was more than I expected, maybe things were looking up. There was a small wood stove in the corner of the kitchen. When I opened the door to the stove and shined my flashlight inside – there it was – another sign that Vince was here; our sign to each other that we used for years - a partially burned ½ of my business card, another sign of hope, and another reason to keep searching. Things were looking up!

It was time to move out. We didn't want to hang around any longer than necessary. Cruz probably had more men somewhere around here. Once the word got out he was dead, there would probably be a power struggle to see who would take his place. There would be no better way to assert that power than to kill the men who killed him. We beat it back to the horses as quickly as we could. Once we reached the horses, I called Raul on the walkie-talkie to see if everything was clear at the campground. Raul replied "No problems here Senor Bill, just me and the dog eating supper."

When we reached camp, Jay and I were both exhausted. Raul said "You guys sit down and rest, I will care for the horses." I think Jay was almost too tired to talk. I asked him what his thoughts were. He leaned back and stretched and said "Billy, we ain't done yet. Them boys think they killed Vince, but how they described him, there's no way it was him. We have to figure he's still alive somewhere." I was relieved he felt that way, because I certainly felt the same way. We would continue our search.

Chapter 10

TIME TO REGROUP

We did not think it was wise to stay at the campground overnight. We loaded up our gear and horses and moved out. Raul drove while Jay and I got a little sleep. My old bones were tired plus the emotions of the day, I was worn out. Raul pulled into a truck stop about 20 miles down the road and we spent the rest of the night there sleeping in the truck. That damn dog snored almost as bad as Jay, but I guess he was part of the team now.

We went into the truck stop and each took a shower. Man, did that feel good. I had a couple of days dust and grime on me I thought would never come off. Jay said "That shower felt better than sex!" I told him "I'm sure it lasted longer."

After showering, we got some breakfast and headed out to the truck to talk things over. I believe we were all thinking "Now what." Jay spoke first "Let's take stock of what we have done. We've killed three men, shot up three more, scared the hell out of few others and probably saved the life of a young girl. We blew up four buildings, one of them a drug factory and a couple of ATV's. Oh, and yeh we also stole a dog. Did I miss anything?" I said "I think that about covers it."

It was time to express my thoughts. "I still don't have Vince. We've eliminated several locations and to some degree, we are back to square one. We've pissed off a lot of people and they will probably be coming after us. We've put a target on our backs and we are going to have to be really careful about our movement from here on out. Jay and Raul, if you guys want to head back home, I understand. No hard feelings, you guys have done all you can to help me."

Jay shook his head and said "You dumb ass, I didn't sign on to do half a job. I'll head back home when I'm damn good and ready. Right now, I'm not ready!" Raul said "I want to stay and help. I want to find Vince and I am not afraid of these drug pushers." I shook both of their hands and was pleased they agreed to stay.

I needed to call Ann and give her an update. I filled her in with what we found and she agreed we should keep on looking. Ann told me "Bob Tucker and agent Hanson stopped by a couple of times asking to speak to you. They both wanted to know where you were and I told them I didn't know for sure." She wasn't lying; she really didn't know where we were. The two of us discussed the very real possibility that the longer it went, the less likely we were to find Vince alive. We agreed neither of us were ready to give up until we knew Vince's fate. I told Ann how much I missed her and I wished this was over. Ann said "I miss you and love you. I also know you will not give up until you get some answers." Ann also said "Kara is fine and the baby is starting to kick her on a regular basis." Her final words were "Be careful."

I thought for a moment maybe we should go back home for a while. But it didn't make sense to do all that traveling. Besides, I would just be restless at home until we found out more about Vince. Jay slapped me behind the head and asked "Are you back? You seemed deep in thought there for a moment." I told him I thought we should get rid of this truck and get another one just in case somebody would recognize it. He thought that would be a good idea.

We headed back into Chihuahua to find a dealer who might have something I liked. After a couple of stops, I found a truck similar to mine but older and a different color. I worked out a deal to lease the truck for a month and to leave my truck parked at the dealership. We transferred all of our gear over and rigged up the lights to work for the horse trailer. We were all set to go.

While Jay and I were working on the truck deal, Raul visited with his friends and got some information from them. They told Raul there was quite a bit of activity around Cruz's house. They saw a number of vehicles in and out of the driveway. Raul said his friends asked him if it was true that Cruz was dead. He told them it was true. Raul blushed and said "My friends think I am a hero for getting rid of Cruz." I winked at Jay and said to Raul "You are a hero my friend, we are a team."

Instead of leaving town we thought we would stake out Cruz's house for a while. Maybe we would get lucky here or be able to follow someone to another location. Raul borrowed a car for us to use while we were in town and we parked the truck and trailer at a little shopping center. We parked across the street from the house and just watched for a while. Raul's friends were right there was a lot of activity. I saw the man I beat our first day out come out of the house. He stood outside smoking a cigarette and taking to another man. Soon there were two other men outside and they were arguing about something. The argument turned into a shoving match and one of the men jumped into a car and took off down the street.

We followed him to the edge of town where he pulled into a bar. He didn't go into the bar but a mobile home parked beside it. After 15 minutes he came out carrying a semi-automatic weapon. Another man came out with him. It appeared the second man was showing the first guy how to use the weapon. I looked at Jay and said "I hope he isn't planning on using that on us." Jay just raised his eyebrows and cocked his handgun. The first man got back into his car and headed back the way he came. Jay said "Guess that answers your question."

We again followed him back into town and back to Cruz's house. He pulled into the driveway, got out and turned the gun on the three men who were still standing outside. He shot them all with a burst of fire at close range. The gunman then got back into his car and took off down the street.

Wow, these are some nasty guys! We were all speechless for a minute. I had no idea why the shooting took place but the three men at the house appeared to be dead. Raul said "Holly shit!" I said "Yeh, me too!" Jay chimed in "That's three guys we won't have to deal with. Now what are we going to do?" I thought out loud "I'm not sure how many guys are in this gang, they ought to be getting a little thin by now. I'd like to get a look inside that house but it's probably going to be crawling with cops before long." Raul turned and looked at me in the back seat and smiled. I looked him in the eyes and said "Don't tell me you have a brother who is a cop." His smile got wider and he nodded his head yes.

We sat in the car and waited, before long we heard sirens screaming and we saw two police cars rounding the corner. Both cars pulled into the driveway and two officers got out of each car with weapons drawn. The three of us just watched. The officers checked the dead men and then checked the perimeter of the house. Another patrol car pulled up with two more officers and all six men entered the house. Raul said the third car contained his brother Rafael. The three of us waited until the officers came out of the house and Raul rolled down his window and hollered "Rafi, over here."

Raul's brother walked over to the car and said "Hey, big brother, I heard you were back in town. Where have you been hiding out?" Raul introduced his brother to Jay and me. Rafael shook our hands and said "I've been hearing some rumors about you guys, are any of them true?" Raul said to his brother "These are good guys, I am proud to travel with them. And besides, this one pays my wages" as he pointed to me.

Rafi asked what we knew about the shootings. We explained what we saw and the reason we were here. He said to us "Look, I know why you are here, I know what you have done so far, and the problem is I can't prove any of it or I would arrest you. In a way you guys have become folk heroes to the local people. I cannot condone what you have done and would highly recommend you go back home while you still can." I told Rafi I appreciated his honesty and we would consider his proposal. Rafi continued "I don't think you understand how much trouble you have created for yourselves. You are marked men and they will keep coming after you." I asked "Who are they?" He told us "Not here, not now, I will speak with you tonight at 7pm at the old campground just west of town." Raul said he knew where it was. Rafi said "Now you guys get out of here before I have to explain who you are to my co-workers."

We left the area and went back to get my truck and trailer. We picked up some food and beer and headed for the campground where we figured we would spend the night. Jay said "Let's see, there's six dead, four crippled, how many more you think there could be?" I said I had no idea but maybe Rafi could help us with that. We made some supper and had a couple of beers around a campfire. We took the horses out of the trailer and let them graze and get some exercise. Old Spook looked around as if to say where the hell are we and then found a patch of grass to munch on.

The sun was going down when Rafi pulled in. We all settled in around the campfire. Rafi said "What you don't understand is these are not some small time hoods you are dealing with. Cruz and his men are just puppets for a much bigger organization. The men you've eliminated were small potatoes, there are many more to take their place. When you blew up that drug house, you crossed the line. You cost them a lot of money. This organization is into drugs and smuggling big time. They have more weapons than we do. They buy loyalty and they kill anyone who turns on them. The kidnappings are another money making scheme and also a way to keep people in line." I asked Rafi "But why did they take my son, my family is not into drugs." Rafi said "I do not know for sure, but maybe your son was taken by mistake or he could have been taken as part of a sex tape business these people run as well." Rafi went on to say they have information concerning other people being taken by mistake and some have been returned.

"You guys are being hunted as we speak. If you don't leave, we cannot protect you." I told Rafi "I understand what you are saying, however I'm not going home without my son. We are not looking for anyone to protect us but we could use some intel as to where we might look next." Rafi said "The shooter today is probably going to take Cruz's place. The gunplay was more than likely a power play for control. It's something that happens all the time with these people. I'm going to put you in contact with someone who may help you, Raul knows him and he can give you more information than I can. Two things you need to remember, we did not have this conversation and if you get your butts in a sling, I can't help you." With that Raul and Rafi hugged and Rafi got in his truck and left.

As we settled in around the campfire, I was thinking about what Rafi said. We needed to be more mobile and be able to move quickly. That meant getting rid of the horse trailer, it really slowed us down. I asked Raul to call his brother Paul and ask if he would care for the horses and maybe hide the trailer for a while and maybe he could keep that damn dog. Raul made the call and told us Paul said no problem; bring them over in the morning. Raul made another call and was on the phone for quite a while. When he hung up he said "We will meet with our contact Eddie tomorrow after lunch. Eddie runs a gambling ring in the area and does not like these drug pushers. Let me do the talking when we meet him, he doesn't trust strangers."

Jay had been unusually quiet the last few hours and I asked him what was wrong. He said "Nothing, it takes all my concentration to try to figure out what these guys are saying in Spanish. Damn, they talk fast!" Raul looked at Jay and asked "Senor Jay, would you like me to translate for you?" Jay shook his head and said "No little fella, I trust ya."

The next morning we took the horses, dog and trailer to Paul's ranch and dropped them off. We didn't stick around too long because I didn't want anyone knowing Paul was helping us. We were off to meet with Eddie and hoping he could help us. Eddie is a big man; he has arms as big as my legs. I guessed him to be 400-450 pounds. Jay thought maybe 500, neither one of us was going to ask him how much he weighed. Raul did all the talking and when they were done, Eddie came over and shook our hands and said "Hope you find your boy. I like what you did to Cruz and his boys, if you need anything, you come see Eddie." Eddie pointed to a long scar on his arm and said "You see this scar, that bastard Cruz gave it to me a few years ago." We all thanked Eddie and we moved on.

Raul told us Eddie gave him the location of two more places to check out. One of them was the trailer beside the bar where we were yesterday. Eddie told him there was a barn behind the trailer where they kept weapons and drugs stored. There was usually someone there guarding the place. Raul told us some of Cruz's men gambled at Eddie's games and when they got too much booze in them, they would get to bragging about what they did. He went on to say the reason Eddie did not like these guys was they tried to take over his business and things got pretty ugly until they agreed to let him alone. Eddie had his own little band of men and most of the bad guys left him alone.

As we were leaving, Eddie had one of his men follow us outside. I asked the man if he was going to follow us all day. He said "I am going to watch your back while you are in town. You guys don't know how much trouble you are in!"

Jay looked at me and said "You know that's the second guy in the last 12 hours to tell us we don't know how much trouble we are in. I don't know about you but I'm getting tired of hearing that. Is it because we are old farts or do we just look stupid?" I said "I guess it's maybe a combination of the two. These guys will just have to learn the hard way; it's not a good thing to piss us off."

We drove back to the parking lot where we left the truck and switched our gear from the car to the truck. The car we borrowed was left in the parking lot for Raul's friend to pick up later. Our plan is to watch the area around the bar and trailer and see what was going on around there. We parked across the street in the parking lot of a restaurant. Our bodyguard pulled in behind us. Jay turned around and looked at the guy parked behind us and said "You know, I don't like him being parked there. How do we know we can trust him?" Jay then looked at Raul and asked "That ain't another one of your brothers is it?" Raul smiled and said "No Senor Jay, not this time."

There were a number of people going in and out of the bar over the course of 2 hours. There appeared to be a guard on the door. While we were waiting and watching, my thoughts turned to my family. I was thinking about Kara and her baby. I thought she would be a very good mother. She was strong willed and intelligent. When she put her mind to do something, she was very determined to complete whatever the task was. Over the past few months, I've watched her read book after book on parenting and planning how she was going to raise her first child. It was amusing to hear her say "I'm not going to allow my children to do some of the things I did as a child. If I have a girl, she's going to be a lady not a tomboy like I was."

A van backed into the barn and two men got out of the front of it. They both walked around to the back of the van and opened the rear door. They each helped a young man with a blindfold over his eyes and a baseball cap pulled down tight to his head get out of the van. Vince! Could it be him? He was the right height and build but I only got a glimpse of him before they took him inside. I looked at the other two guys with me and asked "What do you think?" My heart was racing a mile a minute. Jay said "It could be Vince but I'm not sure." Raul echoed Jay's response.

I looked at Jay and said "You know I'm going in there, how do you want to play it?" Jay thought for a moment and said "Let's talk to our friend behind us and see what he thinks." I motioned for the man to come up and get in the truck with us. I explained the situation to him and he said to sit tight, he was going to call Eddie and see what he wanted to do.

Eddie told us to wait; he had an idea that might work for all of us without any violence.

We waited for about 30 minutes and Eddie pulled in with another man beside him. Eddie told us this man owed him some money and worked with Cruz and his men. He could get inside without any trouble and maybe get a look at the boy for us. I showed him a picture of Vince and he agreed to go inside and take a look. Eddie reminded the man what happened to some other people who crossed him in the past. He told Eddie "No problem Senor Eddie, you help me with my money problems, I will help you and your friends."

Eddie winked at me and said "It will be ok Senor Bill."

I wasn't comfortable relying on people I didn't even know. Apparently Eddie felt he owed us one for getting rid of Cruz. I told the man Eddie called Yogi "I need to know how many men are inside, how many exits there are and where the boy is located inside." Yogi nodded his head yes. I also told him "If you screw us over, I will hunt you down and kill you, do you understand?" Yogi responded "Si, Si Senor."

Yogi walked across the street to the barn and talked to the guard at the door. I was watching them with my binoculars to try to see any strange movements between the two. The guard knocked on the door and another man answered and talked with Yogi and then left him in. He was in the barn for 45 minutes and finally came out. It seemed a lot longer to me and I was getting anxious. Yogi came over and said there were two men in the barn and the boy was still wearing the blindfold and cap. He thought the boy looked like the picture I showed him but it was hard to tell. He told us the boy was tied to a chair in the middle of the barn and there was one other door at the opposite end from where he went in. Yogi said he was told they were keeping the boy there until they figured out what to do with him.

I asked Yogi if the barn floor was open enough to drive a truck through. He said it was and they drove trucks in there all the time. We calculated the barn was about 100 feet long. The doors were made of wood and didn't appear to be reinforced. Eddie and Yogi got back in Eddie's car, our bodyguard got in the backseat of the truck with Raul. Jay looked at me and asked "You're gonna' do it aren't you?" As I started up the truck and put it in gear I said "If you mean we're going in that barn, yeh we're gonna' do it!" As we crossed the street I told Jay "When we get in the barn you grab the boy, chair and all and throw him in the back of the truck. I will take out the guard at the door; Raul and Paco, you guys try to take the two guys in the barn. This is gonna happen fast, so it's lock and load time."

I pulled up slowly to the barn and about 40 feet away floored the accelerator and drew down on the guard at the door. I emptied my gun at him and he was down. When we crashed through the door there were pieces of wood flying everywhere. As quickly as we entered the barn I slammed on the brakes and slid sideways on the barn floor. I was trying to keep the truck under control and not run over the boy. I could hear gunfire from Paco's gun and saw Jay jump out the passenger side and in one motion pick up the chair with the boy in it and they both disappeared into the back of the truck. Jay hopped back in and said "Go, go, go, get out of here!!" We crashed through the opposite end of the barn with splintered wood flying everywhere. There was a dirt driveway leading around the trailer and back onto the street and we took it. I headed out of town to the old campground and didn't stop until we got there. I parked the truck behind a row of trees and we all climbed out. I ran around to the bed of the truck and checked on the boy Jay threw in there. Ever since we left the barn, I was hoping upon hope it was Vince in the back of the truck. I was hoping my son would have some smart remark about my driving or Jay's physical prowess.

Once again, my heart sank. It was not Vince. I asked him if he was ok and he said he thought he was. I removed the blindfold and he asked "Who the hell are you? Are you the police? Where the hell am I?" I told him my name and where I was from. I explained to him why we were here and how we found him. He told me his name was Thomas Martinez and he was from Phoenix also. He was taken from his home two days ago and he has been blindfolded ever since. I assured him we would help him get back home as I helped him get untied from the chair. Thomas asked me who threw him in the back of the truck? Jay walked around the back of the truck and said "That would be me son, my name is Jay" and Jay offered his hand to Thomas. Thomas said "You are one strong S.O.B. sir to be able to throw me around like that." Jay said "Aw that was nothing son, I used to throw 400 pound steers around like that just to wake up in the morning before breakfast."

Raul and Paco came around the back of the truck and I asked them if they were alright. Paco said "The rumors are right Senor Bill; you are a little bit loco!" I asked them if they took down the two men inside the barn. Paco said he did shoot one man but I took out the other one inside the barn. I asked him what he meant; I didn't fire my gun inside the barn. He told me "One of the men must have been right inside the first door we crashed through because I saw a man flying through the air as we entered the barn." I must have been focusing on my driving, I never saw that man.

Paco's cell phone rang and it was Eddie asking where we were. He told Paco to have us lay low and to ditch the truck. He would send someone to pick us up after dark tonight. Eddie told Paco the barn and trailer were crawling with people and they had a description of the truck. The radiator on the truck must have gotten a hole in it because it was pushing water out pretty bad, it would be of little use to us now anyhow. I looked at Raul and he seemed a bit shaken. I asked if he was ok and he just smiled and shook his head. He asked if it would be ok to use my phone to call his brother Rafi and arrange for him to pick up the boy. I thought that would be a good idea. Thomas would be a lot safer with the police than with us right now. I'm sure our hit and run tactics were pissing off these guys more and more.

Raul took Thomas across the ridge to a friend's house to meet with his brother. The three of us would meet up with him later at a place down the road a mile or so. When we reached the place Paco agreed with Eddie for us to be picked up, it looked like it would fall down any minute. Paco said it was an old mining shack. It was definitely old. It was located off the main road about a ½ mile. We took some branches from the nearby brush and scratched out our footprints leading into the shack, just in case anyone came looking for us. Two hours later, Raul came back and said Thomas was safe with his brother. We had to sit tight until someone came to get us.

I wasn't comfortable sitting in this tiny building, I felt like a rat in a trap. I went outside and found a hiding place above and behind the shack. It wasn't long before the others came out as well. They spread out around me to watch and wait. After a few hours, it finally got dark. We could see the lights from a vehicle coming in the old dirt road. We all stayed put until Paco identified the driver. We jumped in the truck and took off back to the campsite to get our equipment out of our truck. Paco and the driver stood guard as we transferred our gear into the new truck and then we headed back out into the countryside. I had no idea where we were headed but I was glad it wasn't back into town.

The driver pulled off at a truck stop and drove to the back of the parking area. He parked the truck alongside of a storage trailer. The driver said something in Spanish to Paco and I didn't understand. Paco said "This is your new home Senor Bill. You may unload your equipment inside." Jay opened the rear door and said "Holy shit, look at this." I looked inside and there was a complete living area fixed up, living room, bathroom, bedroom and kitchen. Paco told us Eddie used this trailer for his guests sometimes and we should be safe here. We unloaded our gear and Paco said he would be back tomorrow with a vehicle for us. The three of us settled in and we were all ready to get some rest.

As I stretched out to relax I couldn't help but think it had been three weeks since Vince was taken. The odds of finding him alive were very thin. I called Ann and we once again discussed the reality of the situation. We both agreed we needed to face the fact that we were probably never going to see Vince again. Ann said "Why don't you come, we all miss you and I don't want to lose you also." I told Ann I would discuss it with Jay and Raul in the morning and would call her with our decision. I missed my family too and my mind was pretty well made up to go back home and regroup.

The next morning I told the guys I wanted to go back home and unless they strongly objected we would head back as soon as I could get my truck back. I explained to them I was feeling increasingly guilty about putting their lives in danger. I felt it was best to get out of here and maybe take some time to think out a new plan. They both agreed if that was what I wanted, they would go along with it. Jay said "You know Billy, I was starting to enjoy this game but these old bones could use a break. I wonder if anybody still thinks we're too damn old for this kind of action. I bet these clowns will really be pissed when they find out they got their asses kicked by two old farts like us." I called Ann and told her we would be coming home today.

Paco pulled in with a car for us to use and I explained our plans to him. He said "I think that is wise Senor Bill; there are a lot of people looking for you right now." I gave him the paper work from the dealer to get my truck back and $5000.00 cash for the repairs to the rental truck. I also asked him to get my trailer and horses from Paul and bring them back here. Paco said he would be back later today. I still had $5000.00 left from the money we took from one of the houses and I planned to give it to Raul when we got back home. Eddie had the refrigerator stocked with food and drinks, so we made ourselves some breakfast. For the first time in three weeks we didn't really have anything to do but relax, after breakfast we all took a nap.

Around 3pm Paco came back with my truck, trailer, horses and that damn dog. Paul didn't want to keep the dog. He said the dealer was upset at the condition of the rental truck but when he gave the dealer $5000.00 cash for the damage, he was happy. Paco told us it would be wise to get out of here as soon as possible, as far as he and Eddie knew the bad guys were still looking for the truck that crashed through the barn. That truck was parked inside the dealer's body shop and would stay there for another day. He told us we could thank Eddie for that. I told Paco "You be sure to thank Eddie for all his help and I may very well be seeing the two of you before too long." We shook hands and I thanked Paco for his help as well. Jay said to Paco "I didn't really trust you at first but you're ok in my book buddy, we'll meet again and maybe I'll have some old war stories to tell ya' then."

We loaded our gear into the truck, I checked on the horses, put the dog in the horse trailer and we headed north for home. It was a bittersweet return, I was happy to get back home, but we had not completed our mission. We didn't find Vince.

Chapter 11

BACK IN THE USA

The trip home was uneventful, with only a routine check at the border. I told them at the check station we were trying to buy some horses but we were not successful. I dropped Raul off at his home and handed him the envelope with the cash in it and told him to open it after I left and I would call him tomorrow. When I pulled into my driveway Ann and Kara came running out to greet us. Ann said jokingly she was even happy to see Jay. John greeted us with a hug at the front porch and the dogs just about knocked me over with their greetings. It was truly good to be home. I asked John if he would please take care of the horses while Jay and I went inside to get caught up with the girls.

Between Ann and Kara and the two dogs, I could barely find a spot to sit on the sofa. Ann pulled a chair close to the rest of us for Jay; he really was a part of our family. I joked with Kara about her belly getting bigger with my grandson and all she could do was hug and kiss me. She wiped away some tears and asked me if I was ok. I said "Sure, don't I look ok?" She said "No, you look really tired." I told her that Jay and I had been through a lot looking for Vince and we just needed to rest for a while. Kara asked "Did you have to shoot anyone while you were down there?" I told her we would talk about that tomorrow, for now I just wanted to hug my two favorite girls. Ann held out her hand to Jay and we had a big group hug. I thanked God for his guidance back home to my family and for the best friend any man could ask for.

John came back in from caring for the horses and said "You forgot to mention the dog in the trailer; he scared the crap out of me when I opened the tailgate. What should I do with him?" Jay and I both laughed. I told John I was sorry, I completely forgot about him. I told John to bring him in and let him meet the rest of the family. Ann looked at me and asked "What dog, why did you bring a dog along home?" I told them the entire story about the dog and said Jay insisted on bringing him home with us. Jay piped up "No way, I don't even like the dog, he doesn't even speak English!" We all had a good laugh about that one!!

John brought the dog in and after the traditional butt sniffing and checking each other out, the two Labs allowed the Rottweiler to move in. Ann asked "Jay, what's your dog's name?" "He's not my damn dog and I don't know what his name is, probably some Spanish name I can't pronounce anyway." We decided to give him a new name and asked everyone to make a suggestion. By now the dog was going around and licking everyone's hand, I was sure he was just glad to get out of the horse trailer. Kara suggested Jose' since he was from Mexico, Ann thought maybe Brutus since he was so big and John said how about Max. By now the dog was licking Jay's hand and Jay was stroking the dog's head. Jay said "Aw hell, if you're gonna' dump the damn dog on me, we'll call him Bud. I used to have a dog named Bud when I was a kid and for a dog he was ok." Bud it is. Ann put her arms around Jay and said "If you like, Bud can sleep in your room tonight." Jay thought about a little bit and said "Well I guess so, but there's no way he sleeping in bed with me. I don't want no mangy dog in bed with me." With that Jay said "Speaking of bed, I'm beat and that's where I'm going right now, goodnight everyone." He started for his room and then stopped and looked around at Bud and asked "You commin'?" Bud looked at me and I motioned with my head for him to go and he followed Jay into his room. We could hear Jay laying down the rules to Bud as they went into their bedroom, no jumping on the bed, you sleep on the floor, no damn snoring or farting and stop licking me. We all got a good laugh and Jay just made a new friend.

John and Kara needed to get back to their home and we made plans to have breakfast together tomorrow morning. As Ann and I were heading to bed she handed me a note to call a Mr. Turner ASAP. She said he needed to talk with me whenever I got back. I asked if it was the same Mr. Turner whose daughter we rescued a few weeks ago. Ann said it was. Ann also reminded me the FBI agents and Sheriff Bob were inquiring about where I was and when I was coming home. I told her I would probably have to deal with them Hanson went on to say "I'm told you guys put a crimp in Jose Cruz's operation and that Mr. Cruz is no longer involved in the business." Jay piped in "That sounds like good news to me!" "On the surface it is good news" said Hanson "But you have also created a lot of trouble for yourselves and that trouble is not going to go away. The Mexican authorities have contacted us and although they have no evidence against you at this point, they are advising us to not allow you into their country in the future. From a legal standpoint, we have no reason to keep you here and they have no reason to keep you out of Mexico. For your own safety and that of your family you should not go back. You have pissed off some very bad people and they will come after you." Jay said "Aw hell, where have I heard that before, when are these clowns gonna' realize they have pissed off some pretty bad people themselves?"

Bob asked if anyone down there could identify us. I told him we left two witnesses behind and maybe they could identify Jay and me. I also said we never mentioned any names including Vince's and I was very sure they had no idea who we really were. Bob said "You know the Mexican police cannot protect you, they do not have the manpower." I explained to both of them we never asked anyone to protect us, we were capable of taking care of ourselves. I asked Hanson if they were going to try to stop us from crossing the border again. He said "No, they had no reason to do that. However common sense should tell us it would not be safe to go back." Hanson was blunt, and I liked that.

I looked at Bob and said "Vince is down there somewhere, we found some evidence of that. I know your hands are tied, but mine are not. I'm not giving up until I find him. I appreciate what you both have done to help us but Jay and I will take it from here. All I ask from now on is please do not get in our way." We shook hands and as the two of them left Bob whispered to me "Good luck."

After Bob and Hanson left, I said to Ann and Kara "I think you should go stay with your parents for a while. At least until we get back from this next trip. Just in case these guys have figured out who we are, I don't want them coming after you." Ann looked at me and said "I guess you've made up your mind, you are going back and there's nothing I can say to stop you." I told her if there was any other way I would take it. But yes, Jay and I were going back for Vince.

After much discussion, Ann agreed it would be wise to stay with her parents for a while and Kara and John decided to stay with his parents until Jay and I got back, hopefully this time with Vince. I decided we would leave for Mexico in two days. It would give me time to get new supplies and arrange for Raul and Mike to look after the horses and dogs while we were all gone. Ann said she would leave for her parent's home the same time Jay and I left. Kara and John would arrange with his parents a time to stay with them.

Sheriff Bob called and asked me what our plans were. I still trusted Bob and explained to him what we going to do as far as Ann and the kids not staying at our place for a while. Bob felt that was a good idea. He told me when he was able he would have a patrol car drive by and check things for us. I thanked him for his help and told him I hoped he and Vince and I would be hunting together this fall. Bob agreed and wished me luck.

I really didn't want to leave my family again but I knew I couldn't live with myself if I didn't try again. Hanson was right, we created a lot of trouble for ourselves and these guys were going to try their best to make us pay for it. This mission was not over and I was determined to see it through. Jay and I could use the next two days to relax and plan our next move. We both agreed it was too dangerous to take Raul along this time; it would be just the two of us. I joked with Jay about taking his new friend Bud along but he shot that down with "I don't want that damn dog going with us!"

I finally got time to call Mr. Turner and he asked if he could meet with me. I told him if he liked he could stop by this evening. He said that would be great and we set the time for 7pm. I guess I didn't realize how out of rest I was; I laid down on the sofa and quickly fell asleep. When I woke up I walked by Jay's room and peeked in – he and Bud were stretched out on his bed fast asleep.

That evening when the Turner's stopped by it was nice to see them again. Maria gave Jay and me a big hug and a kiss and Mrs. Turner called me her lone ranger again. Ann got a good laugh out of that. She winked at Jay who was standing beside her and said to him "You're my Tonto, Jay." Mr. Turner expressed his family's disappointment that we didn't find Vince. He went on to say that he'd been in contact with a number of other victim's family's and they all wanted to share their appreciation for what Jay and I had done to put a dent in the kidnapper's ring. He pulled out a large manila envelope and handed it to me. He said "Go ahead, open it." When I opened it, the envelope was full of cash! I looked at him and asked "What's this for?" He told me "We all know you lost a considerable amount of money to those thieves and we hope it helps to ease some of you pain and cover some of your expenses. In addition we have formed a committee to continue raising money and community awareness to help you and any others in fighting these thugs."

I told Mr. Turner "I don't know what to say, I'm speechless, thank you!" We hugged each other and the rest of our family's joined in a big group hug. I felt so humbled by this gesture I asked if we could all pray to God thanking him for bringing us all together. We asked for continued spiritual strength to end this reign of terror on our community. It truly was amazing what a group of people could do when they put their minds to it.

We ended the evening with some food and wine and my family and the Turner's became friends for life. I informed everyone Jay and I would be leaving in another day to continue our search for Vince. Jay asked the Turners if they would continue to pray for us while we were gone. I almost fell off my chair!! In the over forty years I've known Jay, I never heard him ask anyone to pray for him. I felt like God was truly going to be with us on this trip.

After the Turners left, Ann counted the money they had given us. She counted it a second time. Ann looked at me and said "Oh my God, there's $40,000 in this envelope!" We were all shocked. I never thought there was that much money in there. We both agreed that first thing tomorrow she would take it to the bank and deposit it. We didn't want that kind of money in the house with no one going to be around. Jay looked at both of us and said "You know I'm beginning to think there might be something to this God stuff. It ain't every day a man walks through your door and hands you $40,000 with no strings attached." I just looked at Jay and said "Amen brother."

We all had some packing to do, so Ann and I went to our room to get started. I looked around the corner and watched Jay walk into his room with Bud right on his heels. It was good to see Jay caring about someone other than himself, even if it was a dog. Tomorrow we had a lot of loose ends to tie up before we headed south.

The next morning I gave my foreman Mike a call and asked him where he was working. I told him I would meet him in an hour at the job site. I picked up Raul and he and I went to see Mike. On the way Raul couldn't thank me enough for the money I gave him. I simply told him he earned it. I also needed to tell Raul that this time Jay and I would be going back alone. I explained that I didn't want to put him in any more danger and that I needed him here to help Mike run the business while I was gone. Along with that added responsibility was a nice pay raise starting today. At first he seemed disappointed at not going with us but when I mentioned the job promotion and raise it eased the sting of disappointment. I told Raul I greatly appreciated his loyalty and help he gave us and would always be proud to call him and his family my friends.

When we reached the job site, I introduced Mike to his new assistant. I trusted Mike completely and told him he could give Raul whatever assignments he saw fit. I took Mike aside and we talked a little business and it seemed everything was going well. I then handed the keys of my truck to Mike and said "Give me your keys; we are going to trade vehicles." He looked at me and said "Are you serious, my truck is 8 years older than yours. It runs good but the body's pretty beat up." I slapped him on the shoulder and said "Exactly, where we're going this beat up old truck will blend in perfectly. Consider this newer truck a perk for taking over for me while I've been gone."

Mike looked me in the eyes and said "So you're going back. I hope you bring that kid back this time, I've got a lot of work for him when he gets here." Mike hugged me and said "Don't worry about anything here boss, Raul and I will take care of business. You and Jay take care of yourselves and kick some ass if you have to." We switched the equipment from our trucks and when Mike saw the grenades, ammo and other equipment his eyes got wide. I simply told him "Don't ask, Raul can fill you in later." I hopped in my "new" truck and headed for town.

I rounded up some more food, water, gas and some other provisions. I went to the garage where we kept our heavy equipment and grabbed two extra spare tires for the truck as well. When I got back home, Jay was outside playing with the dogs. I couldn't help but think how much the labs must miss Vince, when he was around he spent a lot of time with them. I sure missed him too.

Jay and I spent the rest of the day going over maps and double checking our equipment. Late in the afternoon I gave Eddie a call and told him we would be coming his way tomorrow. Eddie said "Don't come by my place man, you guys stirred up a hornets nest down here. There are a lot of bad dudes looking for you and they mean business. You gotta' be careful where you go down here, I'll meet you at the old mine shack, call me when you get here." I told Eddie we would see him tomorrow.

John and Kara joined us for dinner in the evening and we all shared some Vince stories. Kara always referred to him as the scientist. As a child he was always experimenting with something, always trying to figure out how and why something worked. Kara recalled how he used one of her dolls to perform an experiment on a "human". Ann remembered how she was constantly cleaning up dirt around the house from his experiments and how he ruined her flower beds with his constant digging and trying to concoct formulas to make the flowers grow better. For me the best memories were the times we spent outdoors, teaching him about the land and animals who lived there. I was amazed how at age 7 or 8 he knew more of the scientific names of plants and animals than I did. Jay remembered a scrawny little kid who was always smarter than he was and someone who was always asking questions. His fondest memory of Vince was how much his wife wished their son had Vince's good manners instead of his father's.

Before we all went to bed that evening, we held hands and prayed to God that we would all have many more memories of Vince in the future. We asked God's to guide us to Vince and allow us to bring him back home. My personal prayer was if it was God's will, to take my life in exchange for Vince's. My emotions were overflowing, I really did not want to leave but I was not satisfied with the answers we'd gotten. I was not sure how God would deal with me. I killed men in my search for Vince and I may have to kill again. From the time my children were born, I felt I would do anything to protect my family and now I have been forced to do so. I really didn't feel any guilt about the killing and deep down I guess there was a fear that I may once again enjoy it. A long time ago, there was an adrenalin rush, a pride in body counts and a feeling of invincibility. I didn't want those feelings again. I also asked God to keep those feelings from me.

In bed that night Ann and I fell asleep with our arms around each other and I hoped we would be able to do it again.

Chapter 12

THE SEARCH CONTINUES

In the morning John and Kara joined us for breakfast. We all hugged and kissed goodbye and I felt the baby kick one more time. It was time to go. Ann went through a checklist of things to make sure we had everything and double checked the satellite phones to make sure they were working. She slapped me on the butt and said you guys be careful and bring my boy back.

Jay and I mounted up and we were on the road. Neither one of us said much for the first hour or so. I asked Jay how he was feeling about the killings we had done. He didn't answer me for a while and then finally said "You know, I was thinking about asking you the same thing. I kinda enjoyed it, not the killing, but the sneaking around and recon stuff. I still like intimidating people and getting results. Do you think we went about it too hard?" I said "No, the bastards took my son!" Jay asked "Are you going to have second thoughts about taking somebody down again if we have to?" "Not if involves getting Vince back or covering our butts" I said. Jay said "Look, we aren't the same guys we were 40 years ago, we've both grown up and found our way in life. Whether we find Vince or not, there's a whole lot of people think we're doing the right thing. Law enforcement can't go where we can go and some of them probably can't do what we can do. You talk about God's will, well maybe it's God's will we were trained to do what we do. Maybe God put us through the experiences we had to prepare us for this mission. You ever think about that?"

Wow, Jay laid it all out for me! I was impressed with that speech! I pulled off the road and looked at him and said "Ok, your right. Enough of this psychological stuff, let's go do what we know best and let shit happen." Jay looked at me and winked and said "Let's do it."

We motored on down the highway and in a couple of hours pulled into the truck stop where we hid out before. I called Eddie and told him where we were. He told me to stay put, he would meet us there. Eddie pulled in about 45 minutes later. He motioned for me to pull around to the back of the truck stop. I noticed there was another vehicle following his and it stopped short of where Eddie and I parked. I asked Eddie if he knew who was in the other car. He said "Ya, those are my boys, they are covering our butts. Right now I don't go anywhere without them. There are too many bad guys floating around here." Eddie looked me in the eyes and said "My friend, I am glad to help you but we must be careful. You cannot trust anyone around here right now. These drug dealers will pay anyone for information about you, they have offered to pay me but I played dumb and said I knew nothing about you. These men I do not like, but I have to play along with them for the sake of business. They spend a lot of money in my place."

Eddie handed me an envelope and said "These men want you dead; you kill them first if you get the chance. I don't know if they have your boy but they are behind everything that goes on around here. Do not contact me until you kill them." With that Eddie shook my hand and said "Good luck, Senor." Eddie crawled back in his car and they were gone. Jay said "Man, that old boy is spooked! He don't want nothin' to do with us right now." I said I kinda gathered that myself.

So here we are, obviously on our own from here on out. I opened the envelope Eddie gave me and there were two names on a piece of paper inside along with a map. Ricardo and Manny Cruz, the older brothers of Juan, the man we killed. The map showed the location of a ranch that appeared to be 300-400 miles south of here. Eddie had written on the map that as far he knew this is where the Cruz brothers ran their drug and kidnapping ring from. Circled on the map was one word in big letters – QUIDADO, Spanish for be careful.

I looked at Jay and said "Well partner, looks like we're heading south." Jay said "Not so fast, I think we should head back north." I asked "What the hell you mean, north?" "Looks to me like this is a pretty big ranch and we don't know a damn thing about it. I'm thinkin' a fella with an airplane could fly over and do some recon rather than just go chargin' in there blind and getting our asses shot up. You still got that fancy long range camera don't ya?" "Yes I do and your right again my friend, guess that's why we make such a good team" I responded.

After talking things over, we decided Jay would rent a car in Chihuahua and drive back to Phoenix to get his plane. I would make arrangements for him to land at the local airport. We had a lot of cash to work with and it probably wouldn't be any trouble to grease the wheels we needed to put things in place. I dropped Jay off to get a rental car and I headed to the airport to make arrangements for him to land. On the way I called Raul's brother Rafi to see if he could be of any help in getting Jay into the airport. Rafi just sighed when he heard my voice. He asked me what Jay was bringing in on the plane. I assured him nothing lethal except Jay himself. I explained we just wanted to do some recon of the Cruz's ranch and then we would park the plane.

Rafi said "Our department has a private air strip just outside of town. If you give me your word there are no bombs or other lethal weapons on the plane I can get you clearance to land there. However, I will inspect the plane once it lands." I told Rafi that would be fine and I would give Jay his phone number and instruct him to call Rafi for the information he would need to land. I thanked him once again for sticking his neck out to help us. Things were coming together easier than I thought!

I called Jay back and gave him the good news along with Rafi's phone number. I told Jay "If there is anything on that plane that resembles a weapon or explosive – get it off or hide it well." Jay answered simply "Not a problem, they'll never find anything." If I knew Jay he already had a few hiding places built into the plane. I decided to go back to the truck stop and wait for Jay to get back down here. It was better to park the truck in plain sight rather than trying to hide it. I settled in and put the seat back and took a nap.

After about 4 hours Jay called and said he was maybe an hour out before landing. I told him I would meet him at the landing strip. Rafi had given me directions earlier and I took off to meet up with my pilot. The strip was surrounded with chain link fence and a locked gate. I assumed Rafi would soon be here to meet us. Right on time I could see Jay's plane coming in and behind me Rafi was pulling up the gate. He motioned for me to pull up to the gate. We both drove up to the plane as Jay was climbing out. Rafi said he was going to put an impound tag on the plane so no one would get suspicious. He then told Jay he was going to check out the plane. Jay winked at me and said "Check her out buddy, the only thing dangerous on that plane just got out."

Rafi spent 20 minutes searching inside the plane. He came out smiling and said "Well, I found no missiles or high explosives inside you must have them well hidden. You guys have until 7pm today to fly this plane then you must be back here and park it. I will meet you here at 8pm to leave you out. The plane will remain here until your business is completed and it will be secure. The next flight out of here for you will be back home. I know why you are here and this is all I can help you with at this time. Once again don't make me regret helping you." We thanked Rafi and he locked the gate behind him as he drove out.

We had about 4 hours of flying time until we had to be back here so we climbed aboard and got back in the air. It was probably an hour flight to get to the ranch which gave us two hours to look around. I looked at Jay and he was smiling from car to car. I asked him what was so amusing. He said "There's a hand held missile launcher under your seat. I built a trap door for it a couple of years ago and mounted the seat on top of it. I actually forgot it was there until Rafi mentioned he didn't find any missiles." I just shook my head and didn't say a word.

As we approached what we thought was the Cruz's ranch we could see a large house with a horse barn and a large metal storage building next to the barn. There was only one road into the place that was probably ½ mile long. We figured we would only get one fly over of the property without drawing attention to ourselves so I got as many pictures as I could. There was a main road that paralleled the property for a mile or so to the east and we could see another ranch to the east maybe 2 miles away. The terrain was pretty open around the ranch with a few rolling hills maybe ¼ mile to the west. It was really open to the north and south of the ranch. I got some pictures of a couple of vehicles parked outside the house, one a yellow ford pickup with brown stripes we could probably recognize later.

We headed back to the air strip to meet our curfew with Rafi and to look over the pictures I had taken. We landed without incident and Jay said "We got time to pull that rocket launcher from under seat until Rafi gets here." He handed me a wrench and told me to take the seat off. When I pulled open the compartment he built under the seat, there it was, a Russian made rocket launcher and three rockets. "Where the hell did you get this?" I asked. Jay replied "At a yard sale a few years ago. The guy I bought it from had no idea it was still functional. He was using it as a decoration in his den and his wife made him get rid of it. Can you believe that Billy?" I just said "No, sorry I asked." We put the launcher in the back of truck and covered it up with boxes of food and water bottles incase Rafi got nosey.

Rafi pulled in at 8pm on the button. He unlocked the gate and we drove the truck out. He told us "You guys are going to be out of my jurisdiction if you're going after the Cruz brothers. You need to know they've put a bounty on your heads for killing their brother. They will keep coming after you until you kill them or they kill you. Are you ready for that?" Jay said "We've had a bounty on our heads before and we're still kickin'. Hell, we might put a bounty on their heads!" We shook Rafi's hand and thanked him again for his help. He left us with "Good luck, Senors."

Jay was right, back in Africa we had a bounty put on our heads by a group of radicals. They offered $500.00 in US dollars literally for our heads. But nobody collected. I wasn't here to kill anyone; I just wanted my son back. Jay and I talked it over while we were flying and we both agreed we would go underground from here on out. Rafi and Eddie were the only people who knew we were here and we would try hard to keep it that way. It meant no eating in restaurants or sleeping in motels, we would rarely leave the truck during daylight. Most all of our work would be done at night.

We found an isolated spot not far from the air strip to park for the night and looked over the digital pictures of the ranch I had taken earlier. The only way in was from the west using the hills as cover. There was a dry creek bed that looked like we could get within 150 yards of the barn. We would have to hike in on foot for 2 or 3 miles to get to the creek bed. I was going over the pictures when I came to the one of that yellow truck.

I looked at Jay and said "That's it, the truck. We'll hole up somewhere outside the ranch and wait for that truck to come out. We'll take the truck and that will be our ticket in; we can drive right up to the front door." Jay said "That'll beat the hell out of crawlin' around in the sand. Sounds like a plan, Billy." We each had a sandwich and rolled out our bedrolls and turned in for the night.

We were on the road by daylight the next morning heading south. Other than stopping for gas and to pee, we kept moving. Jay had some elk jerky and dried fruit that we munched on and it felt good to be working a plan of action again. We passed through several small towns and it was tempting to stop and get a hot meal but we didn't. Eddie told us about a bar called "Rita's" where these guys hung out sometimes; it was located in a little town about 5 miles from the Cruz's ranch. We thought we would stake out the place and see if we could spot the yellow truck. As we drove into town it was easy to find Rita's. The bar was in the center of town on the main street. This town looked like one of those places where everybody knew each other. Not a very big place so we couldn't spend very much time here until somebody noticed us. We parked in a parking lot beside the bar where we could see the main street.

We both left our beards get pretty scruffy and our hair grow longer. Our clothes were dirty work clothes and our beat up truck helped us to blend in. We both had dark complexions from spending a lot of time outside. We didn't look like a couple of rich "Gringo's" as we heard we were called. Looking around the parking lot our truck definitely blended in. I told Jay if he improved his Spanish maybe we could pass for locals. He just growled at me.

We settled in for what could be a long wait. There was not a lot of activity here right now and we had no sign of the truck we were looking for. It was the only lead we had to these guys for the moment. Jay took the first watch. I got my handgun out and stripped it down and cleaned it, I went through my backpack making sure I didn't forget anything, I cut my finger nails and then cleaned some of the trash from the truck. That was the first hour. I decided to take a nap for the next hour until it was my turn to watch. We sat there for 8 hours and no yellow truck.

Jay and I reminisced about the old days, sitting and watching for days, many times waiting for one shot. Hours spent in the rain, heat and humidity. Bugs, snakes, mud, sweat and lousy food, if we had any, were just a few of the fine working conditions we had back then. I remembered what a treat it was if we happened to shoot a wild pig and roast it back at the firebase. It was amazing how fast a roasted pig could disappear around a bunch of hungry Army grunts. Suddenly sitting in this soft truck seat all day didn't seem so bad.

We spent the night in the parking lot with no results. At least while it was dark we could take turns walking around outside and get the kinks out of our old bones. We even fired up the engine and got it warm enough to fry some burgers in aluminum foil on the manifold. We were both getting antsy and had to convince each other to stay put. A few times we had people ask us if were broke down or needed a jump. We just thanked them and said we were waiting for some friends.

Time passed slowly, it was nearing 24 hours in this spot and we would soon have to move before somebody got too curious about us. Then there it was – that ugly yellow truck with the brown stripes pulled into the front of the bar. Two guys climbed out of the truck and went in the bar. Now our adrenalin was flowing again. The two guys didn't fit the description of the Cruz's brothers we had. We debated on our next move and decided that would depend on how long they spent in the bar. The longer they stayed; the easier our job would be. I considered going into the bar and see if I could get any more information but Jay talked me out of it. He said "We've waited this long; a little while longer won't make any difference. I know you're getting anxious, so am I." I told Jay I would wait two hours after that I was going in the bar.

Two hours passed and the two men were still in the bar. I looked at my watch and then at Jay and he said "Yeh, yeh, now what are we gonna do." I reached behind the truck seat and pulled out a duffle bag. In the bag were some wigs and fake moustaches and beards along with eye glasses, hats and small pillows to make my belly bigger. I asked Jay "What color hair you want and do you want to be the fat one or the skinny one?" Jay smiled and said "I want to be a fat redhead." He became a fat redhead with a beard and I put on a dark, long haired wig with a dark beard and dark horn rimmed glasses.

I went in the bar first and sat at the bar close to the two men who were in the yellow truck. Jay would wait a few minutes and come in by himself so we would not be associated together. He would sit somewhere away from me and be my backup if I needed some. This was like any local bar; all the regulars looked me over and mumbled to each other about who I was. I nodded at the bartender and asked for a draft beer. The two men were talking pretty loud with two other men. I was all ears. It appeared the booze was loosening their tongues as we expected. I saw Jay walk in about 10 minutes later and sit at a table in the back of the bar. Jay was a big man to start with but with the big belly he now looked huge. I overheard one of the four men comment "That's one big Hombre!" All the rest of the people in the bar checked Jay out just like they did me.

I overheard the men complaining about their boss and all the crap they put up with. What a mean bastard he was and how badly he treated them. Much the same conversation one would hear in any bar anywhere in the world. While nursing my beer, I heard one of the two men we were interested in say they each had the next two days off. The second man said "We will not have to do any babysitting for two days. I wish we could get on the crew that makes pick up runs down south. Those guys make good money. I am sick of this job we have now."

My ears really perked up. Could it be this guy was referring to babysitting kidnap victims? Neither one of them looked like someone a parent would hire to babysit their children. I ordered another beer hoping to get more information. I could understand Spanish pretty well but was not fluent in speaking; so I just kept my mouth shut. After two more beers I finally heard what I needed. The first man said "I am tired of looking after these rich kids and waiting for their parents to pay up. We get paid peanuts and our bosses make millions."

Bingo, now I knew they were part of the kidnapping ring and there was a good chance there may be some kidnap victims at the ranch, hopefully Vince would be there. Jay and I would wait for these two guys to leave the bar and take their truck. I hoped they would soon leave before I got drunk.

Finally, I heard one of them say "OK, let's get out of here and go to my place." I nodded my head to Jay to head for the door. We got in the truck and followed them across town. They stopped in an alley behind a feed mill and both got out to take a leak. Jay looked at me and said "Let's take um." We pulled up behind their truck and jumped out and the two guys never knew what hit them. All that booze slowed them down and their reaction time was slow, even against two old guys. We tied them up and gagged them and put them in the bed of their truck. Jay drove their truck and I followed him until we were a mile or so out of town. We pulled over and unloaded our passengers into a drainage ditch along the side of the road. Somebody should find them in the morning.

We headed towards the Cruz ranch and found a place to hid our truck and pulled in to talk things over. We decided to drive into the ranch house with our new truck and hope nobody would pay much attention to us. When we flew over earlier there seemed to be a bunk house next to the main house with a few vehicles parked in front. We would pull in there and park. When we pulled into the ranch lane there was a guard at the gate and he just waived us on through, so far so good. We pulled up to the bunk house and parked in front of it. A man came out and said "Hey what are you guys doing back here, you forget something?" I opened the window a bit and said "I forgot my jacket and it might get cold tonight." The man walked over to the truck and I stuck my handgun in his face. I asked how many men were in the bunkhouse with him. He said he was alone. Jay went in to check. The man was right. I asked him how many people were in the ranch house. He said he thought there were two men and two other people. I asked him "Who are the other people?" Two boys, Senor, I don't know who they are." I asked him if the Cruz brothers were here right now. He said "No Senor, they are away and will not be back for another week."

I followed the man to the main house with my gun in his back. Jay went around to the side of the house and eased up to the front door. I told the man to call the men out of the house saying he needed help. One of the men came out the front door and Jay took him out by hitting him over the head with his gun butt. Then things turned bad. I heard a pistol cock behind me and then another and another. Someone said "Drop your gun Senor." I looked at Jay and there was a man with a gun pointed at him as well. We both dropped our guns, we'd been had.

We were marched to the metal building and taken inside. There was a trap door in the floor and one of the men opened it. We were both thrown down into a hole. One of the men asked what we were doing here. We did not answer. He asked if we were looking for someone. Were we the two Gringos' who caused so much trouble for him and his friends? Did we have any idea how much trouble we were in right now? Did we realize the only reason we were still alive was there were people who wanted to see us before we died? Did we have anything to say? We did not say a word. They slammed the trap door shut and we were in total darkness.

Jay said "I guess we underestimated these guys a bit." I said "Ya think!! By about 5 men we underestimated!" I lit a match and looked around. We were in a hole in the ground about 8 feet square and 10 feet deep. The only way out was through the door above us. I was sure someone was guarding the door. They were probably going to keep us here until the Cruz brothers came back. That was a week according to the man at the bunkhouse. I dug a small flashlight out of my pocket and realized they hadn't searched us before throwing us in this hole. I had a pocket knife and a small .32 caliber pocket handgun stuck on my belt. I looked at Jay and smiled "They screwed up, what do you have on you?" Jay had a small fanny pack around his waist and opened it up. "Well looky here, I got a tiny little gun like you, a big old Rambo knife, some fuse, a small detonator, a tin can, a length of rope and a couple of candy bars." I looked at him and asked "What the hell's the tin can for?" Jay pulled the duct tape that was serving as a lid off and said "Well I'll be damned; somebody put some C-4 in this can." Leave it up to Jay; there was about 4 ounces of C-4 plastic explosive in the can.

At least we had some tools to work with. Now we needed to figure out what to do with them. Jay grabbed his Rambo knife and started digging hand holes in the dirt to climb up to the trap door. He checked the door and it was locked so he climbed back down. I decided to crawl up to the door as I was smaller than Jay and wait until somebody opened the door. I dug my feet into the dirt to support my body weight and held onto the frame around the perimeter of the door. We had no idea how long it may be until somebody came to open the door. I hung there for an hour and my legs and arms were starting to cramp. I crawled down and Jay took a turn. He hung there for another hour and still nothing. I changed places with him and was wondering if maybe we wouldn't see anyone for a week.

After 5 hours of switching back and forth I heard someone walk on the wooden floor above. I could only hear one set of footsteps. The trap door was wiggling a bit and then it was open. A man was bent over looking in the hole right in my face. I grabbed his shirt and pulled him down into the hole with Jay. I heard a couple of thumps and the man gasp for air and then it was quiet; except for the gurgling sound of a man dying. Jay whispered "He's done." I looked around the room and couldn't see anyone else as I climbed out. Jay was right behind me coming out of the hole. Jay wiped the blood off his knife on his pants leg and stuck it back in his pack. I whispered to him "Should be 6 more plus the guard at the gate." He nodded his head yes.

We moved over to a window that faced the ranch house. I could see 4 men seated inside playing cards; that left 2 men unaccounted for. We needed a diversion. Jay winked at me and said "The C-4, let's use half of it and blow the side out of this building out. That should bring those fellas outside and we can take them down." I looked at Jay and said "Rig it." While Jay was rigging the explosive, I crawled over to the house to look around. I found the other two guys in another room playing video games. I felt better knowing where everybody was. I went back to Jay and we decided to each take a position on opposite sides of the house and get them in crossfire. Jay slapped me on the back and said "Ready when you are Billy." I nodded yes and we moved into position.

When Jay hit the switch, there was a huge explosion. Men came running out the front door of the house with guns drawn. We took down the first 4 men before they hit the steps off the porch. The last two hesitated and dove for cover on the porch. They were hollering to each other where they thought we were. I only had 2 rounds left in my gun plus the 9 rounds in the gun from the guy in the hole. I wasn't sure if Jay was out or not. I could see bits and pieces of the two men but didn't have a good shot. There was a plastic bucket lying beside me on the ground. I threw the bucket as hard as I could behind me and when it hit the ground both men raised up and fired in the direction of the bucket. I was able to hit them both and they were done. It was eerily quiet. I could hear nothing in the house. Then I remembered the guard at the gate; where was he. I moved around the back of the house to get to where Jay was located. I gave him our old signal so he wouldn't shoot me. Jay said "I'm out of ammo man, what you got?" I had the two rounds in my gun and then I would be out. I said "Let's wait for the guard to come to us. He got to be wondering what's going on."

Jay was trying to crawl up on the porch to get a gun one of the dead men dropped. He got his foot caught in the porch railing and was pulling and pulling and couldn't get loose. I grabbed his boot with both hands and he pulled his foot out of his boot and then he was free. Jay flipped me a gun with some ammo in it and he slithered back to me with another handgun for himself. We had six dead men on the porch and one more to find. We waited 15 or 20 minutes and I saw something move by our truck. I poked Jay in the ribs and he whispered "I got 'em." The truck was about 50 feet away. I could see two legs at the back of the truck. Jay was easing around to my right to try to get behind him. I laid down a burst of fire at the man's legs and he hit the ground moaning. Jay got to his feet and moved around the back of the truck and with one shot the moaning was over.

Now it was time to check out the house. According to the two men whose truck we borrowed there should be someone in the house they were guarding. We searched the main floor and found nothing; the second floor was the same. There was a basement door in the kitchen and I went down the stairs first to check it out. There was a small room in the back with a light on. I eased the door open and inside I could see a young girl lying on a small bed with one arm chained to the wall. She looked like she was sleeping. In the opposite corner was a young man lying on a bed that was also chained to the wall and appeared to be sleeping. My heart was racing, could it be? I shook the boy and rolled him over. It was Vince!! I was overjoyed!! I hugged him and kissed him and told him he was safe; I was here to take him home! But something was wrong. He didn't say a word. He was breathing but his eyes were turned up in his head, his lips were moving but he wasn't saying anything. What the hell did they do to him? I hollered for Jay to come down. When Jay stepped in the room he said "Oh my Lord, its Vince. How is he?" I said "I don't know, something's wrong, maybe drugs but we got him."

I told Jay to check on the girl. She appeared to be in the same shape as Vince. Jay looked at me and said "We got to get them the hell out of here, now." I shielded Vince and Jay shot off the chain holding him to the wall. Then we did the same for the girl. He picked up the girl and I picked up Vince and we made it out of the basement to the truck. When we laid the two of them in the back seat we could needle marks on their arms. I could feel Vince had lost a lot of weight when I was carrying him he felt skinny. I sat in the back seat with the two of them and Jay drove. Our plan was to go get my truck and head back to Chihuahua. They both seemed to be in a drug stupor and only semi-conscious. They both had a hollow, blank stare in their eyes. I could only get soft mumbles out of them and could not understand anything they said. I was both extremely happy and concerned at the same time.

When we got to my truck we quickly loaded them in the back seat and headed north. Jay and I talked it over and decided to call Rafi and see if he could arrange to get us some medical care for the two of them when we got to the city. When I called Rafi he said "Si, Si Senor Bill, I will arrange for you to take them directly to the medical clinic. I will meet you on the highway outside of town and escort you to the clinic." I told Rafi "I will call you when we are closer to you."

It was a long drive and it seemed to take forever, we only stopped for gas. Jay was rooting around in his pocket and found the leftover C-4 and said "Aw hell, I shoulda blew up that pretty truck before we took off." We both laughed and it felt good to laugh. For so long I held on to a thread of belief that Vince was alive. I had plenty of doubts and thought many times I was just kidding myself. I was beginning to accept that I was going to have to face the reality that Vince was dead. My emotions were overflowing right now there were moments when I cried uncontrollably and others when I was grinning from ear to ear. I thanked God for not allowing me to give up, for protecting Vince and for giving me the best friend a man could ever ask for. Even grouchy Jay was in a good mood.

An hour outside of Chihuahua I called Rafi. He gave us a location where we would meet him. The kids were still out of it in the back seat and hopefully they would both be alright with some treatment. Rafi was waiting for us when we pulled in to the little turn off in the road. He asked if we wanted an ambulance and I said "No, let's just get going." We followed him about two miles to the medical center and there were two stretchers waiting for us when we got there. They took Vince and the girl into the ER and we followed them as far as we could. We were escorted to a waiting room where a nurse came out and asked us questions. I gave her what I could about Vince but I knew nothing about the girl; not even her name.

I decided to wait to call Ann until I knew what condition Vince was in. While in the waiting room Rafi was asking us where we found them. He asked "Did you find them at the ranch? How did you get in there? Didn't they have the place guarded?" I simply said "Yes." Rafi asked "Are there more bodies?" I nodded my head yes. I said "Look Rafi, I will be glad to explain it all to you later. Hell you can even take credit for it but right now I want to take care of my son, ok?" Rafi said "Sure, we will talk later, I will pray for your son and the girl." I thanked him for his help and he left saying he would be back in an hour or so.

Over an hour later a doctor came out and asked if I was Mr. Wright. I said I was. He said "We have your son and the girl stabilized. They have both been heavily drugged with cocaine and they are both dehydrated. We've got some fluids in them and their vitals are stabilizing. That's all I can tell you, right now they are both very ill. Tomorrow we should know more. You may see him now and stay with him if you like."

Jay and I went back to be with Vince. He was sleeping soundly and it was sure good to be by his side. I held his hand and just stared at him thinking of better times. There were times when he ran with the dogs and times when he was small and full of questions. I remembered a time when he found a fossil in our pasture and he thought he had made a major discovery. He didn't know at the time there were hundreds of the same fossil in that pasture.

Jay put his arm around me and said "He's gonna be alright Billy. We'll get him the best damn doctors' money can buy if we need to." I thought it was time to call Ann and give her the good news. It was 2am in the morning but I knew she wouldn't mind. When she answered the phone I said "Honey, we got him. He's alive, our boys' alive!" Ann was crying and mumbled through the tears "Is he alright?" I explained the situation to her and she said "I'm coming down there and don't you tell me I'm not." I told Ann "Look, I know this ace pilot and I bet if you talked to him real nice he may come and pick you up." I held the phone away from my ear and Ann said "Jay, I know your standing right there, you get some sleep and get your butt up here and pick me up at first light, you hear me?" Jay replied with a big chuckle "Yes Mam, I will be at the airfield by 8am and you better have your buns ready."

Wow, here we are actually joking around with each other. It seemed like such a long time since we had done that. I felt truly blessed again. Jay said "Well Billy I'm going to get some shut eye like the boss said. I'll be stretched out in the waiting room if you need me." I went out to the nurse's station and asked about the girl we brought in. The nurse told me they found a necklace in her pocket with the name Jillian inscribed on the back. I asked if they could check with the police to see if they could find out who she was. The nurse told me they had already called the police and they were working on it. I told the nurse if there was any question about paying her bill I would take care of it. I called Ann back and asked her to contact the Turner's and get them working on identifying this girl. She said she would but not at 2:30am. I gave her Rafi's phone number for Mr. Turner to contact.

All of a sudden I could think of a lot of things that needed done. I was tired but I was not going to sleep until I knew Vince was going to be ok. I knew we were in deep trouble once somebody found what we did at the Cruz's ranch. We needed to get out of here as soon as possible. Jay could handle four people in his plane. That meant Ann, Vince and the girl could go with him. I would have to drive my truck back home. To my knowledge the Cruz's did not who we were yet and I'd like to keep it that way.

As I was sitting in the waiting room, Rafi came in and sat down beside me. He asked how Vince was doing and I told him "I guess as good as can be expected for what he's been through." He asked me "How many bodies are at the Cruz's ranch?" I told him "Seven." Rafi shook his head and said "I guess I under estimated you guys. I'm really glad you got your son back; it doesn't usually turn out this way. I guess you know you are marked men and the Cruz's will not stop until you are dead." I told him I was just thinking about that. Rafi told me that they were probably holding my son and the girl to be used in a sex slave ring. They would probably have sold them to someone in Europe or Asia after they had them hooked on cocaine. They keep the kids on drugs to control them and eventually the kids will do anything for a fix. Rafi said they auction the kids off over the internet to the highest bidder. He went on to say many of the kids end up dying of an overdose or murdered after the buyer gets bored with them. What a hellish life for these young people!

I realized how close Vince was to disappearing forever into that life. Rafi asked what we were going to do next. I told him "We are going to get out of here as soon as we can. I would appreciate if you could clear Jay for takeoff tomorrow morning to pick up my wife and come back here and pick up the two kids later in the day." Rafi said he would do that. He asked "Senor Bill, what about you?" I said "As soon as they are in the air I'll take off for home in my truck. Of course all this will depend on the kids being healthy enough to fly." Rafi said "I have talked to some federal officers and they have agreed to not pursue you if you leave the country immediately and don't come back." I told him "No offense, but I have no intention of ever coming back here again." Rafi said jokingly "If you do come back; the feds might give you a job cleaning up these crooks!" He told me he was going to leave and get some rest and he would handle getting Jay in and out of the airfield in the morning.

I went back to Vince's room and he was still sleeping. I dozed off for a while myself. About 6am someone squeezed my hand. I looked up and Vince said weakly "Hi Dad." Those words sounded so good!! He asked "Where are we?" I told him and he asked "What about Jillian?" I said she was ok and in another room. I asked Vince if he knew Jillian's last name. He said it was Marks, Jillian Marks. I told him I needed to tell the nurse about Jillian; I would be right back. I gave the nurse the news and she said she would pass it on to the police. I went back to Vince's room and called Ann. I told her there was someone here who wanted to talk to her. Vince cried and I know Ann was crying as well. I let them talk and walked over to Jillian's room and I could hear two people talking. Jillian was talking to the nurse in her room. I knocked on the door, opened it slightly, stuck my head in the door and said good morning. Jillian screamed and pulled the blankets over her head. She screamed at the nurse to not let me in the room. I closed the door and stepped back into the hallway. I wasn't sure what to do.

I could hear them talking and the nurse was telling Jillian to calm down that was the man who saved you and brought you here. At that point I took a look at myself. My clothes were dirty and dusty, I had some blood on my pants, I had not shaved for a few days and I'm sure I smelled really bad. I'm sure I looked like a crook.

I went back over to Vince's room and he was still talking to his Mom. I reminded her she better not miss her flight this morning; she knew how grouchy the pilot could be. She told me she was ready 30 minutes after I called her the last time. Vince told his Mom he loved her and would see her soon and he hung up. Jay walked in and Vince said "I knew you had to be here; good to see you Uncle Jay." They hugged and Jay was so choked up he couldn't speak. But it didn't last long. Jay said "Boy, you're a sight for these old eyeballs. You're Daddy and I bin lookin' all over for you."

A nurse came in the room with a light breakfast for Vince and took his vital signs. They were good. Vince said he was hungry and the nurse said that was a good sign. I could see some bruises on Vince's legs and arms and when he sat up there was a big bruise on his back. It angered me and at that moment I was not feeling the least bit guilty for killing those men. Jay said he was going to get something to eat and then head to the airfield to go pick up Ann. I would stay at the hospital until they got back.

The nurse who was in Jillian's room came in Vince's room and said Jillian would like to talk to me now. I walked into her room and she started to cry. She said she was sorry for being rude to me earlier. I told her "Don't think twice about it, the way I probably look, I can only imagine I looked scary to you." She held out her arms and said "Please come here, I want to hug you for helping me." We hugged and she said "So you are Vince's Dad. He kept telling me you would come and find us. He told me not to give up; his Dad and Uncle Jay are a couple of bad asses who were not afraid of anything." I simply told her I was glad I could help her. I told her if the doctor said it was ok she would be flying back home later today with Uncle Jay. I said "By the way; where is your home?" Jillian said "I live in Flagstaff." I asked her if she remembered her home phone number and she said "Sure I do." I handed her my satellite phone and said "Here you go call your parents." She grabbed the phone from my hand and dialed the number. Tears streamed down her face when her mother answered. "Mom, Mom, I'm ok, I'm alive!!" Two men rescued me yesterday and I'm in a hospital but I'm ok. I love you Mom!" Jillian handed me the phone and said tell her where we are. I explained the situation to her mother and gave the phone back to Jillian. It was great to be a part of such a joyous time.

I met the doctor in the hallway and asked him if it would be possible to take Jillian and Vince home on an airplane. The doctor said "They seemed to be stabilized and I don't think a few hours flight would do them any harm. Mr. Wright you need to know they will both go through some withdrawal symptoms for several days. They will both get pretty sick for a while but I believe they will be fine. I can arrange for them to be released later today." I thanked the Doctor and asked if there was some place I could take a shower and change clothes. He took me to a staff shower room and told me to help myself. I went out to my truck and got some clean clothes and my shaving kit and headed back in to take a shower.

As much as I enjoy the outdoors and roughing it at times; a good hot shower always feels mighty good. This was no exception. I went back to Jillian's room to get my phone after getting cleaned up and the nurse said "Boy, you clean up pretty good." Jillian was sleeping but left me a note to call her mother. I called and Mrs. Marks answered, she asked my name and we introduced ourselves. I told her as far as I knew Jillian would be flying back to Phoenix with my family later today. I gave her directions to the airfield and she and her family would be welcomed to meet her there. I told her I would call her with a time later this morning. She said "You bet we'll be there; thank you, thank you so much for bringing her back."

I was on cloud nine; finally everything came together. An old instructor of mine told me a long time ago — patience and persistence will take you wherever you want to go. I've found that to be true throughout my life. There is one more aspect I added to it later in my life — faith. Those three added together are mighty tough to beat.

When I got back to Vince's room he was sleeping. I thought that might be a good thing for me as well. I dozed off for about three hours and my phone rang. It was Ann calling to say they were taking off to head back down to Chihuahua "See you soon." I touched Vince's hand and he jerked his head up and I could see the fear in his eyes. I said "I'm sorry son; I didn't mean to startle you." He said "It's ok Dad, it's just going to take me while to realize I'm safe now." I told him "Well, you might want to think about getting dressed, I just spoke to your Mom and she is on her way to get you." I gave him some of my clothes to put on because his were pretty much rags. While he was getting dressed he looked at me and said "You know Dad, these clothes smell like you and it really smells good." We both laughed and hugged. Jillian came into Vince's room and she was dressed nicely in some clothes one of the nurses gave her. She hugged both of us and the three of us sat on Vince's bed. They both complained about a headache and feeling a bit unstable. I said "Look, you two have been through quite an ordeal. You both are going to have some withdrawal symptoms for a while and you need to take it easy." I could see some bruises on Jillian's arms and legs but did not want to mention it. I knew in their own time they would need to talk about what they went through. For now I wanted them to enjoy the moment and the anticipation of getting back home.

The nurse came in the room with the discharge papers for both of them and a set of instructions for when they got back home which included to see their family Doctor right away. I stepped outside the room with the nurse and asked where I could pay the bill for the two of them. She directed me to an office. I went in the office and told them who I was and a lady asked me to wait a minute. She brought out some papers and said it was taken care of earlier today by a Mr. Turner from Phoenix. I raised my eyebrows and thought to myself, that guy is really on top of things.

I went back and got the kids and we went down to the lobby to wait for Jay and Ann to get here. I told them I would be driving my truck back home and not flying with them as there was only room for 4 people in Jay's plane. Jillian asked me if she would ever see me again. I told her "You can count on it." I kind of sensed she and Vince had a special bond that would bring them together again. As the two of them talked I could hear them making plans for what they do when they got home and it made me feel that in time they would be able to move on with their lives.

It wasn't too long before I saw that old truck pull into the driveway of the clinic. Ann came rushing in and hugged Vince and kissed him over and over. She had her little boy back! Jay came through the door like "Marshall Dillon" who had just saved the day. He looked at Jillian and said "Well little lady, if I was 40 years younger I'd be looking to take you to a dance tonight. You look a lot better than you did yesterday." Jillian hugged him and said "You're everything Vince said you were." Jay said "He's a smart boy." Ann asked "Can we go get something to eat before we leave?" I told her "As much as I'd like that; I would prefer all you get out of here as soon as possible." Jay agreed. We all climbed into the truck and headed back to the police airfield for one more flight out of here. I dropped them off at Jay's plane and said I will see you later tonight. I waited outside the airfield to make sure they got off ok. When the plane was airborne; I let out a big sigh of relief. It was a big weight off of my shoulders. One more leg to this journey and it was over. I only had a few hours' drive and I would be back home with all of my family.

Chapter 13

A TURN IN THE ROAD

I was feeling relaxed for the first time in a month. Driving out of the city
I was thinking about all the crap Jay and I went through the last few
weeks. We had some invaluable help and made some new friends. We also
made a lot of new enemies and hopefully I was leaving them all behind. I
was really uneasy about having all of us in one place at the clinic. It made
it too easy for someone to find us. I felt more comfortable after Jay's plane
took off. I was looking forward to seeing Kara; she was 6 months pregnant
now and I was anxious to kid her about my new grandson.

About a mile outside of the city I could see flashing lights ahead of
me. It looked like an accident with a car stopped partially in my lane and
a wrecker trying to hook up to the car. I pulled up short of the car and was
waiting for the road to clear. I had my window down and was enjoying the
cool breeze outside while I waited. My eyes were partially closed when I
felt the cold steel of a gun barrel jam into my neck and someone said "Do
not move!" The truck door ripped open and two men dragged me out of
the truck, threw me on the ground and stuck a gun in my face. "Do not
move Senor or I will shoot you" one of the men said. They rolled me on
my belly and tied my hands behind my back and put a gag in my mouth.
They picked me up and put me in the back seat of the car.

I knew at that point I'd been set up; there was no accident. Somebody
must have recognized me or rolled over on me. Maybe it was the truck they

recognized; I didn't know. I did know I was in deep shit. They drove me back through the city and we headed south. After an hour or so we turned off onto a dirt road and drove to a house about a mile off the main road. The two men took me inside an old barn and threw me onto the floor. One of them asked "Where is your friend; the big man?" He took the gag out of my mouth so I could speak but I did not answer him. He said "I ask you once more where is your friend?" I did not answer. He hit me in the face with his fist and kicked me in the belly with his foot. For an instant I saw stars. The man grabbed my hair and jerked my head back and said "You have killed many of my friends and now I will kill you." The second man grabbed his arm and said "Not now, we must wait until Senor Cruz gets back or he will kill you."

I'd made up my mind I was not going to say a word to these men. They wanted me to plead with them for my life and I would not. If the man from two days ago was right the Cruz's wouldn't be back for 5 more days. I knew if I wasn't back home by tomorrow morning Jay would come looking for me. I'd been in this situation before. I got captured by some rebels in South Africa a long time ago and a man we called Bear came to my rescue. My hope was the same scenario would happen again with a man called Jay.

The men dragged me into a boarded up room, tossed me into it and locked the door. This time they didn't leave me with any weapons. They searched me and cleaned out my pockets before they put me in the car. However they didn't find a small 2 inch blade folding knife that was duct taped to the inside of my belt. Jay and I learned a long time ago to put a piece of duct tape inside the length of our belts; it came in handy several times before. It might help at some point again. I don't know who invented duct tape but I'd sure like to shake his hand someday.

I could see through some cracks in the boards someone was sitting outside the door. I looked around the room for something I could use. All I could find were a couple of 2x4's maybe 3 feet long. I remember seeing a second floor above the room before they threw me in it. I couldn't quite reach the ceiling in the room; it was about 6 inches above my reach. There were old wooden boards on the ceiling that maybe I could knock out with a piece of 2x4 as an escape route if I could reach them. But it would make too much noise with somebody seated right outside the door. I'd have to wait and hope they would leave me unguarded for a while. The wooden boards on the walls were old and I thought I could probably break through them with a good lunge. At least I had something to work with.

I could hear another man come in the barn and he said to the one guarding me "Hey Richie, look at this." Looking through the cracks in the boards I could see him holding Jay's rocket launcher. Richie asked "Where did you get that? Is it a real one?" The other man said "I just took it out of the back of the gringo's truck and yes it is real. He has a lot of weapons in there." The man walked closer to the room I was in and said "Hey Gringo, maybe I use this on you one day!" He laughed and said "Boom!" I could see him walk out of the barn into the dark. Richie hollered to me "Hey gringo, what's your name, you some kind of tough guy? You with the Army or something?" I didn't say a word.

I was smiling to myself. They must have brought my truck back here with them. That was a good thing. These guys didn't know it but there was a GPS tracker attached to the undercarriage of the truck. Jay would know exactly where I was. We were basically low tech guys but some of this stuff was pretty cool. I pulled together the little bit of straw that was on the floor and made myself a bed and tried to get some sleep.

I got a few cat naps during the night but never really slept soundly. My mind was racing about how to get out of here and cussing myself for letting my guard down. I could see it was daylight outside and heard someone walk in the barn. Through a crack I could see him carrying a burlap bag. The door opened and he looked in at me and smiled and said "I bring you breakfast Senor." He grabbed the two pieces of 2x4's laying on the floor and took them with him. He opened the bag and threw three rattlesnakes at me saying "Hope you enjoy your breakfast Senor!" He and Richie laughed loudly and he locked the door. I could hear the two of them giggling outside of the room. The snakes were obviously mad. Living where I do I had some experience with rattlesnakes and despite what most people think, they are not normally aggressive. If left alone they will try to hide. I was going to try to let them calm down before dealing with them. They were coiled and focusing on me. I tried my best to not move and after a few minutes they started to calm down. They separated and each one tried to find a place to hide. One of them slithered close to me just inches from my right boot. After his head passed my boot; I stomped his head into the floor. The noise of stomping agitated the other two snakes and they coiled again.

I remained motionless for a few moments (it seemed like an hour); the two snakes relaxed out of their coil and continued looking for a place to hide. I slowly took off my left boot and laid it on the floor with the open top next to the floor. I hoped the warmth from my boot would attract one of them. It worked; one of them crawled in the boot. I slid the open end of the boot against the wall to keep the snake inside. The remaining snake was stretched out along the opposite wall. I took my shirt off and threw it over the third snake. Then I took off my other boot and clubbed the snake under my shirt to death. I went back to my boot with the snake in it and moved the boot slightly away from the wall just enough for the snake to stick his head out. His head came out slowly and I grabbed the snake behind its head and pulled it out of the boot. While I was holding the snake in my hand; I had a thought. I decided to fake being bitten by the snake and maybe draw these guys into the room to check me.

I screamed out in pain and fell to the floor with the snake positioned so they couldn't see it. I hollered help me, help me, I've been bitten. I still had a grip on the snake behind its head so it couldn't bite me. I was moaning and pleading for help and I heard the door open. They were both laughing and Richie said "You are not so tough now are you Gringo." I was lying on my side and someone grabbed my shoulder. I rolled over and jammed the snake's mouth into his arm. The snake clamped down on his arm and I let go of the snake. It was Richie and now he was screaming and hollering "Get it off me, get it off me, the snake is biting me!" He ran out of the room with the snake hanging on his arm. The second man slammed the door shut and screamed at me "I will kill you; I will kill you, you bastard!"

I said under my breath "Not if I kill you first." I felt energized and was ready to deal with this situation on my own. I was sure I would be made to pay for the snake biting Richie and needed to prepare for whatever was next. I could hear Richie moaning in pain and two men talking about taking him to a doctor. One of them said he would take Richie somewhere to get treated. I heard car doors slamming and the car start up and drive away. That meant two less men to deal with. I wasn't sure how many men were left. I took out my little knife and skinned one of the snakes down its backbone and sliced off a couple of strips of meat. I liked rattlesnake meat fried but I wasn't sure about eating it raw. I wasn't sure what if any superstitions these guys might have but it was worth a shot. I took a small bite of the meat and it was to say the least – not tasty! My plan was to act like I was crazy and hope these guys would be afraid to come near me. I stuffed some of the meat under a loose floor board to make it look like I ate a lot of it. I smeared blood on my face and clothing, ripped my tee shirt open down my chest, peeled the rest of the snake skin off the carcass and wrapped the skin around my neck.

I heard two men talking as they walked into the barn. One of them said "I am going to teach this Gringo a lesson." The second man said "Don't kill him yet." The first one said "Do not worry my friend; he will wish he was dead when I am through with him." I was pretending to be eating the snake when the door opened. I could see the shock on the man's face when he looked at me. He called his buddy over and said "Look at this guy he's crazy!" I took two quick steps towards him swinging the other dead snake above my head. He slammed the door shut and said "He is crazy. He ate the snake raw; he's a mad man. I'm not going in there!!" I chuckled to myself, it worked. I bought myself some time and for now didn't have to take a beating. The two guys were talking about what they were going to do with me and one of them said "The hell with him; the Cruz's can deal with him when their plane lands. We'll just keep that crazy bastard locked up for four more days. Maybe we can find his buddy by then." I again thought to myself "You're going to meet my buddy before those four days are up."

I really was hungry but not hungry enough to eat raw snake meat. What I really needed was something to drink. After about a half an hour I could see 3 men walk into the barn; the two who were here earlier and one guy I had not seen before. I jumped up and pounded on the wall and growled as loud as I could "I want water, give me water!!" I just gritted my teeth and snarled at them as mean as I could. The third man said "You are right; he looks like he is going crazy. Maybe we should give him some water to keep him alive." They all left the barn and in a few minutes they came back with a bucket of water. One of them opened the door and ordered me to get back or he would shoot me; a second one sat the bucket of water inside the door and quickly slammed the door shut. I stuck my head in the bucket and acted as wild as I could while drinking the water. I then wrapped my arms around the bucket, looked at the men and growled like a dog protecting his food. One of them said "The snake has made him loco." As they left the barn I sensed they were afraid of me now.

I was pretty sure the three men were the only ones here right now. I reasoned if there was any one else here they would want to come and see the crazy man in the barn. The man that took Richie to the doctor would probably be coming back so that meant there were four guys to deal with. Even if Richie came back he would be pretty sick and would not be a problem. I felt pretty confident these guys were going to let me alone. I could see one of them seated by the barn door which was about 20 feet from where I was. He was still too close for me to try to break out of the room; he would hear anything I tried to do. According to what they said I had 4 days until the Cruz's got back. I sat down to rest and think about what my next move was. I slept for a few hours and the heat of the day woke me up. I noticed there was still someone seated at the barn door.

A car pulled up and I heard the driver tell the man at the door Richie would be ok but he would stay in the hospital for a couple of days. He asked how I was behaving and the man at the door replied "The hell with him; he is out of his mind; stay away from him." The driver asked him if they gave me anything to eat or drink. "We gave him water; if he's hungry he can eat snakes" was the reply. I guess I knew what was for supper tonight.

I pulled up the floor board where I hid the snake meat earlier. Underneath was dirt. I got to thinking and took my belt off and peeled off some more of the duct tape and I'll be damned there were 3 barn burner matches. They had been there for years and I'd forgotten they were there. Now I was curious what else I had stashed under that tape. I found a small piece of steel wool soaked in Vaseline wrapped in plastic for fire starter and 12 M&M's wrapped in plastic. Guess what I did with the M&M's. I pried up another piece of floor board and found a few white grub worms in the dirt and laid them on the floor beside me. I dug out a hole in the dirt and put some of the dried straw in it and broke up the floor boards, laid them on top of the straw and made a small fire. The man guarding the door must have smelled the smoke and came over to see what I was doing. I jumped across the room and growled at him and he backed off. He stood and watched me from outside the door. I stuck the grub worms on a stick and roasted them over the fire. I'd eaten them before in Africa and Australia and once you get past the idea of what you're eating they taste good. They actually taste like scrambled eggs. These tasted fine. I then roasted some of the snake meat over the fire and had myself a fine meal. The man stood outside the door watching me the whole time. He hollered for one of his buddies to come and see this. The other man said "As long as he doesn't burn down the barn; let him eat that shit. Then we don't have to feed him."

All in all it wasn't a bad meal. I could feel the strength coming back into my body. I shoved the fire to the base of the back wall and let it burn some of the framing along the floor. I hoped it would weaken it enough that if the time came I could kick my way out through the back wall. The fire started to burn up the wall and I had to put it out. I kicked at it a little and it seemed to give way. Hopefully it would give enough for me to break out of here. But as long as there was someone guarding the door I was stuck here.

I was expecting Jay to show up after dark tonight but just in case he didn't I needed to come up with some kind of a plan. The four men were taking turns guarding me about every 4 hours and I was hoping one of them might fall asleep when it was his turn. I put my back against the back wall and just kept pushing on it. I could feel it give a little bit at a time. After a couple of hours of pushing on the wall and digging with my heels in the dirt, I had a hole big enough to crawl through. It was dark outside and the only light was a small lantern by the door. I waited until there was a change in guards and watched the new guy for any sign of sleeping. After an hour or so I could see his head starting to nod. I knew I had probably 3 hours until a new guy came out. I eased through the opening I made trying to be as quiet as possible. I moved just a few inches at a time and finally got myself free. I had maybe 30 feet to crawl across the wooden floor to get to the guard. I crawled on my belly maybe 12 inches at a time. I could see the guard was sleeping but one creak from this wooden floor would probably wake him.

I really wanted to jump up and rush him but I knew that would make too much noise. He had a gun and all I had was a 2 inch knife. He was seated on a chair facing outside of the barn with his back to me. Finally I was able to crawl right up to the back of the chair he was sitting on. I eased up to my knees, grabbed his head with both of my hands and with one hard twist; I heard the unmistakable snap of his neck. His body went limp and I eased his lifeless body to the floor. Both my legs were asleep and for a moment I couldn't stand. When I could I dragged his body to the corner of the barn. I put on his shirt and hat and stuck his gun in my belt then went back to sit in the chair. My plan was to wait for the next guard to come out to relieve me and take him down. I figured I had close to two hours to wait.

After a while I stood up and walked to the side of the barn to take a leak. I felt the barrel of a gun poke me in the back and a voice said "Don't move." I knew that voice. I said "McMurray, I think we're on the same team." Jay grabbed me by the shoulder and turned me around and said "Billy, what you doing in that get up? I damn near shot you!" I told him "I've been sitting here waiting for you." "Hell, I've been watching you for the last ½ hour trying to figure out how to get closer. I didn't know it was you." Jay said. He asked if I was ok and I told him I was fine. I explained to him there were three more guys in the house.

We kicked around what we wanted to do next. Jay said "Let's not dick around, there probably relaxing inside, let's just rush 'em." I agreed I was ready to kick some ass. We eased over to the house, kicked the door in and both hollered nobody move. The three men were seated around a table with a big bag of weed in the middle. It looked like they were breaking it down into smaller bags. We disarmed them and told them to stay seated. I found a roll of duct tape and while Jay kept them at gunpoint, I wrapped the three of them to their chairs with the tape. When they were secured we looked around the place. Jay found a stash of bags filled with white powder. He tasted it and said it was cocaine.

Jay looked at me and asked "Now what?" I was thinking what these guys did to Vince and all the other kids they took. I said "Let's look around and see if we can find some needles. We're gonna give them a taste of their own medicine." I found some needles in a cabinet and a butane burner along with some large spoons. I asked Jay "You remember how to do this?" He winked at me and said "I remember."

We cooked down more than enough for the three of them and filled three needles. They each got a full dose. In less than an hour they were all dead. We removed the duct tape and let them fall on the floor. Maybe the Cruz brothers would think they did it to themselves, maybe not. I really didn't care.

Jay said "I know that look on your face; do you want to stay and finish this?" I said "Yeh, if we don't we'll always be looking over our shoulder. I don't want these bastards coming after my family again. The brothers are supposed to be back here in three days, let's set up a little welcome home party for them."

Chapter 14

THE HEAD OF THE SNAKE

Jay said "You know if we leave now, we could be back home by daylight." I said "I know, but I think Rafi was right, these guys are just going to keep coming at us." "Do you think they know who we are?" Jay asked. I said "I don't know. If I knew for sure they didn't, we would head out of here right now. I just don't want them coming back after my wife and family. We need to cut the head off of this snake and it sounds like the head is the two Cruz brothers."

I asked Jay how Vince and Jillian were doing. He said they were both pretty sick when they got home. He told me Jillian's parents picked her up at the airport and they were going to take her back home to see their doctor. He told me Ann took Vince to see our doctor yesterday morning and he gave Vince some medication to help him through the worst of the withdrawal. Speaking of Ann, I thought I'd better give her a call. When she answered the phone she said "Thank God you're alright! Now don't you think it's about time you get your butt back home? I want my family all in one place for a change." I told her my plans and explained why. She didn't like it but I think she understood. I told Ann I loved her and I would call her again when it was all over.

I asked Jay where he parked. He said "One hill over to the north. That GPS is one handy gadget; it lead me right to this place. I knew when you didn't show up the next morning you got your ass tied in a knot somewhere. What the hell happened?" I explained the whole thing to him including the snakes and we both chuckled about that. He said "hell, you didn't have to pretend to be nuts; you are. Everybody thinks I'm the crazy one but they don't know some of the shit you pulled over the years." I told him maybe that was because I didn't feel the need to talk as much as he did. Jay said "I prefer to think of it as being more entertaining than you." "That you are my friend that you certainly are."

We looked around the place some more to see if we could find anything useful. There was a desk in a back room with some drawers on each side of it. I looked through the drawers and found a couple of hundred dollars, a notebook with some names written in it and another small notebook with a lot of phone numbers and initials behind the phone numbers. There were also two handguns in one of the drawers. There were some pictures on the wall and I recognized Jose Cruz in one of them. He was standing with two other men who I assumed were his brothers but I didn't know for sure. Jay found some food in the kitchen and a bottle of wine. We took all of this stuff with us.

We took my truck and drove out to the main highway to pick up Jay's vehicle. Jay told me he flew his plane back down to the Chihuahua police airfield and rented a car in town to drive down here. He told me Rafi wasn't too happy that he came back and Rafi told him he just knew one or both of us was going to end up dead. Jay said he told him maybe if the Mexican police would do their job we wouldn't have to do it for them. I suggested to Jay that wasn't the smartest thing to do; we may need Rafi's help later. Jay said he knew and he would smooth it over with Rafi when he saw him again. He laughed "I'm going to have to kiss his butt to get my plane back."

After finding a place to pull off the road we decided to get some sleep. I was really tired; I hadn't slept much the past two days. I stretched out in the back of the truck and was out pretty quickly. Jay slept in his car. At daylight we woke up, had some breakfast and sat down to come up with a plan. The Cruz brothers were due back in two days. We didn't even know what they looked like for sure or what kind of vehicles they drove. We assumed they lived at the ranch where Jay and I were thrown into the hole in the ground but we didn't even know that for sure. We needed information as quickly as possible.

We went through the things we took from the house last night. Jay found some more pictures in a small box and one of them had writing on the back identifying the three brothers standing in front of a blue Ford Expedition. I was going through the notebook with names and addresses in it and didn't really find anything useful. I looked through the notebook with phone numbers and initials and some of the phone numbers were the area code for Phoenix. There was one number with the initials S.B. that seemed familiar to me but I couldn't I couldn't place it. We had a start; we knew what they looked like and possibly what vehicle they drove.

Our plan at that point was to go to the nice stone ranch house and wait for the brothers to come home. It only made sense they would live there as it was a beautiful house inside with all the luxuries one could want. Maybe we would take advantage of some of those luxuries. We figured there would be some cleaning up to be done from the last time we were there.

After pulling in to the ranch, it looked like somebody beat us to the punch. I expected the bodies to be lying on the porch but they were gone. There was some "police, do not cross" tape on the front of the porch and a police seal on the front door. Apparently the federal police were here and collected the bodies and whatever else they wanted. I wondered if the federal agents were watching us now. I pulled my truck around the back of the steel building so it wouldn't be visible from the driveway. We walked over to the house and took the police tape off and removed the seal from the front door. Inside the house the bodies we left earlier were gone as well.

Throughout this whole deal Jay and I wondered who we could trust. We decided from the start we would trust no one, including the police. Jay sat down on a chair and said "You know Billy, I don't like this. It smells like a setup. It's too easy. You would think somebody has tipped these brothers off that we are coming after them." I told him "I agree; it doesn't smell right. Everybody expects us to be here; we don't have the element of surprise and that's the one thing we've had in the past. With all the shit these guys are into they've got to have some Fed's on their payroll. Let's get out of here and go to plan B.

As we were pulling out of the driveway onto the main road Jay asked "Just what is plan B?" I said "I don't know." I was mad at myself for not thinking this thing through well enough. I stopped about a mile down the road, turned around and headed back to the Cruz's ranch. I stopped short of the driveway and told Jay to get his rocket launcher out, load it and I asked "How close you gotta be to hit that house?" Jay said "I don't know maybe 100 yards." Jay got on the back of the truck with the launcher and I pulled up to about 100 yards from the house. I told him "Whenever you're ready." I watched him line up the sight and he pulled the trigger. There was a big explosion and it wasn't a nice house any longer. There were pieces flying everywhere. Jay jumped down off the back of the truck laughing and said "Man, now I know this sucker works!" I felt better; now we knew the Cruz brothers were not going to be staying here. If the Feds were watching us maybe they would know we meant business and leave us alone.

We drove back to the highway and parked in a secluded spot. I was sure the Cruz's had a landing strip somewhere close by; we just had to find it. I dug out the pictures we'd taken from Jay's plane earlier and we both poured over them looking for signs of a landing strip. Jay pulled one out and said "I think this is what we're looking for." We could see the wheel marks from a plane and some marker flags along each edge of the strip. It was a dirt surface and not easy to pick out from the air. It was located about a ½ mile south of the ranch house with a one track road leading to the house. There was a rundown building where they probably housed the plane at the end of the runway.

Between the map and our pictures we found a place to hide the truck that would leave us about a mile walk to get to the airstrip. We loaded up our packs with enough gear to do the job and headed down the road to stash the truck. Hiking into the landing strip was no problem. There was an old jeep parked in the building which they probably used to travel back and forth to the house. We settled in to wait for the boys to come back. We debated how we were going to handle this and Jay said "I can rig this jeep with the little bit of C-4 I have left or we can just whack 'em when they get off the plane." I told Jay "I don't care how they die but I want them to see who is going to kill them and know why." After discussing a few different scenarios we came up with the idea of waiting until they left the plane and take them at that point.

Obviously when they flew over the ranch house they would know we were here. However they wouldn't know exactly where we were. I don't know how many men we killed but I was thinking there couldn't be too many left. It was our hope that it would only be the two brothers and a pilot coming in on the plane. I was hoping the plane would come in today and we could end this.

Jay looked at me and said "Seems like we been here before Billy, waiting for somebody to show up so we can whack 'em. Remember that time in the Nam we sat for four days in the rain waiting for some officer to show up. Then the C.O. called us off and told us to abort the mission. The crazy bastards." I said "Yeh that was one of the highlights of my tour."

Jay laughed "Remember the time we were in Laos, when the Army had no military presence in Laos and we waited for days to be picked up after a mission. Charlie set up a camp 100 yards from us and stayed for two days. We could hardly take a piss for two days with those clowns so close." I nodded my head yes, I remembered. We sure had a lot of close calls over the years; hopefully this situation would be something we could reminisce about in the future.

It was getting dark and it looked like there wouldn't be any plane coming in today. We would be spending the night in this old shed, waiting again. It was really quiet, only an occasional coyote howling. The events of the past few weeks were passing through my mind; some of them seemed a long time ago. Some of them happened so quickly, I had trouble remembering what happened where. I had an uneasy feeling in my gut that I couldn't shake. It wasn't guilt for all the lives we took; I could justify that in my mind for what they put my son through. I was feeling we were pressing our luck. Jay and I had a chance to get out of here and we didn't take it. I was feeling maybe we wouldn't make it through this one. These were bad ass, ruthless people not unlike people we dealt with many years ago. I was feeling maybe this time I let my ego over power my common sense. We not only had the Cruz brothers to deal with, there were probably a good many so called law enforcement personnel who the Cruz's paid off to deal with as well.

After an hour or so of not saying a word Jay looked at me and asked "Ok Mr. Thinker, you been quiet for a while, what's on your mind?" I said "Well you know me; I was trying to think everything through and wondering if maybe we should just get the hell out of here while we can. I'm afraid we may have run out of luck and bit off more than we can chew." Jay looked me straight in the eyes and said "Bullshit, you know it wasn't luck that got us here. It was teamwork and knowing what we are doing.

Don't you think we have these guys running scared? Hell man, they don't even know who we are for sure. For all they know we could be looking to take over their business. They don't know there are only two of us. You said it yourself a while ago; let's finish this and cut off the head of this snake! Now get your head out of your ass, quit thinking so damn much and let's do what we do best and end this here and now!"

I joke a lot about Jay stretching the truth but when it comes down to pulling off a mission there's nobody else in the world I trust better than him. I acknowledged he was right and admitted maybe I was getting soft and too philosophical in my old age. Jay simply said "Damn straight."

We settled in and I took the first watch as Jay got some sleep. Before Jay fell asleep he said "Think about how we're gonna' take these guys out if you have to think about something." I threw a stick at him and told him to go to sleep.

It was a quiet night, no plane, nobody in or out of this place all night. As the new day was dawning I admired the sun rising over the mountains. It was quiet and peaceful. Jay woke up and said "Maybe we got some bad information Billy, it doesn't look like these guys are gonna' show." I said "I don't know what to think. Guess we might as well eat a little breakfast." I asked Jay if he wanted a granola bar or a granola bar. He said he guessed he would have a granola bar. While we were eating our breakfast I thought I could hear a plane off in the distance. I got out my binoculars and sure enough there was a light plane coming in off in the distance. We hunkered down in the old barn and waited for it to land. Our plan was to wait until they taxied up to the barn and got out of the plane and then jump them.

As the plane was just about to touch down on the dirt landing strip, there was a loud explosion and the plane turned into a ball of fire! We looked at each other with wide eyes and Jay said "What the hell?" The plane was in pieces and tumbling down the runway right at us. It stopped about 150 yards out with the tail section completely separated from the cabin. I could see the top half of a body hanging out the passenger window. The passenger compartment was on fire and I could smell the aviation fuel burning. It was a smell we both knew well. We were both shocked!! I looked at Jay and said "Somebody just shot that plane out of the air!" Jay said "No shit, who?" I had no idea. "We best lay low and see who comes to take a look. Let's go out the back of the building in case they want to blow up this barn." Jay said "Sounds like a plan to me." He started kicking out a couple of half rotten boards and we both slipped out the back of the building and climbed through some brush on our hands and knees to the top of a small hill behind the barn. We both got reintroduced to the local cactus while crawling.

We sat back to back so we could see in all directions and both glassed the area. The air was filled with thick black smoke from the burning plane and it actually made a good cover for us while hiding. We saw no movement from inside the plane and I could not imagine anyone surviving that explosion and fire. After about 45 minutes we could see a tan SUV driving in from the old ranch house. The wreckage was still burning as the vehicle got closer. I could see an emblem on the front door through my binoculars. It was a Mexican Federal Police vehicle. The vehicle stopped a couple of hundred feet from the plane and two men got out. They both got out and approached the plane with automatic rifles in their hands. One of the men sprayed the wreckage with his weapon while the other took pictures. They high fived each other and got back in the vehicle and drove back the way they came.

Jay said "Well partner looks like our suspicions were right the Feds are involved. You think these were good guys or bad guys?" I told Jay "I don't know and it doesn't matter, good or bad we've got to steer clear of them. Somebody just did our job for us. Let's back out of here, it's time to head home. I don't want to get in a battle with the feds."

We worked our way back to our vehicles and after glassing the area I was relieved to see there was no one waiting for us. While walking out, I was thinking to myself the same people who blew up the plane might have spotted the hiding spot where we parked yesterday. I followed Jay back out to the main road and we headed north. We didn't stop until we were half way to Chihauhau. We pulled off at a little gas station to fill up and get something to drink. Jay wiped the sweat off his brow and said "You know Billy, I been thinkin', we're pretty damn lucky to get back up here without any trouble." I agreed and said "I'll feel a whole lot better when you get that plane off the ground and I cross the border into the good old USA." Jay said he would drink to that and we headed north again.

I called Rafi and made arrangements for him to meet us. When we reached the airfield, Rafi was waiting for us. He said "I don't mean to be rude Senor' Bill but I hope this is the last time I see you two for a while. You guys need to disappear and let things cool off." I thanked Rafi once again for all his help and assured him it was our intention to do just that. I gave Rafi money to pay for the car rental for Jay and we both watched as Jay fired up his plane and took off. We shook hands and it was my turn to leave. Before I pulled out, Rafi gave me some directions to drive around the city saying it would be safer for me to take some back roads.

I was off and real glad to be back on the road. I still had an uneasy feeling that probably wasn't going to go away until I got across the border. I had a lot of weapons and ammo in the back of the truck and didn't want any more trouble. I called Ann and told her where I was and asked her to find out if our friend was working at the border crossing tonight. I was three hours from the border and would need his help one more time. She told me she would check and call me back. After about 20 minutes Ann called back and said he wouldn't be working until 6am tomorrow morning. I told Ann I wasn't going to risk it and would lay over at the truck stop on this side of the border until morning. I asked her to let our friend know I would be coming through around 6:30am and would have a red handkerchief tied to my antenna along with a description of the truck.

It was a little past one am when I reached the truck stop. I was tired and hungry and went inside to wash up and get something to eat. While I sitting in a booth eating a man stopped at my table and asked "Senor Bill, is that you?" I wasn't expecting to know anyone here and it took me by surprise. I looked up and it was Eddie who had helped Jay and I earlier and put us up in his trailer for a few days. I stood up and shook his hand and said "Hey Eddie, nice to see you again. I wasn't expecting to see anybody I knew here." Eddie said "This is one of my truck stops where we do a lot of business. What are you doing here?" I told him to sit down and I would fill him in. I told Eddie I was waiting for morning to get some help to cross the border. Eddie said "There are a lot of people that want to shake your hand for what you did to the Cruz brothers today. They were bad people and deserved to die. How did you blow up their plane?" I told him we didn't blow up the plane. We watched it blow up but we didn't do it. "Well you got credit for doing it and everybody thinks you did it. If you didn't do it, who did?" I told Eddie I didn't know.

I asked Eddie "How do you know about this, it just happen this morning?" Eddie said "It's our business to know these things. The Cruz's have been hard on our businesses for a long time, you and your buddy Jake, is that his name; are heroes around here. Where is your buddy Jake?" I laughed and said "His name is Jay and I hope he's back at my ranch relaxing about now."

I explained what happened this morning to Eddie and said all I wanted to do was get this behind me and get home. Eddie asked "You need help getting across the border?" I told him I had to wait until after six am to get across at which time my friend would help me cross. Eddie laughed and asked "What you drivin'?" I told him my old pickup. "How wide is it?" I said "I don't know." "Well let's go see; maybe I can get you home a little earlier." I paid my bill and we walked outside. Eddie looked at my truck and said "Yeah, it will fit. Drive your truck around the back to that white car hauler and we'll load you up and get you home tonight." I drove to the back of the parking lot and one of Eddie's men opened the end gate of the trailer and motioned for me to drive inside. I parked the truck inside the trailer and climbed out. Eddie's driver hooked up the electric to the dual wheeled pickup hooked to the trailer. While his man was hooking everything up Eddie pulled me aside and said "You don't know this but there are Federal Agents waiting for you at the border. They don't know for sure who you are but they have a description of your truck and they are planning to take you out before you cross over." He went on to say "We've been following you for quite a while and we were almost ready to pull you over if you hadn't stopped."

I looked at Eddie and asked "Are you shittin' me? How do you know all this?" Eddie said again "It's my business to know this stuff. The Cruz's have some of the Fed's on their payroll and there is a contract out on you and Jay. Your one of us now man, you see all these trucks parked here? We own them and this truck stop." I could see six tractor trailers, two wreckers and two car haulers. Part of our business is getting people across the border when they need help. They pay us real well for our services but for you my friend there is no fee."

I looked at Eddie and said "Sounds like you just saved my butt." "That's what friends are for Senor Bill." I asked Eddie what happens if the border guards checked the trailer. Eddie winked and said "My trucks don't get checked; the Cruz's aren't the only one's paying people off." Eddie put his arm around my shoulder and said "One more thing my friend; there are people on your side of the border who will kill you if they find out who you are. Now let my men take you across the border and be safe my friend." I hugged Eddie and said "Thank you, I will see you again my friend."

I climbed in the back seat of Eddie's truck and we took off for home. It was only a short distance to the border and sure enough when we pulled up to the crossing guard he motioned us right on through. We pulled off in the parking lot of a truck stop on the US side and backed into a spot at the back of the lot. The driver motioned for me to get out and he opened the end gate on the trailer. I climbed into my truck and backed out of the trailer. I asked the driver how much he would normally charge to make this trip of 5 or 6 miles across the border. He smiled and said "$5000.00 Senor Bill. That Eddie ain't no dummy!"

I again thanked the men for their help and started on the road home. On the way I called Ann and told her I would be home in an hour or so and would explain everything to her when I got there. Ann told me Jay was back and everything went well with him.

The strain of this long day was starting to hit me. The stress of uncertainty was with me all day. Throughout the day I was thinking something was going to go wrong and without Eddie's help it probably would have. I just had to suck it up for a little while longer and maybe this whole deal would be over.

While I was driving I thought about all the people who helped us. Without them we would never been able to rescue anyone. I said a little prayer to God; thanking him for keeping us safe and asked him to watch over all the folks who helped us along the way. I also asked for his forgiveness for the lives I took and the anger that boiled up inside me. I'd been taught that God will forgive all sins but in the back of mind I had some doubts as to whether he could forgive me for some of the nasty things I'd done. I thought to myself time will tell.

I know I was speeding and it didn't take that long until I was pulling into my driveway. Before I got parked, Ann, the kids, Jay and the three dogs were at my door to greet me. Man it felt good to be home! They all hugged me and Vince took a step back and said "Well Dad, this makes the second time I've seen you cry!" He knew the first time was when we found him in Mexico. I looked at Kara and thought to myself her belly had gotten bigger before I said "Honey, how's my grandson doing in there." She smiled, patted her belly and said "He or she is kicking to get out of here." Jay asked me if I had any trouble along the way. I told him no; thanks to Eddie. They all wanted to know what happened and Ann said "Let's all go inside and you can explain it to all of us." I agreed.

We all sat around the kitchen bar and I related to them the events of the day. After I was done, Jay said "You know Billy, I guess I was wrong. I never really trusted that guy Eddie. But it sounds like he really had your back." I told them all "I think Jay and I underestimated Eddie. He seemed to know everything we did soon after it was done. By us eliminating part of the Cruz brother's operation life was going to be a lot easier and profitable for Eddie." Ann looked me in the eyes and asked "Is it over, can we put this behind us now and get on with our lives?" I kissed her and replied "I sure hope so." But in the back of mind I wasn't so sure.

We were all exhausted and agreed it was time to get some sleep. I can't remember a time when my own bed felt so good and to have my wife beside me again made this day complete.

Chapter 15

GOOD TO BE HOME

The next morning I did not want to get out of bed. The two dogs had other plans for me. By 9am they were both in bed with us and they wanted to resume the walk I usually took with them in the morning. They were not going to take no for an answer, both of them pulled the blanket off of me and were licking my face. I got up, took them outside and after a short walk I paused and looked around the property. It was so good to be home. Everything smelled good; even the horse manure. There were a couple of mule deer feeding in the pasture and it was so peaceful.

I went back to the house and Ann had breakfast ready. After breakfast Jay, Ann and I went out on the front porch to talk and have some coffee. Ann said "Ok, I didn't want bring it up in front of the kids, do you guys really think it's over." I said "Probably not. There is still somebody in Phoenix who is involved in this kidnapping ring; more than likely more than one person. We have the initials SB and a phone number, but nothing else." Jay asked "Billy what are thinking? Do you think they made us? Do you think they will be coming after us here?" "I don't think they've made us for sure or they would have tried taking me out traveling up the road yesterday. We have to consider we may be dealing with somebody who knows us here and we have got to be careful who we talk with. Until we find out who we're dealing with it's probably best not to trust anyone."

Jay said "You know them FBI Agents are gonna' come snoopin' around.

What about Bob; you think we can trust him and his boys." "Like I said, I don't think we should trust saying anything to anybody, including the law, are we all agreed to that." I replied. We all agreed. "For now we will all just go about our business as usual and do our investigating on our own. Ann, you can try to track down that phone number and Jay and I will do what we do best to find these guys."

In my heart I really hoped this whole thing was over but common sense told me it wouldn't be that easy. The connections the Cruz brothers had in the Phoenix area are still here and there was the big "if factor" of them being aware of Jay and I. I met with my foreman Mike and it seemed everything was going well with the business and it didn't appear anyone made the connection there. I expected if they would have made us; my equipment or building projects would have been an easy target.

Jay was right, around noon the FBI agents stopped in to talk with us. Agent Hanson said "We heard you boys were back in town. How were things in Mexico?" Jay said "Mexico, hell man we were up at my ranch in Idaho! Billy was helping me do some remodeling." Hanson smiled and said "Well then you guys will be glad to know the Cruz brothers are no longer with us. Somebody blew up their airplane with them in it two days ago." I in turn smiled and said "That's the best news I've had so far today. Who do you think did it?" "Well until now I figured you two did it, but if you were in Idaho at the time, I guess it must have been somebody else who didn't like them" he replied. I smiled again and said "Guess so." Hanson stuck out his hand to me and said "I'm glad you got your son back and quite honestly I wish we could have done more to help you, but our hands were tied once they crossed the border. If you boys need any more help on this side of the border; please give me a call." I nodded my head yes, both men shook Jay's hand and got in their car and left. Jay looked at me and laughed "Them boys might as well had fishin' poles on their shoulders; 'cause they were sure enough fishin'." I chuckled and we went out to the barn to check on the horses. Vince was busy cleaning out the stalls and asked what those guys wanted. Jay explained everything to him as only Jay can do.

We both sat down with Vince and explained to him we didn't feel this was over yet. I wanted him to stay close to home until we tracked down whoever else was involved. Vince asked "What about going back to college?" I said "I know you want to go back but I'm not sure it's safe.

Maybe you could look into doing your classes online until we get this sorted out. I know it's not what you want to do but maybe try it for the first semester." He agreed to check it out.

Now we needed a plan to keep Kara and John safe. It was only three weeks until her due date for the baby. I went back to the house to talk to Ann about them and she said "It's already settled; I told them they had to stay here until this was over. They will be coming over tonight when John gets out of class. They will stay in Kara's old room. You know Bill you're not the only one who plans things. Who do you think ran this place when you were away?" I just said "Thank you dear" and headed back outside.

Jay and I were standing on the porch talking when I saw the sheriff's car pull into the driveway. Bob got out of his car with a big smile on his face, hugged me and said "Man it's sure good to see you guys!" He and Jay shook hands and Bob asked "Where the hell have you guys been? On second thought, don't answer that. The less I know the better." I told him "It's no secret; I've been up at Jay's place doing some remodeling. How did you know we were back?" Bob laughed and said "Well you know what it's like around here; everybody knows each other's business. I thought you would want to know somebody took out the Cruz brothers a couple of days ago." I told Bob the FBI agent's just left a bit ago and told us the same thing. Bob winked and said "Everybody sort of figured you two guys had something to do with that. But if you were in Idaho at the time; I guess that wasn't the case. At any rate, I'm glad you're back home and now maybe your life can get back to normal."

I asked Bob if he got any inquiries from the Mexican authorities from our little escapade in getting Vince back. He said he did not. "Speaking of Vince; is he here? I just want to say hi to him." I told Bob I thought he was out in the barn. We shook hands and Bob headed for the barn. Jay looked at me and said "You know sometimes I'm a little slow on the draw but the initials S.B. have been eatin' at me for quite a while. You thinkin' what I'm thinkin?" "It scares the hell out of me. From the first time I heard it I've been thinking about it. To think that a man I considered to be a good friend could be involved in this turns my stomach. For now, we need some proof but I'm not letting him alone with my son" and I headed for the barn. I walked into the barn and Vince was talking to Bob about his ordeal. Vince glanced at me and I gave him the sign to cut off the conversation (my fingers across my throat.) Apparently he got the message and told Bob he'd be glad to talk to him later but he had to get some work done before he got fired. Bob looked at me and said with a laugh "Yeh, your old man's a slave driver and I got to get back to work as well." When Bob left the barn Vince asked "What's that all about? Don't you want me talking to Bob?" I said "I hope I'm being overly cautious; but right now I just don't trust anyone." "But Dad, you and Bob have been friends forever. Do you really think he's involved in this stuff?"

We sat down on a bale of straw and I said "Look son, we can't afford to take any chances right now. Jay and I pissed off a lot of people and we know there is a connection in this area. Until we know nobody is on to us we all have to be careful who we talk with. I'm hoping the things we did to get you and the girls back they may let slide. But if they find out it was us who took out the Cruz's operation; that won't slide. Right now they are not sure and we want to keep it that way. That's why I want you, Tara and John staying close to home for a while." Vince asked what he could do to help. I told him to just be smart if he talked to anyone and maybe try to extract information from them as well; including Bob. For now, stay close and be careful. I handed him the Glock handgun I had on my belt and told him to use it if necessary. I trained him to respect firearms from the time he was a child and knew he would handle it responsibly. "Let's try to get back to a normal life!" Vince shook his head in agreement.

Jay rode with me to one of our job sites to see how things were going. A few of the Mexican workers came up to us and shook our hands. They told us we were heroes to their families still living in Mexico. I asked them to not repeat that too much because we didn't want any more trouble. They all said it was not a problem; it was only something that was discussed within their families. I thanked them and asked how the job was coming. They were building a new sewer plant for the area and everything seemed to be going well. It looked like they didn't need my help so we moved on to the next site. Mike, my foreman was at this site. They were working on an addition to a car dealership just outside of Phoenix. Mike and I hugged and he welcomed both of us back. He told me everything was on schedule and only a few minor problems getting some materials. Mike and I went inside the work trailer and I asked him to have the men not discuss my recent trips away with anyone. If anybody asked; I just got back from Jay's place. He agreed. I spent some time talking with the men and looking over the project and then we headed for home.

On the way back after a long silence Jay said "I guess maybe I ought to be getting back to Idaho and see if I still have a ranch left." "That's fine partner, I hope you know you're welcome to stay as long as you like. I don't know how I can ever repay you for all your help." "Billy, it pissed me off something awful hearing Vince got kidnapped. Gettin' him back safe was all the payment I need. I don't want you thinkin' I'm running out on you. You know I'll be back in a hurry if there's any more trouble." I told Jay I knew that and I said "You know I tell other people all the time I'm blessed to have a friend like you but I don't think I ever told you that." Jay just smiled and said "The feelings are mutual my friend. Someday you'll be able to tell your grandkids about this episode and laugh about it." We both laughed.

When we got back home John and Kara were moving in again. Kara was grumbling this would be the last time she was going to do this. Jay said to her "Well little momma I got this big ranch house up in Idaho; it's just me and a bunch of cows. If you don't like it here I'm fixin' to leave in a day or two. Wanna go along? You can bring this young fella with you if you want." Kara just mumbled something and walked into the house. "Guess that probably means she's not interested" as Jay took off his cowboy hat and scratched his head. The three of us grabbed some things and headed to the house; none of us daring to laugh out loud for fear of Kara hearing us.

When we got inside Ann asked Jay "What's this I hear you're leaving in a day or two?" "That's right Annie. I figured I pretty much wore out my welcome here. Used to be if me and Billy were together for more than a week you'd get a little riled up that I was gettin' him in trouble. I been here way more than a week!" Ann walked over to Jay and got in his face and said "You're right there was a time when I really wasn't crazy about you two going off somewhere together. The lord only knows what you two have done this time. But I know you risked your life to save my son and help my husband. I also know Bill could not have done it without you." Ann hugged Jay and started to cry "But you big lug, you're family now and I love you." It's only the second time I ever saw Jay cry and we all had a group hug. Kara even softened up and said "You know Jay after the baby's a little bigger I'd like to come and visit for a while."

The next morning Jay started gathering up his things and decided he and the dog would take off later in the afternoon. We made plans for him to come back after the baby was born and help us celebrate the arrival of our first grandchild. I sure was going to miss him; we'd spent a lot of time together and he'd always been someone I could rely on no matter what. Around 3pm everyone said their goodbye's and Jay and I were off for the airfield where his plane was parked. He reminded me 3 or 4 times that he was only a few hours away if I needed him. I told him to just go home, relax and take care of his cows. He called his ranch foreman and told him to expect him home by early evening.

When we got to the airport they had Jay's plane all fueled up and ready to go. I helped him load up and he strapped the dog in the passenger seat. What a sight, I took a picture of he and the dog with my phone, we hugged and he said "See you soon, grandpa!" There were tears in my eyes as he wheeled the plane around and took off down the runway. As I drove back home I was chuckling to myself about all the experiences we'd shared over the years and wondered what might be in store for us in the future.

When I got home Vince had two of the horses saddled up and said "Thought you might enjoy a ride to relax a little." I just looked at him and said "You always were a smart kid, let's go!" The ride was just what I needed, a chance to forget about things and just enjoy the fresh air and the smell of leather and horse sweat. Vince and I stopped to give the horses a rest and talk. It seemed like a lifetime since we spent this kind of time together and it felt great. We'd spent an hour or so talking and my cellphone rang. It was Ann, she asked where I was. I told her and she said I needed to get back to the house as quick as I could. I asked her what was wrong but she wouldn't say. I told Vince we needed to get back; something was wrong. The horses were rested and we pushed them hard to get back.

When we got close to the house I could see Sheriff Bob's car parked in front of the house. When we rode up to the house I could see Ann and Bob on the porch, Ann seemed upset. Bob came out and said "I got some bad news. Jay's plane went down a few miles away from the airport. It looks like there might have been some kind of explosion. He didn't have a chance. I'm really sorry Bill; I know you guys were close." I felt numb; Ann and Vince both put their arms around me; I couldn't speak. In my mind I was thinking no, no, no not Jay! Why not me; I dragged him into this and now it's my fault he's dead.

I wiped the tears from my eyes and asked Bob "Are you sure he's dead?" Bob asked if there was anyone else in the plane. I said no, just him and the dog. Bob replied "We found one body in the wreckage." I asked him why he thought there was an explosion. Bob told me an eyewitness saw what he thought was an explosion towards the rear of the plane before it went down. When he and a deputy looked over the plane most of the rear half was in pieces like it was blown apart. He said the authorities would be checking over the plane to determine the cause of the crash but he felt something didn't look right. I asked Bob where Jay's body was and if he needed me to identify it. He told me his body was taken to the county morgue and they would need me to stop by later today to make the identification. Bob said "This thing is on my turf; if anything turns up I will be on top of it and keep you posted. If you guys need anything, please call me." Bob left to go back to the crash site.

I felt weak in the knees and sat down on the porch. Ann wiped the tears from her eyes and asked "Do you think someone blew up the plane?" I said "That's my first thought and we have to go with that assumption until the investigators find out otherwise. I guess I won't believe he's dead until I see the body." Vince asked "What about Bob? He seemed sincere while he was here." "Now more than ever we cannot trust anyone until we find out what brought down Jay's plane. The two of you go inside and Vince you keep that Glock handy. I'm going to see if it is Jay's body and no one leaves this house until I get back."

I drove by the crash site but couldn't get close. The FAA already had things taped off. I could tell it was Jay's plane and the reality was starting to settle in. I continued on to the coroner's office. They asked if I was the next of kin and I told them I was the closest thing to family he had left. We walked into the exam room and there was a body on a cart covered with a sheet. The doctor said "I need to warn you; the body been badly burned and may be difficult to look at." When he pulled the sheet back it was bad. I could not recognize the face. The body seemed to be the right size. For a moment I had hope; maybe it wasn't Jay. I told the doctor Jay had a scar on his right calf about 12" long and the middle toe on his right foot was missing from an old combat injury. When he lifted the sheet to expose the right leg; I took a deep breath. It was Jay; dam it; it was Jay. His lower legs were not burned which to me indicated a hot, quick flash like an explosion. Seeing those old wounds brought back a flashback of memories from a long time ago.

We'd been through so much over the last 40 years and now it was over. I could hear him say "Damn it Billy, don't cry over me! I've had one hell of ride through this life!" The doctor brought me back to reality when he asked "Is this the body of your friend?" I said "Yes sir it is, please treat him with the respect he's due." The doctor covered him up and we left the room. I sat down in a waiting room to compose myself a bit. After sitting there for 15 or 20 minutes Bob came in the room. He asked how I was doing and said "You need to know the preliminary investigation has turned up signs of explosive residue. At this point I am going to treat this as a homicide. I'll wait for the final results to be sure but for now that's the way it's looking." I thanked Bob for the information. "That's not all" Bob continued "I'm assigning one of my deputies to watch your house until we sort through this. I feel bad I couldn't help you more before; this time it will be different. Whether you guys took out the Cruz's or not the word on the streets is you did. If this is what this is about I'm not going to let them harm you or your family." I shook Bob's hand and we hugged but I still wasn't convinced. My best friend lay dead in the next room and somebody on this side of the border was responsible.

Chapter 16

THE FINAL STRAW

I went back home to think things through. I asked my family to give me some time alone. I went into my office and tried to sort through what my options were at this point. I didn't ask for any of this. I'd thought I put my former lifestyle behind me. All I wanted was for my family to be safe and secure. I planned to retire in a few years so Ann and I could travel and enjoy life. Now it appears these bastards were going to be coming after me and my family as well. Was all of this my fault? Maybe I should have let the authorities handle everything instead of taking matters into my own hands. Jay would more than likely still be alive if I would have done so. I'd have to wrestle with that decision.

I called Ann, Vince and Tara into my office. I told them "First things first; we need to arrange for Jay's funeral. I'm sure he would want to be buried next to his family in Idaho. Ann could you and Tara please make those arrangements?" They agreed. "As of today there will be a sheriff's deputy posted on our property until we know for sure how Jay died. We all need to stick close to the house for safety's sake. I've decided to bring this situation to a head. These people want me; so they are going to get what they want. I'm no longer willing to put the rest of you in danger. The only way I can see to end this now is put myself out there for bait. I will work with law enforcement as much as I can to accomplish this but I promise you it will end!"

Ann asked "What do you mean you'll put yourself out there for bait?" I told her I would need to work out the details with the law but my intention was to make myself more visible than the rest of my family. Vince's asked "What about me, Dad, what can I do to help?" I told Vince he and I were going to set up a perimeter around the property and he was in charge of securing what the deputies could not cover.

John came home from school and told us all that his father and a lot of other people in the community were all very upset over Jay's death. They were all asking what they could do to help. I told John I didn't know what to tell him. Perhaps his father should contact the authorities and see how they could help.

It was getting dark outside so Vince and I gathered up some galvanized wire and aluminum cans and strung a perimeter wire with the cans attached about 100 yards behind the house. We put stones in the cans so anyone tripping on the wire would make a lot of noise. We also put some loosely coiled barbed wire about 2 feet inside the wire just to tangle up anyone coming in from that direction. Vince said "You know Dad if I put a motion sensor light and a camera on each side of the horse barn we could cover the whole front of the property." "Good idea Son, let's see if Bob's as good as his word; give him a call and see if he would bring us the equipment we need. He can put it on our account at the hardware store. I don't want you going into town on your own." Later we put dead bolt locks on the barn doors; the house already had them on the doors.

By now it was dark and when we left the barn I could see 3 cars driving up the driveway. I asked Vince if he had the handgun on him and he said yes. I drew mine and we waited just outside the barn door. When the first car got closer I could see it was Bob. The other two vehicles were Mike my foreman and Pete my equipment operator. Vince and I met them outside the house. Bob said "I drew the first watch tonight. Besides I want to look around and see what we can do to tighten up security around here." Vince said "Me and Dad have been working on that. Come on out back and I'll show you what we've just done." As we were all walking to the back of the house I asked Mike and Pete what they were doing here. Mike said he and Pete would like to put a steel gate at the end of the driveway and tie it into the fence that was already there to keep just anybody from driving in here. He said they would put a digital lock on it and I could give the combination to whoever I wanted. Pete said "The gate won't cost you anything; Tom down at the tractor supply donated it and the lock."

Mike said "Bill, the whole damn town is behind you guys; it's time to put an end to this shit. Me and the boys are going to rotate shifts patrolling your place. I already got a work schedule set up and we don't want any shit from you about doin' it. You got to let us help. You and Jay did so much everybody wants to do what they can to help!" I hugged Mike and Pete and simply said "Ok, do it."

Bob thought the trip wire would be fine and liked the added effect of the barbed wire. Vince told him about his idea of the motion sensor lights and cameras and he agreed it would be a big help. I told Mike he and Pete could pick up the lights and cameras tomorrow morning and put the gate up tomorrow as well. Mike said "No, we're doin' it tonight." My only response was "Ok." The boys left for town to get the lights and cameras and Bob, Vince and I went to sit on the porch. I asked Ann, Tara and John to join us.

Bob told us the FAA told him there was definitely some type of explosive used on the plane. It was no accident. Their lab as well as the FBI lab were working on it. Bob looked me in the eyes and said "You know their coming after you." I told him "We already talked about it and I've decided and explained to my family that I want your people to use me as bait to draw out these bastards. I don't want them coming here. You know I can take care of myself but I could use your help." Bob told us "The FBI is raiding two known hangouts right now as we are speaking hoping to find a weak link; somebody who is willing to talk. My men have arrested 2 men today on suspicion of arson and murder and we will be grilling them as well. Since the news of Jay's death has gotten out my office has had 50-60 phone calls today from people who are now willing to give us information about this kidnapping ring. These are all people who we knew could help us but were afraid to say anything before. The community is fed up; they can sense a change coming. Right now you take care of burying your friend and let us do our job."

I looked around and it seemed everybody was looking at me waiting for an answer. I have to admit I am used to being in charge but I know I was out voted now. I just took orders from my foreman and now I guess

I'm taking orders from the sheriff. "Ok Bob, you're right. I need to take care of Jay first."

Ann told us all she and Tara made the arrangements for Jay this evening. His body will be prepared by a local funeral home and flown back to Idaho in three days. Jay's ranch foreman was taking care of the arrangements in Idaho and the funeral would be in five days. The burial will be in Jay's family cemetery with his wife and son. They also made airline arrangements for all of us to fly to Idaho for the funeral. We would be leaving the same day as Jay's body and spend a few days at Jay's ranch. My wife in her own way was going to make sure I wasn't going to offer myself as bait for a while.

The phone was ringing and Ann answered it. She said it was for me; a Roy Wilson who is Jay's attorney. Mr. Wilson introduced himself and told me he got my number from Harry, Jay's ranch foreman. Mr. Wilson explained "The reason I'm calling is to find out how long you might be staying in Idaho. We have some very important business to discuss and I was hoping we could meet sometime after Jay's services." I explained our schedule to him and suggested we could meet perhaps the day after Jay's funeral. "That would be fine. I'll clear my schedule for the day and will look forward to meeting with you and your family. Jay has always spoken very fondly of you and it will be my pleasure to finally meet you."

After I hung up I explained to everyone what the conversation was about. Naturally, everyone was speculating about what Mr. Wilson needed to talk to us about. Speculation ran from inheriting the ranch to how much money Jay might have had to how eccentric Jay was and his sense of humor. We would just have to wait and see.

I was exhausted and had not had much time to grieve for my old friend. I went to bed and got a little sleep as did everyone else.

The next couple of days went pretty fast as we were all preparing to travel and finishing up last minute things. Everyone was worried about Tara flying; except Tara. She was only three weeks away from her due date. She assured us they probably had hospitals in Idaho if it came to that. John was trying to do everything for her and we could all see it was annoying her. I liked John a lot but he was going to have to develop some more backbone and be more assertive around Kara or he was going to have a hard time with her. She is my daughter and I love her but she is very head strong (not sure where she gets that.)

It was time to go catch our plane at 8am. Mike and the boys assured us they would look after things until we got back. Sheriff Bob would be stopping by as well. I didn't say anything to anyone else but I was a bit uneasy about flying after what happened to Jay.

When we arrived at the airport the funeral director met us at the departure gate. He told me they would be loading Jay's casket shortly. As I looked out the terminal window I could see the casket being loaded into the cargo bay. It hit me like a kick in the teeth; that was all that was left of my best friend. I had to sit down. I'd been holding them back but now the tears just poured out and I couldn't stop them. I knew from past experience there wasn't much left of Jay after the explosion and his casket would never be opened. I had so many memories and he was such a strong and fearless man I just expected him to be ok; another one of his pranks, but not this time.

It was a pretty somber flight and when we landed I saw Harry waiting for us at the gate. When I hugged Harry, I cried again. He worked for Jay for almost 30 years and I could see in his face Jay's death was very hard on him. Harry seemed glad to see all of us again and he was especially pleased to see Kara and meet John for the first time. Harry introduced us to the local funeral director who was waiting with him. Vince and I helped to load Jay into a hearse while John and the girls went to pick up our luggage. We stowed our gear into Harry's van and we all left for the 40 mile drive to Jay's ranch.

When we started up the steep road to Jay's ranch house I felt at home. I'd been here so many times, it just felt good. The steep mountains were always a beautiful sight to me. Everything looked the same, the sprawling two story house with the big wrap around porch, the big red horse barn and horses and cattle feeding in the pastures. I asked Harry how many head of cattle they were running right now. He replied "You want my figures or Jay's?" We both laughed, knowing that Jay's figures were always a little high. "Yours will be fine" I told him. "Right now we have between 300 and 350 head. I know we have some up in the high country we haven't seen for a while and we do lose some of them to the mountain lions and wolves." John asked if we might see a wolf. Harry said "I hope not; they are nothing but trouble. There is a pack that moves through here every now and again so you might get a look at one."

I told John he would be hard pressed to find a rancher in these parts who would have anything good to say about wolves because they do kill some livestock and they kill a lot of elk calves which has had a negative effect on the elk herd in this area. John nodded his head and said "Understood, it's a subject we will discuss later."

When we pulled up to the house, Ruthie the cook and housekeeper was waiting for us at the front door. Ruthie was a big woman, not fat but close to six foot tall and what Jay called "big boned." I guessed she was in her mid 40's and had been with Jay for 15 years. Jay always suspected when he was away Harry who was around 50 and never married and Ruthie who was also never married had a thing going on. Both of them always denied it but some of the other ranch hands claimed to have seen them together. Jay always likened it to a Saint Bernard and a terrier dog getting together. Although Harry was a tough and wiry guy he was 5'5" and maybe 120lbs. soaking wet. I chuckled to myself when I saw Ruthie and remembered how Jay would go off on a tangent about the two of them.

Ruthie said "I'm happy to have some female guests here but I wish it was under different circumstances." She patted Kara's belly and said with a laugh "Maybe that little baby will come out to say hello while you're here." Kara just smiled and said "maybe." Ruthie lamented "This place just won't be the same without old Jay here to grumble and complain about things. You know he was more of a father to me than my own father. He took me in and gave me a job when I had no place to go. He was a fine man and just like you folks; I'm sure gonna miss him."

We all agreed; we sure were going to miss him. Ruthie said to me "You and Ann can sleep in Jay's room if you like or take one of the guest rooms. There are 4 other bedrooms." I said to Ruthie "I think we will stay in the bedroom next to Jay's; I just wouldn't feel right staying in his room." We all got settled into our rooms and then went for a walk outside to take in the scenery outside. John said "Wow, this is a beautiful place. The mountains look like they go on forever. The air is so fresh and clean; I think I could live here!" Kara said "There's probably not much call for a lawyer up here." I could see the wheels were turning in John's head and he mumbled "You're probably right."

Ann said "Maybe you boys can take the horses up into the mountains tomorrow and you can show John how big this place really is." John asked "How many acres are deeded to this ranch?" I told him I thought there were 8000 acres deeded and another 5000 leased. Tomorrow we'll take a look at some of it. Vince pointed a rock slide off in the distance to John and told him right under that rock slide was where he killed his first elk. He winked at John and said "Who knows maybe we will see a wolf tomorrow."

The kids were hungry and headed back to the house to find something to eat. Ann and I walked over the horse corral. I saw Jay's horse, Bob walking towards us. Bob was a big buckskin who was getting old himself. Jay talked about him a few weeks ago and how he might have to put him down. I could see Bob was getting a sway in his back and he walked pretty stiff legged. We both rubbed his muzzle and stroked his dark mane and I knew I wouldn't have the heart to put him down. Jay had mostly quarter horses with a few mustangs mixed in. I knew he had 5 or 6 mules they used for packing but I didn't see them anywhere. It could be the two ranch hands he had working here full time were using them to fix fences or move equipment somewhere.

Ann looked me in the eyes and said "You're going to have to talk about this sometime. Why not now?" I told her I just feel responsible for Jay's death. We'd been friends for over 40 years and I thought we would grow old together. Ann grabbed me by my chin and said "You're wrong. Can you imagine how hurt Jay would have been if you had not asked him to help. Look at all that explosive stuff he brought down on his plane. You made him feel alive again. The two of you did things neither one of you thought you could do again. Hell Bill, for a while you two were Pauncho and Cisco again. Jay lost his life saving others and as much as he annoyed me over the years; I loved him too. I know you have to finish this but dammit there are people who want to help; so let them. It's not just your fight anymore!"

Through the tears I acknowledged Ann was right. All I could say was "You've always been the smart one and I love you."

The next morning Vince, John and I saddled up some horses and headed out for a ride. I loved this place; it was so quiet and peaceful. The smell of moist fir trees and moss, the sound of a trickling stream, the clatter of horse's hooves on the rocks, my body started to relax. We stopped a few miles out to rest the horses and take in the scenery. John was truly impressed; he must have said 10 times "It's so beautiful here." We rode to a small mountain meadow and stopped to have the lunch Ruthie made for us. While we were eating Vince said "You know Dad, we ought to buy this place." I smiled and said "It's a nice thought but I'm afraid we don't have the kind of money it would take to buy this ranch. It is a working operation; Jay managed the timber real well and made some money running cattle and horses. Plus they do a little outfitting in the fall hunting season. But to make the payments on this place would be tough. Remember, Jay had everything paid for. I think the best we could hope for is for somebody to buy it and allow us to come and visit when we wanted to."

It was supper time 'til we got back and my butt was glad the ride was over. It was a great day spent with the boys and very relaxing for me. Ruthie made a great supper for us and she seemed pleased to have the company. We treated her by doing the dishes and allowing her to relax for a bit. After we finished the dishes, Ruthie pulled a bottle of scotch out of a cupboard and poured a round for all of us except Kara. She told Kara "I don't want that little fella comin' out of there drunk!" We talked a while and enjoyed a drink and Ruthie said "Well tomorrow's the big day and I need to try to get some sleep. See you all in the morning." Ruthie had her own small quarters in the back of the house that Jay built for her probably 10 years ago.

Ann poked me in the ribs and asked "You think Harry's back there waiting for her?" I just smiled and told her to mind her own business. Harry normally stayed in a bunk house with the other two men Wes and Dan who just got back from fixing fences soon after we did. Ann and I went to bed as well; that long ride tired me out.

Jay's funeral was scheduled for 11am at a local church. There was a viewing scheduled for 10am prior to the service. We decided to get there around 10 as there were a few local people I learned to know over the years and would like to see them. When we pulled into the parking lot at the funeral home, it was overflowing and people was lined up outside. The funeral director allowed us to enter a side door so the nine of us would not have to wait in line. We all were given seats in the front and I was able to talk to a few people I knew. It was a nice service; a few people said some nice things about Jay including his generosity and sense of humor. I was asked to speak but could not. Poor Ruthie sobbed throughout the service and I noticed tears on the three tough old cowboys seated with us.

At the lunch reception following the service stories about Jay were flowing much more freely. A group of 4 men about my age or older approached me about serving with Jay in Viet Nam. They each had questions about what Jay told them he did over there. I told them all I could assure them he was a hell of a soldier and if it were not for him; I would not be here right now. One of the men looked at the others and said "Hell, maybe the old bastard was telling the truth!" Then they all laughed.

I talked briefly with Roy Wilson, Jay's attorney and we sat up a meeting for tomorrow morning at 9am for all of us to meet with him, including Harry, Ruthie, Wes and Dan. He informed me Jay had a will and everyone at the ranch is named in it. He also indicated he would like to meet with me privately after the reading of the will.

Back at the ranch speculation was flowing as to what Jay might have in his will. He only had an older brother left and he was in a nursing home with a serious case of dementia. I reminded everyone although Jay liked to clown around he was a very astute businessman. I was sure he gave a lot of thought to what would happen when he died. Whatever decisions he made I am sure he had the best interests of all of you in mind.

The following morning we all ate breakfast and headed out to the attorney's office. We met in a large conference room. Mr. Wilson opened the will and the first thing he read was a trust fund Jay sat up for his brother to take care of any needs his brother may have. Next was Harry, Jay wrote "To my good friend and loyal foreman I give 100 acres of land that is already surveyed and deeded in his name at the base of Cold Foot Mountain along with the cabin and outbuildings already situated on the property. In addition I give him 10 head of cattle of his choosing to start his own herd. To Wes and Dan; two fine cowboys and also good friends I have deeded 50 acres for each of you. Wes your land is located in the Sweet River bottom along with the cabin I know you always liked and hope you will enjoy. Dan, your 50 acres is at the head of switchback trail with the cabin overlooking your favorite spot, the bluffs.

My dear Ruthie, the closest I ever had to a daughter. I leave to you the two rental properties I have near town; one of which I know you always admired. Also my Dodge truck so you have some wheels of your own to get around.

For each of the four of you Harry, Wes, Dan and Ruthie I leave

$50,000.00 cash each to add your own personalities to your properties. After the reading of this will you will receive a check from my attorney Roy Wilson.

Now for the ranch that I so dearly loved. I've given a lot of thought to what I was going to do with this place and since my own son has passed away before me; I can only think of only a few people who would care for this land like I did. Vincent Wright and Kara Harris, I'm giving you this ranch of now 7800 aces and all that goes with it; with some stipulations. One, if they wish to stay, the current staff of Ruthie, Harry, Wes and Dan retain their jobs with the ranch. Two, this ranch will remain a working ranch; it will not be subdivided into a bunch of 20 acre lots for city slickers for a period of no less than 30 years. Three, your mother and father can come and go as they please.

To my best friend and his dear wife, Bill and Ann Wright I leave to you the sum of $250,000.00 to enjoy the rest of your life together. You might need to loan the kids some until they figure out this ranching business!

Any assets remaining will be donated to local charities as I have instructed my attorney to distribute."

The room was quiet; I think we were all a bit shocked. Mr. Wilson asked if anyone had any questions. He said he was sure there would be plenty of questions after we all had time to digest this and suggested we meet with him perhaps next week to sign all the documents. He assured us he had been Jay's attorney for almost 35 years and was very familiar with the ranch operations and his office staff has done all the deed work so everything should be a smooth transition. Since it was Friday; he suggested we meet again Monday morning to get everything signed. We all agreed. Mr. Wilson gave checks to the four staff members and Ann and I agreed to a bank draft to our bank at home. He excused everyone except me and we met alone in his office.

He asked "Bill, did Jay mention anything to you about an attorney in Phoenix that may be involved with this drug trafficking ring?" I told him no. "Well, I spoke with Jay on the phone two days before he died and he asked me to check out this guy. My investigator got some pretty good information and it's pretty clear this guy is involved." "Who is the guy?" I asked. "Well, I think the reason Jay didn't mention anything to you is because he wanted to make sure the information was good before he told you. The attorney is Greg Harris, your son-in-law's father." "Holy Shit!" was all I could say. "Are you sure it's Greg Harris?" Wilson said "Look, I've had several people I know from that area confirm there have been suspicions for some time." "Damn Roy, you've thrown me two huge curve balls in the last few minutes; I don't know what to say." Roy suggested I contact my friend the sheriff and see if he could verify any of this.

I asked to use his phone and called Bob right away. Bob said everything was fine there and what was on my mind. I asked him if Greg Harris was someone they were looking at. Sheriff Bob asked "Why do you ask?" I said "Please Bob; just answer my question." "Yes Bill; we are looking at Greg Harris. How did you find that out?" "I'm sitting here with Jay's attorney right now. Two days before Jay died he asked his attorney to check out Greg Harris. Two minutes ago is the first I knew anything about it! Why didn't you tell me about this before?" Bob replied "First of all Bill; the fact that Greg's son is married to your daughter really complicates things, secondly we do not have any hard evidence against him right now and finally I didn't want you going off halfcocked without some proof. I need to ask you; do you think John could be involved?" "I just don't know Bob; I've gotten a bunch of stuff dumped in my lap today and I need to sort through it all. I guarantee you one thing – I will have a talk with John and see what I can find out. I won't be home for at least 4 or 5 days, please keep me posted if anything happens." Bob assured me he would.

"Well Roy; you sure gave me a lot to think about today. Did Jay mention how he got this information about Greg Harris?" I asked. Roy said "Jay mentioned a guy from Mexico named Eddie something. I don't remember his last name. Is that someone you know?" "I'll be damned, yes I do know Eddie; he helped Jay and I quite a bit down in Mexico. As far as I know he never steered us wrong with the information he gave us. We will talk again on Monday; after I've had some time to think through this." We shook hands and I left the office.

Ann asked me what that was all about and I just told her we would talk about it later. Let's all go back to the ranch and relax and see what plans the new owners might have in store for the place. That's if we are invited to stay a little while longer.

It seems while I was meeting with Roy Wilson the kids and the ranch staff already struck a deal for them all to stay on and run the ranch. On the way back to the ranch each side was explaining their arrangement to me and we had to stop and look at the properties each of them had just inherited. They all seemed very pleased and there was an air of excitement in everyone; except me. I was happy for all of them but also apprehensive as to how I was going to handle the information I just received. I decided I would wait until tomorrow to talk to John and allow him and Kara some time to contemplate their new venture. John, who was normally very quiet, was especially talkative and full of ideas and questions. He asked me "Bill do you think we should form a corporation among the three of us?" I said "Hell John, you're the lawyer in the group; why are you asking me?" We all laughed about that one.

I told everyone "Tonight we are all having dinner at the Steakhouse and it's on me. I know Jay would want us to have some fun with all the money he left us today; so let's go do it!" Ruthie couldn't decide whether she should cry or be happy. I asked her what Jay would say to her if he was here right now. She laughed and said "He would grab me by the chin and say "Girl, quit your damn bawling' and enjoy the rest of your life!" We spent a few hours at the Steakhouse and had a good time; on the way home we were all singing to the country music on the radio.

That evening I told Ann what Roy and I discussed and she found it hard to believe. I asked her advice on how she felt I should talk to John. "You need to go easy on him; maybe he doesn't know anything about this deal. Think what this could do to their marriage and the baby is only a couple of weeks away. I think you should wait until we get back home before you talk to him. Besides, you said Bob doesn't have any solid proof at this point. I know you Bill Wright; you want to go bulling right into this without thinking things through. Let Bob do his job." It was hard for me to admit but she was right, again.

The next couple of days Ann and I spent with the kids talking about the ranch and how they might run things. Vince was seriously thinking of moving up here. It didn't really surprise me; he always liked it here. He said "You know Dad I could transfer my college credits to the university up here and still get my degree. 7800 acres is a lot of dirt to dig in!" "It sure is son but remember you have a partner to share all that land with." It seems they decided to form an LLC (limited Liability Corporation) with John's legal advice. I was a bit apprehensive about John being involved right now but did not say anything. Actually it was Kara's idea to make it a 50/50 partnership with Vince and not give John any shares for now. I thought to myself "That's my girl!"

We met with Roy Wilson on Monday morning and all the documents were signed and the ranch was officially Vince and Kara's. I was really getting antsy and it was time to get back home. I know Kara wanted to get home as well. The baby could show up anytime. Ann made our flight plans two days ago and we were scheduled to leave at 4pm tomorrow.

While we were packing Ann said "You know the events of the past week are somehow going to change our lives." "Yeh, I was thinking the same thing myself. Plus we are going to be grandparents pretty shortly."

Chapter 17

WHEN ONE DOOR CLOSES ...

On the flight back home everyone else was sleeping after what was an exhausting several days. I had time to reflect back on the remarkable friendship I'd had with Jay. We'd been friends for almost 45 years. In that time we became brothers, best friends and I was sure going to miss him. He was the one person in my life other than my wife that would always listen and help in any way he could. I was sure he felt the same about me. I helped Jay deal with the death of his wife and son and saw a little piece of him die each time. He was bold, brash, and tough as nails but underneath all of that he had a heart of gold. It was tough for him to say he cared for someone or loved them but the results of his will sure indicated he loved those people. I remember him telling me over the years "I don't want to be too nice to the people who work for me or they'll think they can slack off a bit." It was eating at me that Jay died because of helping my family. I know he wanted to help and I have to admit I never could have accomplished what we did without him. Life will be different without him. I wiped a tear from my eye and settled back to try to get a little nap myself.

When we landed at the Phoenix airport Mike and Raul were waiting to take us all back home. The kids were excitedly giving them all the details of what transpired the last several days. Mike joked with them that they'd better save a week out of the year for him to hunt at the ranch. Vince assured Mike he would save him a spot and then laughed while telling him "You know, it will come with a fee!" We all got a good laugh out of that.

When we got back home the dogs almost knocked us over with their welcome back greeting. It was good to be home. Mike and Raul told us there had been no problems while we were gone and that was a relief. We thanked the guys for picking us up and I told them I would see them tomorrow.

As Ann and I were unpacking I let out a big sigh of relief. She looked at me and said "Me too, I'm really glad to be home." I told her "That's part of it but mostly I'm relieved we had no problem with the plane. Before we left, I had some reservations about flying after what happened to Jay. I'm glad we got back ok but to my way of thinking it solidifies Greg being involved in Jay's death. His son was flying with us and even though he might be crook; I don't think he would have blown his own son out of the air."

We both sat down on the bed and Ann took my hand and said "I had the same thoughts but didn't want to scare anyone. What are we going to do? The kids are so happy I don't want to burst their bubble. Like you, I want this to end, if Greg is involved I want him put away." I suggested we both go and talk with Bob tomorrow and hopefully get some information. I told Ann I would call Bob later and set up a meeting with him away from the house.

Although Ruthie is a good cook, I was looking forward to a meal prepared by my wife. She didn't let me down; dinner that night was great. The kids agreed and most of their conversation still revolved around plans for the ranch. They were asking our advice and it seemed Vince was seriously considering moving up there. I told Vince "I really want you to get your degree whether it is here in Arizona or in Idaho so I feel your first step should be checking to see if Idaho has the courses you need. If they do, you can transfer up there and complete your studies. If they don't have the courses you need then you're going have to stay here for two more years. Does that make sense?" Vince nodded his head and said "Yes it does Dad. I'll start checking to see what courses are available and go from there."

Ann looked at Kara and John and asked "What are you guys thinking you're going to do?" Kara laughed and said "Well, first I'm going to spit this baby out and then we'll talk about the ranch. Vince and I have agreed that I'm better at managing things and he is more hands on. I can manage the ranch from here so moving up there right now is not an option until the baby is older." John said "I believe I could live up there but right now I want to finish law school and I don't see how I could make a living in the middle of nowhere; besides my Dad expects me to join his firm when I graduate. However Vince and Kara have agreed to have me be their attorney for a fee of course!" We all laughed at that. John continued "My Dad talks about retiring and doing some traveling after I learn the business and I can take it over. Ever since he and my mother divorced he talked about traveling to Europe. So I do have a commitment to take over his business here in Phoenix."

I just swallowed hard and didn't say a word. Ann broke the silence and said "Well great, I wasn't looking forward to having a long distance relationship with my grandchild. Your Dad and I will be happy to help you guys figure things out and after all the years of business we've been through; I can assure you all it will all work out. Your father and I came out here with nothing; you guys have been given a tremendous gift from Jay and I'm sure you will do fine, with our help, if you want it."

We talked a while longer and it was getting late so we all headed off to bed looking forward to sleeping in our own beds. When in our room Ann said "I'm proud of you; you didn't jump on John about his father's business" and she gave me a hug. "It wasn't easy but it seems to me right now John is not involved in his father's drug business. Maybe Bob can enlighten us more tomorrow" I replied. I kissed Ann and tried to crawl in bed with my wife and two labs taking up most of the bed. I'm sure the dogs got used to having the bed to themselves while we were gone and they were not too crazy about sharing any space. For now I didn't mind.

The next morning Ann and I said we were going to do a little shopping and we left the house around 8am. We really didn't want to alarm the kids by telling them we were going to talk with Sheriff Bob. We exchanged small talk with Bob and his staff then headed to his office. Bob sat back in his chair and said "You must be getting old my friend; I figured I would have gotten a call by now that you just beat the tar out of your son-in-law!" "You can thank Ann for that not happening" I replied. "Ann and I are pretty sure John is not involved. Either that or he is one hell of an actor. Through the course of conversation with him the last week or so neither of us has seen any indication he knows what's going on." Bob said "I sure hope that's the case because I'd sure hate to see Kara get hurt by all this. Now as far as Greg is concerned, you're just going to have to trust me to handle it. I can't tell you a lot because the FBI in heading up the case and it is an ongoing investigation. What I can tell you is that there is some proof that Greg had some business dealings with the Cruz brothers. Between the FAA and the FBI investigating Jay's murder and political pressure being put on them to clean up this drug and kidnapping ring shit is starting to happen." Ann asked "What proof do you have against Greg?" "All I can say is there is proof that money exchanged hands between Greg and the Cruz brothers. Since someone took care of the Cruz brothers the investigation is focusing on Greg. The FBI has already taken down four people from this area who we know were involved in the ring."

I looked Bob square in the face and said "Bob, I'm embarrassed to say this but at one point not too long ago I suspected you might be involved. I want to apologize for that right now." "No apology necessary; if I was in your shoes I would not have trusted anyone either. Sometime after this whole thing is over you and I need to sit down up in the mountains and I need to hear from you just what the hell you and Jay did down in Mexico. Now, one more thing – I need you to promise in front of your wife and me – you will keep your nose out of this investigation and let us do what we do best. I promise both of you I will keep you posted when I have more I can tell you." I shook Bob's hand and said "We have a deal."

Ann and I left Bob's office agreeing in principle we felt a little better that things were being handled. She grabbed my hand and asked "You sure you can keep that promise?" "Only with your help, dear" I smiled. "That doesn't mean I can't ask some questions and maybe put some other people on Greg's trail. Remember all those people who wanted to help when Vince was missing; now it's time to call in those markers and see who was serious about it." Ann just shook her head and said "I know you're going to do this whether I approve or not so let me help. You've done enough and I see how it has worn you down. Let me make the phone calls and do some of the leg work; you know I'm better with people than you are. I'm just as angry as you are and if that bastard is guilty I want to see him pay. Besides you've got at least one business to run and maybe two until Vince and Kara get on top of things." "OK, I know when I'm whipped; get on the phone today when we get home and see who we can count on. I've got to get out to the job sites and see how things are going."

I dropped Ann off at the house and took off to the first of two jobs my men were working on. It was a hot day, 105 according to my trucks outside temperature gauge so I stopped and picked up some cold Gatorade for the guys. I talked with Mike who was heading up this water and sewer line job and he told me everything was on schedule. I walked over to where the men were working and told them to shut it down for a few minutes I wanted to talk to them. I passed out the Gatorade to everyone and said Mike tells me you all are doing a great job and I want to thank all of you for doing so while I was gone. Mike tells me we are on schedule and if we finish this job on time there will a $100 bonus for all of you when it's done. I shook hands with all the guys and pulled Mike aside and asked to keep his eyes and ears open for any information concerning Greg Harris being dirty. I filled him in a little bit and headed off for the other job site.

Raul was the foremen on this restaurant remodeling job and he greeted me at the door when I walked inside. There were three other men working with him at this site. I shook hands with the guys and asked them to all sit down for a few minutes I needed to talk with them. As before I passed out the Gatorade and thanked them for doing a good job while I was gone. I offered them the same $100 bonus if the job was done on time and the quality was good. It was especially important for this job because the restaurant was closed until we were done with the interior work. Raul walked with me outside to my truck and asked if I needed anything. I told him "As a matter of fact, yes there is something." I explained the situation to him, his eyebrows raised up and he said "Senor Bill, I hear things about this Greg Harris but I didn't want to tell you because your daughter is married to his son." "Tell me what you know Raul it's very important." "You need to talk to my cousin Juan; all I know is he has done some work for this man and Juan does not like him." "What kind of work?" I asked. Juan is an accountant for a firm in Phoenix and he travels to different business places in this state and even out of state to help them with their bookkeeping. You need to talk to Juan to get things straight. I will call him now on his cellphone if you like and you can speak to him." "Call him!"

Juan's cellphone went to voicemail and Raul left a message in Spanish that I could loosely translate into call me back as soon as possible; it's very important. I asked Raul to have Juan call me as soon as he called back. He assured me he would. I asked Raul if he had some work for me to do today. He laughed and said "Well, sure you're the boss you can do what you want. Jimmy could use a hand installing the new exhaust hood in the kitchen." I spent the rest of the day helping Jimmy and it felt good to be working with my hands again. Around 4pm Raul came to me and said he had Juan on the phone and he would be glad to talk to me. I grabbed the phone from Raul hand and introduced myself to Juan. Juan said "That's not necessary Bill, Raul speaks very well of you as an employer and you've become somewhat of a folk hero around here." I thanked him and said "I understand you may have some information that may be useful to me. I don't want to discuss it on the phone but will be glad to meet you anywhere anytime at your convenience." Juan said "I have appointments tomorrow morning but could meet you around 2pm tomorrow." I asked if he knew of Rosa's Café just outside of Phoenix and he said he did. We agreed to meet there tomorrow at 2pm. After I hung up Raul said "See Senior Bill, we all want to help you." "Thank you Raul, thank you very much. I guess I'll gather up my tools and head home." Raul said "Oh by the way boss; you did good work today!"

I was feeling pretty good about today's events as I pulled into the driveway and couldn't wait to talk to Ann. When I walked in she hugged me and said "Have I got some news for you. I spoke with Maria Turner's father today and he wants you and I to stop by his home tonight. He feels he has some information for that will be useful." After I kissed her I said "Great honey, you're taking this sleuthing job seriously. What time tonight?" "8:00, I got directions and we should leave here about 6:00 because you are going to take me out for dinner tonight because I've been on the phone all day and didn't have time to make dinner!" I told Ann "I am proud of you and I'll be happy to take you to dinner." I didn't want to steal her thunder so I decided to wait until later to tell her about my meeting tomorrow. Kara called me from the kitchen to the living room and said "Daddy can you please help me get out of this chair. My ass and belly are getting so big I can't get up." I could see she was getting frustrated and I grabbed her by both hands and pulled her up and hugged her and said "your ass and belly really are getting big but I still love you." She slugged me on the arm and laughingly said "Thanks, I guess. I'm never having another baby and waddled off to her room mumbling something about if John wants another baby he can have the next one. Ann came around the corner smiling and said "It's getting close, our little momma is getting awfully grumpy."

I got a shower and we were off for dinner. We actually stopped at Rosa's, it was a small, local place that was built by Rosa's family in the 1970's and we have been eating there for years. Rosa actually passed away two years ago and now her daughter Tina was running the place and the food was always good. I believe every town I've ever been in has a place like Rosa's where most of the locals hang out.

When we arrived at the Turner's house it was a beautiful, large two story Spanish style house with red tile roofs and very well maintained landscaping on the outside. Mr. Turner met us at the door along with his wife. Maria came running over to us and gave us each a big hug and told us how good it was to see us again. They all expressed their sympathy for the loss of Jay. We had a drink and some small talk and George and Iris asked how they could help. I explained the situation to them and asked them if the name Greg Harris meant anything to them. George rubbed his chin and said "I own several car washes and apartments around Phoenix and one of my tenants was late with his rent regularly and I had to put pressure on him to pay up. After 7 or 8 months of this the guy started to pay regularly always in cash. Now don't get me wrong; that's a good thing. I was talking to the tenant that lives beside him one day and mentioned that his neighbor must have gotten a job. The guy laughed and said "I guess if you consider selling drugs a job; yeh he got a job." So I asked him how he knew the guy was selling drugs. He told me the guy is a user himself and he spends everything he has on drugs. He also told me the guy bragged to him one day he just made $1000.00 in two hours one night. The man I was talking to asked if I knew anywhere in Phoenix a man could make $500.00 an hour other than selling drugs. I had to admit I did not."

Ann and I agreed but I asked "What does this have to do with Greg Harris?" George said "I'm getting there." Ann poked me in the ribs and said "Be patient, dear." George continued "I didn't like the idea of one of my tenants being a drug dealer so I followed him for a couple of days. On the second day I saw him get in a car with two other men and they drove to an old cattle auction barn just outside of town. When they went inside

I sneaked over to a window and saw my tenant give the two men a rolled up grocery bag with money in it. One of the men dumped the money on a table and counted it and gave a portion of it to my tenant. He also gave my tenant a number of small plastic bags filled with a white powder. At that point I got back to my car and drove to the end of the street where they would have to drive out and waited. When they drove out they took my tenant back to his place and dropped him off. I followed the two men to see where they were going. The men pulled into a Laundromat took three paper bags into the Laundromat, went into a back room and after a few minutes came back outside empty handed and left the parking lot. A few minutes later a different man, well dressed carrying a briefcase came out, got in his car and drove off. I followed this man to the law offices of Greg Harris and Associates. I later found out the man with the briefcase is a junior attorney with the Harris law firm."

I asked George if he took any of this information to the police. He said he did not because he wasn't sure who he could trust. Then when he heard Jay was killed he was waiting to talk to me first. George continued "I want these assholes brought to justice as much as you folks do. I've talked with my attorney and he wants me to go to the police with this information but I trust you and wanted to talk to you first. All of this has happened in the last few weeks and I'm sure no one spotted me following them."

"Well George, I believe you can trust Sheriff Bob and if you take this information to him he will use it wisely. I can tell you the FBI is watching Greg Harris and building a case against him and the Sheriff is working closely with them. I would normally be glad to go with you to talk to Bob but I made a promise to him I would keep my nose out of this investigation. Actually you spoke to Ann first and she did not make such a promise to Bob so I feel like I'm just advising you. How's that for semantics?"

"Oh, one more thing you need to know; Greg Harris owns the old cattle barn and the Laundromat where these transactions took place" George remembered. Ann said "Well George and Iris you've been incredibly helpful, this information should help this case along nicely. Please let us know how you make out in your meeting with Bob." George said "I told you some time ago when you brought my daughter back I would help in any way to catch these bastards and I meant it." We all hugged and were in accord we were doing the right thing. We thanked the Turner's for their time and as we were leaving Maria came out the door, hugged us again and then asked Ann "What's it like being married to the Lone Ranger?" Ann laughed and said "Well, it's never boring."

When we got to the truck I gave Ann a big kiss and told her I was really proud of her, you did good! This is sure going to give law enforcement a big boost in their investigation. On the way home I mentioned to Ann that Raul set up a meeting with his cousin who is an accountant to get some information about Greg tomorrow afternoon at 2pm. "You see Bill, people are really glad to help us after what you and Jay did for them. Some of them see hope that things can change. "It's corny but you are my Lone Ranger too! Let's do something we haven't done for a long time – let's go parking!" And we did.

When we got back home it was 12am and Kara and John were waiting up for us. Kara barked "Mom, Dad where have you been? We were starting to get worried. You should have called us." Ann hugged her and said "Well, if you have to know; we went parking!" "Oooh, really, at your age" Kara said disgustingly as she shook her head; John just laughed. We both snickered like a couple of teenagers and went to bed.

Vince and I got up early the next morning and went to work on the restaurant remodeling job. I worked until noon and went back home to get a shower and get ready for my meeting with Juan. When I got home Ann said she just got off the phone with George Turner and he had just come back from meeting with Sheriff Bob that he said went very well. "Great" was my response. "Hopefully my meeting with Juan will have the same results." Ann said she was going to continue to make some more calls while I was gone.

I met Juan at Rosa's at 2pm. Juan explained to me he worked for an accounting firm and part of his job was to perform audits of various companies either by request of the companies themselves or by the local regulating authority. He told me he performed such an audit on Greg Harris and Associates about four months ago. This audit was ordered by the local District Attorney's office. Through the course of his audit he found what he thought were exorbitant fees. He knew from auditing other local firms the average hourly fee was $175. Juan said he found some charges of $400-500 per hour for similar average services. This threw up a red flag to him. He said he also found real estate holdings the corporation held that were not justified by the corporations cash flow.

Juan continued he took his findings to his boss and expressed his concerns. His boss took his findings and said he would look them over and get back to him. After two weeks of no contact from his boss, Juan said he asked his boss if he had time to review the audit. His boss replied "Yes I did and I made a few minor changes and sent if off to the D.A.'s office. I knew they were in a hurry for it." Juan said "I personally performed this audit and I should have signed the report according to procedure. In four years of doing this job no one else every signed my reports and sent them out." Juan said all of the audits they perform are on the computer so he went in and looked over the report for Greg Harris and Associates and none of his questionable findings were in the report. The report found no irregularities and gave the Corporation a clean report. It was signed by his boss.

Juan said he didn't want to lose his job so he did not confront his boss. However he did not like what happened. When he talked with Raul the other day he thought it might be a way to get this monkey off his back. In his opinion and experience there is some kind of money laundering going on. I suggested he take this information to the FBI they have the resources to perform their own audit. I gave him agent Hanson's phone number and told him to call him, he could be trusted. I also asked that he not mention speaking to me about this case. He agreed, we shook hands, I thanked him and we parted ways.

Strike two, it seemed like things were coming together. Maybe I could keep my nose out of this investigation technically speaking. I have no idea what the FBI has on Greg but I was pretty sure they didn't have any of this stuff because both the people we talked with were afraid to talk to the authorities. I decided to head home and share what I just learned with Ann. I stopped to get gas on my way and my cellphone rang. It was Ann and she said excitedly "It's time Bill; it's baby time! I'm leaving with Kara right now to go to the hospital; where are you?" I told her I was closer to the hospital than she was and I would meet her there. When I got to the hospital John was already there and nervous as hell, already pacing the floor. He looked at me and asked "Where are they Bill, I got here as fast as I could." I grabbed him by his shoulder and said "Calm down man, they have a 20 minute longer drive than you do. They will be here shortly. If Kara goes into labor it could be a few hours so try to relax, everything will be ok." A nurse named Carol came over and asked John if he was Mr. Harris. She told him she just spoke with his mother-in-law on the phone and they would be here in about 10 minutes. She told him she will meet them at the door with a wheelchair and he could accompany her to meet his wife. The nurse smiled and said I will explain to you what's going to happen when they get here. The nurse looked at me and asked "Are you the grandfather?" I told her yes I was, I hope before too long I will be grandpa Bill. She laughed and said "You can come along too, Grandpa Bill."

Nurse Carol told John she did this almost every day and everything will be fine. I didn't calm John down a bit. Ann pulled in a few minutes later and John ran out to meet them. They put Kara on the wheelchair and Carol pushed her down the hall to an exam room. Another nurse escorted us to a waiting room. She explained that after the doctor examined Kara and they prepped her for delivery we could go into the delivery room if we wanted. Ann put her arm around John and said "This is why you went to all those classes so in a few minutes you need to be strong for Kara." John took a deep breath and said "Ok, sorry I kind of flipped out; this all happened so fast, I'm good now." In 20 minutes nurse Carol came out and said Kara was starting labor and we could come in the delivery room after we put on gowns and masks.

Two and a half hours later, to our extreme joy our grandson was born. Mom and baby were fine and Dad was beaming from ear to ear. After the nurses checked out the baby, they both were moved to a regular room and we went to see them. When we walked into the room Kara was lying in bed holding the baby. She and John kissed and hugged. Kara said, "Mom and Dad, John and I would like to introduce to your new grandson, Jay William Harris." My emotions overcame me and I broke out into tears. Ann and I hugged and she cried as well. After pulling myself together, I told them I was so proud of them and deeply honored with the name they chose. The baby was beautiful and I felt uncomfortable holding him; he was so tiny – 7 ½ pounds. I looked Kara and John in the eyes and asked "You guys knew all along the baby was a boy didn't you?" They both laughed and Kara said "Yes, we knew if we told you right away you'd be buying guns and ponies and all kinds of stuff for him. We wanted it to be a surprise."

"So now it's ok if I go buy a bunch of stuff for my new grandson?" Kara said "Sure Dad, knock yourself out." Ann asked Kara if she would like her to stay a while and Kara said "I'm fine Mom, I'm really tired and I'm sure I'll be asleep soon so you go along with Dad and make sure he doesn't go crazy buying stuff for Jay. Besides John will be here if I need anything." We both hugged and kissed Kara and left the room assuring her we would be back tomorrow morning. John followed us out of the room and down the hall a bit and told both of us how glad he was we were both here. You guys have been more like parents to me than my own parents. He said he left a voicemail message for his Dad but has not heard back from him yet and he wasn't sure where his mother was. Ann hugged him and told him "We are proud to have you as our son-in-law and you'll make a great father. We will see you later tonight."

When we got outside of the hospital I exploded "Can you believe that asshole Greg; he could not even be here for the birth of his grandson! I should go down to his office and punch him in the mouth!!" Ann looked at me and said "That would be an incredibly stupid thing to do. Maybe he is out of town and will call John later. For now forget about Greg and let's enjoy our new grandson." "You're right again Annie; I just hope the day comes when I can lay my hands on that bastard and give him what he deserves. So what do think I should get first for Little Jay; a gun or a pony?" Ann shook her head "How about some clothes and diapers and things he needs right now." So off to the baby store we went. I was shocked at how expensive baby clothes were but nothings too good for my grandson!

When we got home Vince was there and wanted to know all the details. We filled him in and he asked if it was ok to take off work tomorrow morning to go see his new nephew. I told him sure it was but he'd better call Mike and let him know he would be late. Vince said he would call him right now. Ann was busy washing the new clothes, stocking up the new supplies and trying to take care of all the last minute details. I had one thing I needed to finish before Little Jay came home. I built a new crib for the baby and just had a few finishing touches to put on it. I bought decals for both a boy and a girl and now I could put the appropriate ones on. After applying the decals I carried the crib into John and Kara's room. Vince looked at it and said "Nice job Dad."

Later that evening John came home and told us Kara slept most of the evening only waking up long enough to fed Jay. The nurse told him if everything was ok they could both come home the day after tomorrow. He said Jay's vitals were good and he seemed fine. John assured us Jay's lungs were in good shape!" I asked John if his father contacted him and he said "Yes, my Dad called me back around 6pm. He is in Denver and will not be back for three more days. He told me he will call when he gets back home." Ann showed John all the things she bought and asked if he thought there was anything she forgot. John said "Thanks, it looks good to me. Where did you find this crib? We've looked all over and never found one like this." Vince blurted out "Dad built this for you guys." John's voice crackled a bit and he said "You guys are the best."

The next day seemed agonizingly slow as we all anticipated Kara and Jay coming home. I went to work and must have looked at my watch 50 times throughout the day. When I got home that evening Ann said the same thing. She was still scurrying around making sure everything ready. When John came home from visiting the hospital he said everything was a go for tomorrow. He would be picking them up around 9am.

After dinner that evening John asked if he could talk to me. I said "Sure, let's go into my office." John started by saying that he was pretty upset that his father didn't think it was an important enough of an occasion to take a few days off work. He went on to say he should have expected it because while he was growing up his Dad's work was always more important to him than any event in his life. John looked me in the eyes and said "Bill, I want you to know I'm not going to be that kind of father. I understand how hurtful it can be for your father to put business before his own family."

I told John I was glad to hear that. It is important for him to be his own person. "John, you don't have to answer this if you don't want to but do you really want to join your Dad's law firm? Is there something else you would rather do?" John paused a bit and said "You know that's the first time anyone ever asked me what I wanted to do. It's always been assumed I would take over the business. I just resigned myself to that's how it was going to be. I really don't like how my Dad treats people; he looks at everyone as some type of business opportunity. He never takes the time to get to know them and honestly I don't want to do business that way. I admire how you treat your customers and employees and that's how I want to do business." I simply told him "Then do it that way. That's what I mean about being your own person!" [In my mind I wanted to say your Dad's a damn crook and if you turn out like him; you and I are going to have trouble. But I didn't.]

"Since Jay left his property to Kara and Vince I've been thinking of how that could give us a new opportunity. Maybe somehow I can use my education to help them and create a practice of my own" John continued. "That's great John, now you're thinking for yourself instead of allowing someone to think for you. I have always believed one can accomplish anything if they put their mind to it." John said "Thanks Bill, I really want to make it on my own, without my Dad's business. Now I have to find the strength to tell him how I feel." I told John "Son, you're a member of this family as long as you make sound decisions we will support you any way we can." We hugged and now I was convinced John was not involved with his father's dirty business.

Ann and I stayed awake most of the night talking and getting things ready for the big day. I shared with her my talk with John and we both felt a bit more comfortable with his situation. We did get a few hours sleep and the dogs woke us up about 7am. Soon John was off to pick up Kara and Jay. Ann made a big welcome home banner and we hung it on the front porch. Ann's sister and parents came by along with a few other friends to welcome the baby home. I'm sure all of them wanted a peek at the baby. Finally around 9:45 they arrived. What a joy to see the three of them walk through the door. John and Kara were proud parents and beaming from ear to ear. Everyone had their opinions as to who Jay looked like, including me. I thought he had Kara eyes and nose but I realize I am prejudiced. After a couple of hours Kara excused herself to breast feed Jay and I was sure they would both take a nap afterwards. Most of the folks took that as a clue to leave. Ann's family was the last to leave and thankfully they did help do some dishes and put them away before leaving.

Now thank God, our whole family was under one roof. I sat down to the quiet in the house and was reflecting on what a good friend told me a long time ago. He said "When one door closes another one opens."

This seemed so appropriate to my old friend Jay dying so suddenly and now a new Jay has entered my life. I only hoped that I could have as good a relationship with this new Jay as I did with the old one. My mind was racing with all the things I could teach this little guy. Somehow I needed to temper my eagerness to match what he wanted to learn and to accept he may not like the same things I do.

Later that night around midnight I got to hear my grandson cry. I thought it was pretty cool. I hoped that it wasn't every night but when babies are hungry, they are hungry. I remembered taking turns with Ann rocking and feeding our two babies at all hours. It got to be a drag after a while. Fortunately Ann and I were only substitutes this time around. I was sure Grandma would be happy to take her turn as long as John and Kara were staying here.

The first night was uneventful and I got to hold little Jay while Mom took a shower in the morning. He was so tiny and fragile my big clubby hands seemed to swallow him up. I know his parents were proud and so was grandpa. Kara came out of the shower and asked "Well grandpa, how does it feel to hold your new grandson?" "It feels great honey; I think I'd like another one of these!" She almost spit her orange juice on the floor when she said "Well, don't hold your breath for that to happen any time soon!" Vince was up and on his way to work but before he left he snapped what must have been the 100th picture of Jay on his cellphone.

Soon after Vince left there was a knock at the front door. I handed the baby back to Kara and answered the door. It was Greg Harris. He said "Well hi Bill, I know it's early but I just couldn't wait any longer to see our new Grandson." I told him to come in. He walked over to Kara and Jay and said, "Oh my God. I can't believe it! This is my grandson. Hi little guy, I'm your Grandpa and someday you're going to be a lawyer just like me and your Daddy." He looked at Kara and asked "How are you doing; are you feeling ok?" Before she could answer He asked "Where's my boy, where's John?" John came walking out of their bedroom and said "Dad, I thought you were going to call when you got back to town." Greg said "I know, I got in late last night and just couldn't wait any longer. I hope it's not too early." Ann came around the corner and said "You're not too early Greg, how are you? Would you like some coffee?" He said "Yes, I sure would but first I want to get a few things from my car. I'll be right back. Nothings too good for this boy; when he gets a little older I'll show him the good life." Ann looked at me and put her right index finger over her mouth to tell me to hold my peace. I just nodded my head yes. Greg came back in with a dozen red roses for Kara and a big stuffed bear for Jay.

Kara thanked him for the gifts and he sat down to have a cup of coffee. Greg asked John how it felt to be a father. John said "It feels great; it's hard to take my eyes off him." Ann asked Greg if he would like some breakfast and he said "Sure if you don't mind; what are you making there Annie?" (Ann hated it when he called her Annie.) Behind everyone's back I put my index finger over my mouth to tell her to keep her feelings in and I snickered to myself. "French toast" Ann replied. "Oh good, just don't burn it" Greg said, attempting to make a joke but he was the only one laughing. I knew Ann was boiling inside; there was one thing she took great pride in and it was her cooking. Those of us who live here knew to never make a joke about her cooking.

As far as Ann and I knew, Kara and John knew nothing of Greg's business dealings; so the two of us needed to try hard to be hospitable. "Great French toast Annie; best I ever had and you didn't burn it!" Greg laughed. "Bill and Ann, I want to offer my condolences for the loss of your friend. Are there any leads in the case?" I told Greg he would have to talk to the police about that. "If there is anything I can do to help please let me know. You and Jay were really close, right Bill?" Greg asked. I told him "He was the best friend any man could ever ask for." "It's a damn shame what happened to him. I sure hope they catch the guys who were responsible. Especially after all you guys did down in Mexico. Taking out those Cruz brothers probably put a chill on their drug business." Greg rambled on. Now he was starting to piss me off! How stupid did he think I was, fishing for information about whether we killed the Cruz brothers? I simply said "We did not kill the Cruz brothers." I excused myself to go tend the horses; I was so angry I was about to burst inside. I shook Greg's hand and said it was nice to see him again and left the house. I stayed out in the barn until Greg left.

Before I could open the front door John came outside and said "I'm sorry for the way my Dad acted today. Sometimes he can be a real jerk." I told John it was ok, he did not need to apologize for his father's behavior. I really wanted to tell John the truth about his Dad but this was not the right time. I wished John a good day and he was off to classes. When I went back inside Kara asked "What was that about? You don't like Greg very much do you?" "Not even a little bit honey. I'm sorry if I embarrassed you." "Not at all Dad, I don't like him either!" Kara kissed me and said she and Jay were going to go sit on the front porch for a while and get some fresh air.

I walked back to the kitchen and Ann was slamming dishes around and obviously totally pissed. She looked at me angrily and said "That SOB is not allowed in this house again. I never want him to touch my grandson again. We need to do whatever it takes to nail his ass!" Ann did not swear very often so I knew she was really upset. She went on "I'm calling Bob when I'm done here and I want to know when they are going to arrest him. The nerve of that man! He's probably responsible for Jay's death and he brings it up in our house. I never thought I'd say this but if they don't throw him in jail soon maybe you can take care of him." She was mad!!

After Ann calmed down a bit we both went in my office, she called Bob and I put it on speaker phone. Bob told her that he's had several people come forward in the last week with information about Greg. The FBI was checking out the information and if it was accurate they felt they would have enough evidence to arrest him. Ann asked how long that was going to take. He said he wasn't sure. What they really wanted was enough evidence to tie him to Jay's murder and they were working on that. Ann asked what evidence they had and all Bob would say was it looked promising. Bob congratulated us on the birth of our grandson and said he would try to stop by in the next day or so. We thanked Bob and told him to stop by anytime.

"I don't know Bill; I don't want these guys fooling around much longer. Greg has enough money he could probably leave the country if he wanted to." I assured her I felt the same way but I was also sure the FBI was not going to let him leave the country now that he was a murder suspect. We made an agreement to give it some more time and not jump to conclusions.

After a week of staying with us John and Kara decided they were going to move back to their own apartment. It was hard for Ann and me to see them go, but we understood they needed their privacy. Things were pretty calm and almost back to normal. For a few days after they moved out, the house seemed very quiet. We both really missed the baby, although I think Ann stopped by their place every day while I was at work.

One evening Bob called and asked what I was doing the next day. I told him just going to work. He told me he had a day off and was thinking about going up in the mountains to relax and invited me along. I told him I would have to check with the boss to see if I could have off. After a 10 second pause I said yes it was ok and I'd like to go along. I told Ann of our plans and she was glad Bob and I could spend some time together. I asked her if she had plans for the day she said maybe she would stop by and see Kara and Jay.

The next morning Bob picked me up early and after kissing Ann goodbye we were off. We parked at one of our old spots and walked a mile or so to a meadow to see if there were any elk hanging around. It was a little later in the morning when we got there and the elk were probably bedded in the timber for the day; we didn't see any. We stopped to rest and soak in the view. It was cool, maybe in the forties with a nice breeze blowing. I've admired the view from this meadow for years. All that could be seen in all directions was nothing but other mountains. The aspen trees were just starting to turn yellow and it was very relaxing.

Bob broke the silence by asking "Well, aren't you going to ask me about the investigation?" I told him "I wasn't planning to today, but since you brought it up, how is it coming?" Bob told me "I'm pretty sure the FBI will be making an arrest for murder in a day or two. They have tied Greg to paying someone to blow up Jay's plane." I told Bob that was great news and I was sure Ann would be glad to hear that.

Bob and I decided to hike over to the next mountain and look for some elk sign. After about an hour of walking Bob's satellite phone rang. Bob answered and said to the person on the other end "I thought I told you not to bother me today unless it was an emergency!" As Bob listened he said "Oh shit, when, where, ok I'm at least 3 hours away but I'll be there as soon as I can." Bob looked at me and said "I guess you heard that. I've got to get back." I asked him what was going on and he said we would talk when we get back to the truck. We humped it as quick as we could get to the truck. When we started down the road in the truck I asked Bob what was going on. Bob looked at me and said "Greg Harris is dead. Somebody gave him a double tap to the back of his head. His secretary found him a few hours ago in his office." "Holy shit!" was all I could say.

I was contemplating what he just told me when Bob said "You know Bill, you're damn lucky you were with me all morning or the FBI would probably be looking at you as a suspect." "Hell Bob, by associating with me maybe we'll both be suspects in the eyes of the FBI; you know they don't trust anybody" I responded. Bob just said "We'll just deal with that if that happens." My mind was racing, trying to think who could have done this. Was I happy Greg was gone – yes? A double tap to the back of the head was customarily a professional hit. It was two shots at close range meant to kill immediately. Probably a small caliber gun to minimize noise and make sure the bullets stayed in the head for maximum damage.

Bob was flying down the road with his siren blaring. He dropped me off at my place and said "I'll be in touch" and he took off for town. It was almost 4pm when I walked in the house and Ann was in the kitchen making dinner. I asked her if she heard the news? "What news?" She asked. "Somebody shot and killed Greg Harris this morning." I told her. "Really!" Was her first response "Where? Do they have the shooter?" I filled her in with the little information I had. "It's a bit of a shock but I can't say I'm sorry. I need to call Kara and see if John knows." Ann said. She got on the phone with Kara and Kara was crying. Kara told her the police had just finished interviewing John and obviously John was very distraught. Ann told Kara we would be right over. We both jumped into my truck and drove to their apartment.

When we arrived Kara was trying to console John and both of us simply put our arms around both of them. Our focus right now was John's welfare. He had no other family close by and this mess was going to fall on his shoulders. We tried to assure John we were here to help as a family. If he didn't mind Ann and I will be glad to help him through this crisis. It was difficult for John to talk but he did say "Oh yes thank you." I asked John if he would like me to handle the initial contact with my friend Harold at his funeral home. John agreed that would be fine, he liked Harold. In my mind I was thinking how ironic all this is. I am making funeral arrangements for a man I despised. Naturally I was doing this for John as I did not care about Greg. I called Harold and he said he was sure there would be an autopsy and he would make arrangements to pick up the body as soon as he could. We spent the evening with Kara and John and it was nice that several friends stopped by to offer their condolences including Vince. Ann offered to spend the night but they both said that wasn't necessary. Around 11pm we headed back home with the promise we would be back tomorrow.

The following morning at 8:30am there was a knock at our front door. It was agent Hanson from the FBI. I invited him in. Hanson said "I'm sure you were expecting me here at some point. Fortunately for you Bill you have a solid alibi for yesterday; is your wife home?" I looked at Hanson and asked "Now wait a minute you don't think my wife had something to do with Greg's death do you?" "We just have to cover all the bases and I need to know her whereabouts yesterday." Hanson replied. Ann walked into the room and told Hanson she left the house at 8am and was in the city yesterday visiting our daughter and then did some shopping and was back home around 2pm. You can check with my daughter and Max at the grocery store. I talked with Max about his family before I left the store. Hanson said "Ok fine I'm just doing my job. By the way do either of you have a .22 caliber handgun?" I said "Yes I have several of them." He said "I'll need to take them with me so we can eliminate them from the ballistics tests from the bullets we recovered from Greg's body." I got the guns and gave them to Hanson. He thanked us and started for the door and I said "Wait a minute, you need to fill us in on some of the evidence you have on Greg. We've both been very patient waiting to hear from you."

Hanson said "You're right, now that Mr. Harris is dead there are some things I can share with you." He went on to tell us that they have a man in custody who they believe is responsible for blowing up Jay's plane and they have evidence that Greg Harris paid him to do it. The FBI also has evidence that Greg Harris has been doing business with the Cruz brothers and others in smuggling and distributing illegal drugs across the border for years. The FBI was on the verge of arresting Harris before his murder. We are in the process of seizing all of his assets and shutting down his business. At this juncture we do not have any evidence of John Harris being involved in his father's business but we have not ruled him out either. I told Hanson "For what it's worth, Ann and I shared the same concerns about John but after spending time with him and talking with him we are both convinced he has no knowledge of his father's illegal activities." Hanson thanked us for that and said "I know you and Jay did what you felt you had to do to get your son back. I also know you were disappointed our agency could not do more to help you. There is nothing I can do about what's in the past.

I will assure you I will continue to be available to your family until this case is closed." "I have one question right now. I asked Hanson "Have you mentioned any of this drug business to John?" He told me he did not. I asked him to please let me handle that. He told me he would and I thanked him for his honesty, we shook hands and he left.

Ann said "Let's sit down and talk about this. It looks like the FBI has confirmed Greg was involved in Jay's death and was doing business with the men who kidnapped Vince. Now we have to sit down with John and explain it all to him. Do you think he can handle all of this right now?" "I don't know" I told Ann "However it will be better for him if he hears it from us than hearing it on the TV. Let's go over there now and just play it by ear on how to handle John."

When we arrived at John and Kara's place John was giving Jay a bath. Kara gave us each a cup of coffee and sighed "Now what's next?" John dried off Jay and came over and sat down at the kitchen table with the rest of us and handed Jay to Grandma. I started by asking John what he knew about his father's business? He said "Well not a lot. I know they do a lot of real estate work and Dad was helping some investors buy properties for development. They also do a fair share of work settling estates. Why do you ask?" I told John this may not be the best time but there are some things we needed to share with both of them. Ann said "John your father was under investigation from the FBI for being involved in drug trafficking and apparently they have a great deal of evidence against him. Does that shock you?" John thought for a moment and said "Sort of, but not really. I know my Dad only cared about money; that's why he and my mother split up. They argued constantly and I recall my mom saying to him "You've got to break free of those people. But I didn't know who those people were. Are you sure, how do you know about this?" Ann said "You know we are good friends with Sheriff Bob and honestly we just spoke with an FBI agent this morning. We've all had our suspicions but no solid proof until recently. We are telling you this now because we didn't want you to hear it on TV or the radio before we could talk it through. In addition, I'm sure the FBI will be talking to you about it and Bill and I wanted to prepare you for that."

John thought for a moment and then asked "So at some point in the past you guys were not sure if I was involved in this part of Dad's business; is that correct?" "That's true John, we did have some concerns," I told him.

"However, over the last month or so as you've opened up to us more, Ann and I are convinced you are not involved. We will support you any way we can and really want to help you through this. That's as honestly and openly as I can make it."

Kara and John hugged each other and we all shed some tears. John looked at me face to face and asked "Is there any more?" I was seeing a strength in John I had never seen before. I looked at Ann and she nodded her head at me to go ahead. I hesitantly said "There is more but it's very difficult for me to say this. The FBI has a man in custody who they believe your father paid to blow up Jay's plane." Kara said "Oh my God!" John hung his head in his hands and said "Holy hell, I knew my Dad was an asshole, but a murderer? I don't know what to say." You don't have to say anything as I put my arm around John "I'm sorry we had to drop all of this on you right now." The four of us hugged and more tears were shed.

John said "Thank you guys for sharing this with me. I know it wasn't easy for you. I guess I'm a little shocked right now and need some time to process all of this." Ann said "If there was any other way John we would not have chosen today to drop all of this in your lap. We simply didn't want some stranger telling you about it. We love you and want what is best for the three of you. There is a lot you will have to deal with in settling your father's estate but we will all be here to help you one step at a time. The next step will be taking care of your Dad's funeral and we'll get through it together."

Ann and I stayed for a while and tried our best to prepare the kids for what was coming. I explained to John there was a good chance the FBI would seize all of his father's business assets because they were purchased with illegal funds. I did not know what would happen with his personal assets. John said he understood, he in fact had studied some laws pertaining to just that. He said he really didn't care about his father's money he only hoped there was a little left to start a nest egg for Jay. I told John "Who knows this could open up a whole new bunch of possibilities for you." John commented "You know Bill, I'm sad my Dad is gone but I do feel like I've been freed from a burden. Like I told you earlier I really didn't want to work for him but I never got a chance to tell him that." Kara came over and put her arm around John and said "You know honey I'm going to need some help with this ranch up in Idaho. When you're finished with law school in a few months maybe we could move up there." Ann interrupted with "That's ok if you two want to live up there but this baby is staying here with Grandma!"

The telephone rang and John answered after a pause John said "Mom it's so good to hear your voice; where are you? Ok, sure that would be great; see you soon!" He hung up the phone and said excitedly "My Mom's in town and wants to come over. Her friend Patty told her about the baby and Dad dying and she just flew in from Seattle a bit ago. I haven't seen her in over seven years. Do you mind Kara?" Of course Kara said no. "Bill and Ann would you mind staying until she gets here; I really want her to meet you both." Ann said no problem we would like to meet her as well.

In less than an hour John's mother Charlotte arrived. It was obvious John got his good looks from his mother; she was tall, thin with dark hair and very attractive. John hugged her and she gave him a big kiss and told him she missed him so much. He introduced us all and Charlotte was drawn to little Jay like a moth to a flame. Tears welled up in her eyes as she said "Oh, what a beautiful baby. May I hold him?" John nodded yes. She couldn't hold back the tears of joy any longer. As she picked him up she looked at John and said "I'm sorry for crying but I didn't know if I'd ever get the chance to hold my grandchild and to see you again. Thank you so much for letting me come here today!" John asked her where she has been and Charlotte told him we will discuss that a little later. Right now I want to get to know your new family. She asked a lot of questions of us and kept telling John how lucky he was to find such a beautiful wife like Kara. Every time one of us would ask a question of her she would deflect it and change the subject.

Finally John said "Look Mom I'm really happy you are here. But you've been gone for over seven years and I haven't heard from you at all. Why is that? These people are my family and you can say anything in front of them." Well son, you recall I had a drug problem." John nodded yes. "What you don't know is your father got me hooked on cocaine. I found out about his drug dealings and he was afraid I was going to turn him in. As you probably recall your Dad and I argued a lot and our marriage was in bad shape. He and his friends forced the drugs on me until I became hooked and then made me out to be an unfit mother. In the divorce he forced me to sign over full custody of you and to sign an agreement to never see you again. In return he gave me a plane ticket to Seattle and a pocket full of drugs. I was so stoned I had no idea what I was doing. For 5 ½ years I was in and out of rehab but never really clean. There were times when I would think about you but getting high was my primary goal. A year ago the only friend I had was murdered and I guess her death scared me into getting serious help. After getting clean I contacted legal services in Seattle to try to get some type of agreement to see you. For the last two months your father and I have been battling over that. In all actuality I am one of the key witnesses the FBI has in the case against your father."

John shook his head and said "Wow, I had no idea." He took Jay from his mother's arms and handed him to Kara. John hugged his mother long and hard and then kissed her on the cheek and said "Welcome home Mom, welcome home!"

For me this was another big piece of the puzzle of Greg Harris put into place. There was a long silence in the room as we all digested what Charlotte has just told us. In my mind Charlotte just became the number one suspect in Greg's murder. After what he had done to her I really wouldn't blame her. This guy was a total control freak and was not going to allow anyone to get in his way. He had to dominate people and if he couldn't he would throw them away like yesterday's newspaper. I looked at Ann and she just rolled her eyes. Kara sat with her hand over her mouth and just shook her head in disgust. Charlotte broke the silence "John, I am here for you. I want to be a part of your life. We have lost so much time, I have made some mistakes and I hope you can forgive me." John looked at her and said "You are my mother and I love you. Dad poisoned my mind against you for a while. I thought you didn't care about me anymore. In the last few days I have learned that I really didn't know my father at all and I'm ashamed and embarrassed by the life he led. I will not shed another tear for him."

Kara asked Charlotte if she had a place to stay? Charlotte said she planned to get a room at the motel just outside of town. Kara said "That's not going to happen; you will stay here. We have an extra bedroom and you are welcome to stay as long as you like, right John?" John agreed. Charlotte said "Ok then I guess I'm staying here."

I told the kids it was time for us to go, I had things I needed to do yet today. We made plans to pick them up later in the evening for dinner. Ann and I welcomed Charlotte back home and told her how nice it was to meet her and we headed out. When we got to my truck I told Ann I wanted to stop by Bob's office and see what information he might have on Charlotte. When we got to the police station Bob invited us back to his office and asked "What's up?" I explained what just happened and I would like any details he might have on Charlotte and if she was a suspect in Greg murder. Bob told us they did check out Charlotte some time ago and it seemed everything she told us was true. She is in fact a witness in the investigation and no, she was not a suspect because she was in Seattle at the time of the murder. She did not get to Phoenix until this morning. Bob told us the evidence they have points to Charlotte being another victim of Greg's dirty dealings. He went on to say at this point we have no suspects and it appears the murder may have been a professional hit. Greg lived a high and fast life and he was probably posing too much of a threat of exposure to someone. He told us the autopsy was complete and the body would be released some time today. We thanked Bob once again and headed home.

When we got in the truck Ann said "I'm glad Charlotte's story checked out; she seems so nice. What an asshole that Greg must have been to live with!" I told her "That's a fact. Somebody did the world a favor by taking him out."

Later that night at dinner John said he made arrangements with the funeral home to have his Dad's body cremated. He didn't want a formal funeral and really wasn't sure what to do with his ashes. He also told us he would be meeting with the FBI in three days to go over the details of what they were going to confiscate and what he would be allowed to claim. I was glad things were falling into place for John and he was taking responsibility for cleaning things up. He seemed to be gaining more self-confidence now that his father was gone.

The next few days went smoothly and life seemed to be turning back to normal. In the back of my mind I was still wondering if someone might be coming after me or my family but with each passing day I thought about it less. Hopefully Greg's death put an end to all of that. John, Kara, Charlotte and little Jay stopped by with the details of their meeting with the FBI. John told us the FBI was seizing all of his father's business assets including any real estate they could prove was purchased with the drug money. That included his father's home and several properties in and around Phoenix, cars, furnishings and equipment. In addition two of his assistants were arrested as being involved in the sale of illegal drugs. There was money in his checking and savings accounts that could not be proven as ill-gotten so that would be released to John as he was the only heir listed in Greg's will. The total from both accounts was $112,000. John sighed and said "That's all that is left from nearly $2,000,000 in assets. I'm glad that part of my life is over. Now maybe we can all start a fresh new life together."

I told John "Son, I'm really proud of you. You've tackled this mess head on and dealt with it very well. You've had a lifetime of bombs dropped on you in a short time and didn't buckle under to the pressure. So what are you going to do with your inheritance?" "Well Kara and I discussed it and half of it goes to my Mom, she deserves it" he said. Charlotte said "Oh John, you don't have to do that." "I know I don't have to Mom; I want to" John continued "So to answer your question Bill; we are going to use it to start to build a house on the ranch up in Idaho when I'm through with school! After all that has happened around here we just feel it would be best if we get away from this area and my father's reputation and start a new life."

Ann's jaw dropped open and she asked "I suppose you're planning to take little Jay with you as well?" Kara laughed and looked at her and said "Really Mom; you think we're going to leave him here?" "Either that or I'm going with you guys. I don't want to be that far away from my grandson!" I thought out loud "Oh boy, here we go. Why don't we just start a little commune up there? Hell, I can't just walk away from my business and move to Idaho." John asked me "Why not? You're the one who told me one can do anything he wants if he puts his mind to it." Ann and Kara were laughing at me being backed into a corner for a change. Charlotte was being smart and keeping out of it although I noticed a smile on her face. I told them I knew when I was whipped; I would give it some thought. I tried to change the subject and asked Charlotte what her plans were. She said without hesitation "I'm going wherever my family goes." I got up and walked towards my office mumbling to myself their all ganging up on me I got to have time to think. The rest of them were laughing among themselves; I suppose even little Jay was laughing.

Just when I thought everything was settling down now they want to upset the apple cart. It was true I didn't want to be separated from family either but sell the business, our home and move to Idaho; I'd really have to think this through. I could hear them all talking and planning through my office door but I just didn't think it was going to be that easy. John knocked on my door and told me he had an idea for me when I was ready to talk about it. I said ok maybe tomorrow.

Shortly afterwards I could hear them making plans to leave and I joined Ann to see them off. John asked if it was ok he would stop by tomorrow morning before going to school and we could talk. "Ok by me, see you in the morning." When Ann and I got to the front porch she laughed and asked "Are you over your little pouting fit now." Yes I am thank you. I just think you guys don't realize how difficult it might be to sell the business and our house. There are a lot of things to take care of. "Let's go to bed and sleep on it. I'm sure if you want to, you'll figure it out" Ann said.

John joined us for breakfast the next morning. He told us he studied a plan in school a few months ago that might work for me to sell the business. That plan would be to sell the company to the existing employees. It would eliminate the hassle of finding a buyer and make a fairly smooth transition. He went on to say I'm sure we could set it up that you will have a nice monthly income from the sale of the business. I asked John if he was confident enough to present this plan to my employees. He said he was. Then we will set up a meeting with the employees for next Monday evening. If they like it and want to pursue it then we will talk to my attorney and see what he thinks. "Sounds like a plan" John said and he was off to school. I felt like I was on a runaway train headed downhill. I'm not sure if I want to sell the business and my home and move to Idaho. Ann and I sat down to talk things over. "So what are you thinking?"Ann asked. I told her "I think I'm outnumbered. It appears both of our children and our only grandchild are moving to Idaho. If I want to see much of them in the future I guess I'm going to have to move up there as well. What bothers me I always planned to sell the business when I was 65 or 66 years old. I'm 7 or 8 years away from that and I'm just not sure I'm ready to sell yet." Ann nodded her head and said "I understand how you feel. Remember when we were packing to come home from Jay's ranch and we both agreed that somehow the fact that the kids inherited the ranch was going to change our lives? If nothing in our family's lives had changed I would be perfectly happy to spend the rest of my life right here. But that's not the case and I am ready to change my life to spend it with them. Are you?" "Damn woman, you laid that out there plain enough for even me to understand. If you're ready to move then so am I! We'll work out the details as we go along."

Agent Hanson stopped by later that morning and dropped off the handguns we gave him earlier and told us none of them matched the bullets they recovered. He also told us they did not have a suspect in custody and their feeling was Greg's killer was probably across the border in Mexico. He jokingly asked me if I was interested in going back to Mexico to find the guy. Hanson said we were right; they could find no evidence that John was involved in the drug business. We thanked him for his help and we all agreed there were no hard feelings towards each other. He left on a positive note.

The next several days were fairly normal and Monday John and I met with all of my employees. John did a fine job of explaining things and I sensed most of them were seriously considering the proposal. We gave them one week to make a decision and if they did not want to pursue this venture then the business would be put up for sale. It only went two days when Mike and Raul approached me on the job and said the men have decided and they want to buy the business. We shook hands and I told them I needed to run all of this by my attorney and then we would proceed.

My attorney liked the idea and would start drawing up the sales agreement; just like John said; things were falling into place. It didn't take long until every time I went to work somebody would give me grief about them now being my boss. But obviously things don't happen that quickly. It looked like it would take at least a month to six weeks for everything to be finalized. In the meantime Vince decided to pack up most of his things and move up to the ranch. He was set to enroll in college up there in another month and planned to commute from the ranch. John had two more months until he graduated from law school so they were staying here at least until after graduation. Ann and I decided to test the market and listed our home with a realtor. It was a bit painful for me, having built the house myself and developed the property. But I guess I can always build another house.

I got a phone call from Roy Wilson (Jay's former attorney) one day and after talking about the kids and their plans for the ranch for a bit Roy asked me if my son-in-law was finished with law school yet. I told him it would be in six more weeks. Roy told me he was talking with Vince the other day and Vince mentioned John and Kara were planning to move up to the ranch sometime after graduation. I told him "Yes that is their plan." "Well Bill" Roy continued "You know I'm no spring chicken anymore and I've been thinking of retiring. Do you think young John might be interested in taking over my practice after he learns the ropes a bit?" I told him "I can't speak for John but I'm sure he would be very happy to talk to you about it." I gave Roy John's phone number and told him to call and talk to John. Roy laughed and said "I hear you and Ann may become residents of Idaho as well." I told him it was quite possible. We hung up and I thought to myself this could be a really good opportunity for John. I didn't see the ranch supporting two families and I didn't think John was going to become a cowboy.

After three weeks on the market we got our first serious offer on our house. It was a bit less than we were asking but the buyers were willing to allow us to stay here until we found another place in Idaho. They were a nice young couple with two small children who lived in the city and they wanted more space. Ann and I debated for a few days and we decided to sell the place to them. I took a big gulp when we signed the sales agreement. I hoped we were doing the right thing. The next day I called Vince and gave him the news; told him we were coming up to do some house shopping tomorrow and asked if he could pick us up at the airport. Not a problem he told me.

Ann and I met Vince at the airport and we all went back to the ranch. We dropped Vince off and took his truck into town to meet with a realtor that Vince made an appointment with for us the day before. Ann and I agreed we would like our own place and not build a house on the kid's ranch. We felt it would be too much family in one spot. We also wanted some acreage for the horses. The realtor name was Sharon and she was very nice. Sharon was a short heavy woman with a really good sense of humor. Sharon had pictures of several properties to show us but there were only two that really appealed to us. The first one was about ten miles from the kid's ranch and was 100 acres with a nice log house that was very open inside. A 24 foot high cathedral ceiling with log beams in the living room, a large kitchen and dining room, laundry room, master bedroom and full bathroom on the first floor. The second floor was a loft with two bedrooms and a full bathroom. What we liked about the house was the living room was the only room with log walls, the rest of the rooms were done in drywall and tile. There was a nice two story bank barn with red steel siding and a corral and plenty of pasture for the horses. There was roughly 50 acres wooded and 50 acres pasture. The house and barn were set back at the edge of the woods with a ¼ mile long driveway. We both liked it.

The second property had 250 acres and it was only seven miles in the opposite direction from the kid's ranch. It was the typical western ranch house, white siding, two story with a big wrap around porch. It was a big rambling house. The living room was finished in natural pine boards and a big stone fireplace. The kitchen was huge obviously designed to feed a lot of people at one time in the large dining room separated by a double door to the kitchen. There was a big family room off the dining room with a full bathroom and upstairs were five bedrooms and a full bathroom. It was an older home but well maintained. Outside there is a nice horse barn and corral, a bunkhouse and a few small implement sheds. Both properties had features we liked. I liked having 250 acres but really liked the log house. Ann loved that big wrap around porch but didn't think we needed five bedrooms. We told Sharon we needed to talk it over and we would give her a decision tomorrow either way. She said that was fine, she had other properties we could look at and there was no hurry. We drove around for a few hours and looked at several more properties but nothing really jumped out at us.

When we got back to Vince's place he asked us if we found anything we liked. Ann said "Yes I found one place I really like and I think I could live there." "How about you Dad, did you find anything you like?" "Yes son I too found one place where I believe I could be happy." Ann smiled at me and asked "Ok Mr. Bill – which one?" "The log house!" I replied. Ann jumped into my arms and said "I knew it, I knew you liked that place and so do I! Do you want to but it?" I told her "A wise person told me not too long ago; let's sleep on it." We both agreed.

The next morning we met with Sharon and looked at several more properties but nothing that really caught our attention. Sharon bought us lunch and we made an offer on the first place we looked at. After lunch we went back to Vince's place to wait for Sharon to call us back. That evening Ruthie made us all a nice roast beef dinner and we talked about expanding the horse business with the boys over dinner. Harry had some good ideas about breeding stock and marketing and I thought they should move forward with his ideas. After dinner Sharon called to say our offer was accepted by the owners of the property and congratulated us on our purchase. After thanking Sharon I called Roy Wilson to see if he would handle the sales agreement and deed transfer and he said he'd be glad to do it. I made plans with Roy to set up an escrow account for the funds to buy the property until the paperwork was ready.

Ann was able to book a flight home for us for later in the afternoon the next day so we had the evening to enjoy the peace and solitude of sitting on the front porch and contemplating our move. Ruthie said to Ann "It sure will be nice to have you as a neighbor." Ann said "Well, we will be 10 miles away." Ruthie laughed "Up here that's a neighbor!" The next day we looked over the horse stock and discussed what characteristics we needed to improve through proper breeding. There was a stallion paint horse that caught my eye and in my mind I was making plans for him. But first things first; Ann and I had a lot of work to do to get ready to move up here.

Vince dropped us off at the airport and our flight left on time at 5:30pm. I was half asleep about an hour into the flight when there was a jolt and a loud noise from the left side of the plane. The seat belt signs came on and the plane dropped slightly. My first thought was son-of-a bitch they found us! Ann looked at me with eyes wide open and fear on her face! She grabbed my hand and said "No, not now! I thought we were done with these bastards!" In 30 seconds or so the captain came on the intercom and said "It's ok folks. We apparently sucked something into one of our engines but we've got the problem solved and I will be taking off the seat belt sign shortly. Sorry for the excitement." This last moment drained me emotionally. I know in the back of each of our minds the fear of retaliation was still there. The idea of not knowing when or where was taking a toll on both of us. We both tried our best to not show it, especially around the kids but it was always there. I looked at Ann and said "We have got to get past this. We can't keep holding this in. You and I need to vow right now to not allow this to rule our lives. Whatever happens, we have had a great life and I wouldn't change a thing." Ann laid her head on my shoulder and said "This time you are right, Mr. Wright. To hell with those bums; let's have some fun!"

When we got home John and Kara were waiting for us and asked how we made out. Ann filled them in and showed them some pictures of the place we bought. John said "I have some good news. I have reached an agreement with Roy Wilson and will be working for him when I get through with school." "That is good news John" I said "now you can start making plans for that new house." Kara said "Wow, everything is set the Wrights and Harris' are moving to Idaho. Little Jay, you are going to be a cowboy and maybe grandpa can build our new house. Grandpa said, "But first I got to get your mother and me settled in up there."

Ann and I started packing and boy did we have a lot of stuff. Things that both of us forgot we even had. We gave a lot of things to a thrift store and a clothing and furniture ministry our church ran. I originally thought about trucking everything myself on a lowboy trailer I had, but when I saw how much it was, I hired a moving van to haul it all. We spent the better part of a week getting everything ready.

We stayed in Arizona until John's graduation. We were very proud of him and how he matured in a short time. Charlotte went with us to his graduation and she was so pleased to be there. Afterwards she asked us if we would look around for an apartment for her when we got settled and we said we would be glad to do that. However she was welcomed to come and stay with us until she could find a place of her own. John and Kara would be staying at the ranch until their house was built and she could stay there as well, there was plenty of room.

The following day the moving van arrived and the men loaded everything up. I had the two dogs loaded in the truck with me and the horses in the trailer ready to go. The bed of my truck was packed full of tools and equipment; with the horse trailer pulling behind I had quite a load. Ann was driving her Explorer packed full of things she didn't trust the movers to haul. Before we left a number of friends, neighbors and family stopped by to see us off and we invited each of them to come and see us. John, Kara, little Jay and Charlotte planned to leave in another week.

It took another week to find a place for all of our stuff but we finally got it done. The view from the front porch of our new home was beautiful. We had the pastures in front of us with the mountains off in the distance.

It was mid-August and the evenings were pleasantly cool. The animals adjusted quickly and seemed happy here. I had a phone call from Sheriff Bob soon after we moved to see how we were doing and to tell me there were still no new leads in Greg Harris' murder. I told Bob he needed to plan to come up and hunt elk with me when he could get away. I would have Vince save a landowner tag for him. Bob said without hesitation "You got a deal buddy; I'll be calling you back shortly."

John, Kara, little Jay and Charlotte got settled in at the ranch. Ruthie was just tickled about having a baby in the house. After a month or so Charlotte found a nice apartment in town, a job working at a grocery store and seemed very happy to be on her own. John and Kara picked out a piece of land to build a house and we worked together on the plans for it. It was too late in the year to start building because winter came early here and hunting season was just starting; so we would start building in the spring.

In a few weeks Ann and I helped with packing some of the hunters into the back country and did some cooking for them as well. It was a very busy time for everyone as new hunters came in and left every week for eight weeks. We all worked very hard but enjoyed it a great deal. We were all so busy none of us had any time to think about the life we left behind.

After the hunting season was over and we had a little free time. Ann and I were sitting by the fireplace having a cup of coffee and just relaxing with the dogs at our feet and enjoying the quiet. I said to her "You know when Bob was up here to hunt elk a few weeks ago; he told me again there were still no new leads in Greg's murder. It seems that case has really gone cold. I haven't given it much thought lately but every now and then I run some different scenarios through my mind and I can't come up with anyone in particular. I'm sure there were a lot of people who would have liked to kill him, including me, but I never got the chance. Do you give it much thought?" Ann looked at me and said "No, I don't think about that bastard at all!" That was the end of that conversation.

I laid awake that night in bed thinking about our brief conversation about Greg's death. It was uncharacteristic for Ann to be so abrupt about anything and I was trying to figure out why. She normally thought things through before commenting on any subject. In our life together she was always the thoughtful and perceptive one while I was most times more spontaneous. Did she hate Greg that much, did she fear for the life of our grandson and son-in-law or so angry over Jay's death that she just put the thought out of her mind and wanted to keep it that way, I just couldn't figure it out. I thought about all the shady characters Greg dealt with that I knew of and anyone of them could have killed him for a multitude of reasons.

Then it hit me like a slap in the face, could she have done this and all this time I never considered it. Maybe the reason she didn't want to talk about it was she knew who did it. She certainly had the knowledge to do the job because I taught her how to handle guns and how to move around undetected in the woods. She was in the area at the time of the murder and she was certainly tough enough and determined enough to pull it off if she wanted to do so. One side of me wanted to be ashamed of myself for even thinking this way but another side of me knew how determined she could be. I looked over at her lying in bed sleeping and knew at that instant I would never share these thoughts with anyone including her. If she killed Greg, so be it, if someday Ann wanted to talk to me about it we would talk. I will never bring up the subject on my own.

Printed in the United States
by Baker & Taylor Publisher Services